COLTON
UNDER FIRE

CINDY DEES

MILLS & BOON

First Published in Great Britain 2019
by Mills & Boon, an imprint of HarperCollins*Publishers*
1 London Bridge Street, London, SE1 9GF

Colton Under Fire © 2019 Harlequin Books S.A.

Special thanks and acknowledgement are given to Cindy Dees for her contribution to *The Coltons of Roaring Springs* series.

ISBN: 978-0-263-27403-5

0219

MIX
Paper from
responsible sources
FSC™ C007454

This book is produced from independently certified FSC™ paper to ensure responsible forest management.

For more information visit: www.harpercollins.co.uk/green

Printed and bound in Spain
by CPI, Barcelona

Chapter 1

Her cell phone flashed.

Incoming text for Sloane Colton Durant from Ivan Durant.

She scowled at the screen. Ivan could keep his last name. She would rather go back to being a Colton, even with all of its notorious implications in Roaring Springs.

This isn't over.

The cell phone flashed another incoming message. Irritated at being disturbed at dinnertime by her ex-husband, she nonetheless touched the screen to see the next message.

She gulped.

I WILL expose what you did and get her back.

A frisson of terror skittered down Sloane's spine. Her ex, a high-powered corporate attorney, didn't make threats idly in court and he wasn't making any now. The custody battle over their daughter had been a bloodbath, and she'd had to resort to blackmailing Ivan with his infidelities and gambling to get him to back off. Her own divorce lawyer had warned her that Ivan probably wasn't done trying to take Chloe from her.

Sloane's gaze hardened. Her ex would get custody of Chloe over her dead body. He didn't care about their daughter at all. Ivan merely saw her as a trophy. The spoils of war.

Sloane winced as two-year-old Chloe let out a piercing squeal, and heads across the dining room turned to glare. It hadn't been her idea to bring a toddler to a family supper at the upscale Del Aggio steak house at Roaring Springs, or The Lodge, as locals called it. She'd tried to talk her adoptive father, Russ Colton, out of this particular restaurant, but the man was a born-again bull in a china shop.

He didn't listen to anyone.

"Is Chloe all right?" Sloane's biological brother, Fox, asked in concern. "She looks flushed."

"Kids always turn red in the face when they're winding up for a tactical nuclear meltdown," she muttered.

"That sounds serious," Fox responded, eyeing his niece warily.

She and Chloe had spent a few weeks at the Crooked C Ranch while she looked for a permanent place to live. Her adoptive brother, Wyatt Colton, owned the ranch and lived there with his fiancée, Bailey. Fox also had a house on the property and helped manage the spread.

They all had a healthy respect for the temper of a tired, hungry two-year-old.

Sloane scooped Chloe out of the wooden high chair, which was probably half the problem. The log contraption might be considered rustic chic, but it looked uncomfortable.

Of course, the other half of the problem was that Little Bug's bedtime had come and gone, and still, there was no sign of dinner.

"Let's go for a walk, sweetie, and look at the skiers."

Chloe felt warm in her arms. And her cheeks were rosier than usual. Poor thing had really had a time of it, getting ripped out of the only home she'd ever known and being dragged to this new town full of strangers who thought they could walk right up to a baby and get in her face or pick her up because they shared the same last name.

Sloane almost hadn't come back to Roaring Springs, Colorado for that exact same reason. She didn't need her entire loud, nosy, raucous family getting in her face, either. It had been hard enough getting through the divorce without the interference of the whole Colton clan.

"Mama. Pitty!" Chloe exclaimed, pointing at one of the floor-to-ceiling glass windows on either side of the thirty-foot-tall stone fireplace in the main lodge.

Sloane looked outside at the white stripes of ski runs between stands of fluffy black pines, the slopes bathed in brilliant light for night skiing. Hundreds of skiers dressed in bright colors zigzagged across the snow like a moving dance of jeweled butterflies.

It *was* pretty. She'd forgotten how much she loved this time of year in Roaring Springs. Ski season was at its peak, The Lodge bursting at the seams with wealthy patrons who'd come in from all over for the world-class ski runs and five-star facilities. She'd missed the laughter and ruddy cheeks, the scent of hot buttered rum, and wood fires burning cheerily. She'd even missed the funny hitch-step rhythm of skiers tromping around The Lodge in their ski boots.

This was why she'd come home with Chloe. To give her daughter stability. Family. A little joy in her life for a change.

From the first moment Sloane had announced her pregnancy to Ivan, he'd been furious about it. Marriage to him had been great provided she gave her undivided attention to him and brought him status and a fat paycheck. But as soon as those were threatened with the imminent arrival of a baby and parenthood, he'd turned on her.

They'd argued constantly through her entire pregnancy. After Chloe had been born, he'd been gone more than he'd been home—betraying his marriage vows and gambling, as it turned out. But when he was home, there'd been only shouting and fuming silences from him.

By the time Chloe was a few months old, she had become withdrawn and silent anytime mercurial Ivan was in the house. It was uncanny how quickly she'd learned to hide from her own father.

But then, Sloane had learned to hide from him as well. His temper was uncertain at best and violent at worst. He'd never struck her or Chloe, but she was certain it was only a matter of time. The morning after he smashed every single piece of her mother's china—one of the few things she had that had belonged to her—

Sloane had filed for divorce. She wasn't sticking around until she or her daughter got hurt. Or worse.

She shuddered and hugged Chloe tightly. Lord, she'd hoped she was done with that nightmare and never had to deal with Ivan Durant again. But apparently, he wasn't done torturing her.

Her brain kicked into lawyer gear. She would save his texts. Collect pieces of evidence to build a case against him, and then she would ask for a restraining order. The Colton name should hold a little extra weight in the local court, at any rate. If she had to live with the negative implications of the name, she supposed she should benefit from its power, too.

"I go, Mama," Chloe declared, pointing again at the ski slopes.

"Would you like to learn how to ski? I can ask about some lessons for you if you'd like."

Chloe bounced up and down so eagerly that Sloane had trouble hanging on to her. She would take that as a yes. Struck again by how warm Chloe felt, she asked, "Hey, Bug, how's your tummy feeling?"

"Rumbwy tumbwy."

Rats. They'd been reading *Winnie the Pooh*, and Chloe might just be repeating that.

"Do you feel sick?" Sloane asked.

Chloe stuffed her thumb in her mouth and twisted to look out the window, seemingly disinterested in the current discussion. She had mostly given up thumb sucking in Denver. But with the move to Roaring Springs, she'd reverted to the habit. She'd also reverted to bedwetting and temper tantrums.

Sloane figured Chloe had some pent-up anger to act out and wasn't too concerned about the regressive behavior. It wasn't as if she could blame her daughter for it when she had at least as much anger at her ex to work through.

She'd been boxing at a local gym for the past few weeks, and she'd been amazed at how much fury rose up in her belly whenever she envisioned Ivan's face on a punching bag.

Sloane laid her palm on Chloe's forehead. The velvet baby skin was burning hot. "I think you're coming down with something, sweetheart. How about you and I go home and climb into our jammies, have a nice grilled cheese sandwich, and I'll read you a bedtime story—your choice."

"Pooh Bea-uh?"

"Sure. *Winnie the Pooh.*"

Sloane ducked into the restaurant to grab the baby bag, which doubled as her purse, briefcase, gym bag and zombie apocalypse survival kit.

"You're leaving? But the steaks are just about to come out," her biological aunt, Mara Colton, protested. They'd adopted her and Fox after their own parents had died in a car accident. Sloane had been five and Fox seven at the time. She loved them for it, but truth be told, she'd never felt like a real part of their family of three boys and two girls of their own.

"I think Chloe's sick," Sloane explained. "I don't want to share her baby germs with any of you."

Her brother Decker, general manager of The Lodge, stood up. "I'll have the chef put your steak in a to-go box and have the valet pull your car around."

Wyatt and Bailey expressed regret that she had to go and promised to come see her new house soon.

Bailey was awesome. She was a veterinarian who'd

recently reconciled with Wyatt after six years of an on-again, off-again relationship and was about to marry him for a second time. Furthermore, Bailey was expecting their first child. She and Sloane had hit it off from the first moment they'd met. Maybe it had something to do with feeling like outsiders in the middle of the loud, overbearing Colton clan.

Sloane followed Decker to the spacious covered portico out front with its huge timbered roof soaring overhead. Stone-clad columns rose to support the roof, and slate slabs stretched away underfoot. This place was solid. Permanent. Safe. The Lodge really was a remarkable resort.

Decker said, "You're sure I can't talk you into coming to work for me here, Sloane? That is why Dad paid for your law school."

"I've told Russ over and over that I have no training for nor interest in corporate law."

"Training or not, you're smart as hell. I need someone I can trust in my legal department." He lowered his voice. "We've had some cancellations after last month's murder, and we've got a big film festival coming up this summer. I could really use your help managing our corporate image and distancing The Lodge from any unpleasantness."

"Then you need a publicist, not a criminal defense attorney. Honestly, Decker. Hiring me would raise more questions, not less."

"You're a Colton. And this is a family business."

Chloe fretted, giving Sloane a convenient excuse to end the conversation. She struggled to put the fussy toddler into a snowsuit, and Chloe kept pushing the hood off her head. As a result, her daughter's fine blond hair stood up in a halo of static. Sloane tried to smooth it down, but Little Bug was having no part of that and threw her head back and forth, shouting, "No way! No way! No way!"

What had gotten into her? She was usually a sweet baby, cuddly and happy when Ivan wasn't around.

"Terrible twos?" Decker asked sympathetically.

"That and she's not feeling well. A deadly combination," Sloane answered.

As her mini-SUV pulled up, Chloe swan-dived off the emotional cliff into a full-blown tantrum and screamed bloody murder.

Women nearby, obviously mothers, threw Sloane sympathetic looks. Everyone else winced and hurried inside to escape the earsplitting screams.

With a sigh, she put Chloe into her car seat and buckled her in around flailing fists and feet. Ahh, parenthood. And she'd thought being a lawyer had been hard. Ha.

Tonight was one of those nights when she wished to be back at the Crooked C with Fox. The adult moral support would help her get through the challenge of dealing with a cranky baby, and her brother would pour her a glass of wine when Chloe finally wound down and crashed.

She'd had no illusion that being a single parent would be hard, but sometimes it was harder than others. Like tonight.

Finally pulling into the garage of the cute craftsman bungalow she'd just bought with a piece of her divorce settlement, she sighed with relief. But the feeling was short-lived because once she extracted Chloe from her car seat, her daughter had gone from rage to even more alarming listlessness. Which was totally unlike her high-energy child.

It took Sloane several minutes to find the box, not yet unpacked, with the baby thermometer in it. She ran the device across Chloe's forehead.

102 degrees.

Oh, my gosh!

After giving Chloe a quick cool bath and putting her into her footie jammies, then getting into her own pajamas, Sloane made a grilled cheese sandwich, Chloe's all-time favorite food, but Chloe wouldn't take even the first bite.

She measured out the recommended medications for a baby with this high of a fever and convinced Chloe to swallow them. Honestly, her Little Bug should have put up more of a fight than she did at taking the medicine. Sloane's alarm spiked a little more.

She made up a bottle—which Chloe hadn't used for months—with an electrolyte drink and rocked Chloe like an infant to feed her the bottle.

Sloane desperately missed baby moments like this, but she hated that her child was sick enough to need one. Chloe fell asleep in her arms, and Sloane dozed with her in the big recliner chair that had been her first purchase for her new house.

Sloane woke with a jerk as Chloe whimpered in her sleep.

Good grief. She might as well be holding a furnace in her arms. Chloe was still burning up. Carrying her carefully into the kitchen, Sloane ran the thermometer across her little girl's forehead again.

103.6.

Oh, no.

She transferred Chloe's head to her shoulder, grabbed the baby bag, stuffed her feet into fleece boots and headed for her car. Chloe didn't fully wake up as she got her buckled into her car seat and tucked a blanket around her. Trying to stay calm, Sloane quickly climbed behind the wheel and pulled out of the driveway.

She breathed a sigh of relief when the emergency room was empty as she carried Chloe inside. A nurse showed her to an examining room and agreed to stay with Chloe while Sloane went out front to fill in paperwork and hand over insurance information.

She rushed through a pair of swinging doors that led back to the check-in station…and plowed face-first into a man's chest. He must have been standing just beyond the doors. Sloane, at five-foot-three and not much over a hundred ten pounds, barely budged the much larger person.

She inhaled sharply, and the scent of pine trees and fresh air filled her lungs. It was as rugged as the Rockies, as big as the endless skies, as free as a bald eagle soaring. She inhaled again, relishing the scent.

Powerful, gentle hands grabbed her upper arms and steadied her. Which was just as well. Suddenly, she was feeling a tiny bit dizzy.

"Sloane? Sloane Colton?" the man murmured in shock.

She looked up into a pair of familiar aspen-green eyes.

"Liam?" she blurted, equally shocked to have bumped into Fox's childhood best friend.

Bookish, but charming. Smart, but self-deprecating. A good skier on the high school ski team. More handsome than he realized… All the girls had loved Liam.

But he'd been oblivious. Suppressing a sigh, Sloane's eyes drifted over him. He had been tall and skinny in high school but had grown taller since she'd last seen him. And had filled out. A lot. In all the right places. *My goodness.*

"Liam Kastor, at your service. I was friends with…"

"Fox. I remember. You two tortured me incessantly in junior high and high school."

"We did not! We just were looking out for you."

She snorted. "You two drove me crazy."

"You studied too much to even notice our hijinks."

Lord, it felt good to smile. She set aside the strange sensation of happiness. "I would love to argue the point with you, but my daughter's here and I need to give these folks my insurance information and get back to her."

"Of course," Liam said quickly, stepping away.

She whipped through a daunting stack of medical history and personal information and then hurried back to Chloe's room. The nurse looked up when she slipped inside. "The doctor has already been in to take a peek at your daughter. He'd like you to try to get a bottle laced with some medicine down her."

Sloane nodded.

Chloe still didn't become fully alert when Sloane picked her up and popped a bottle in her mouth. Little Bug only glanced around the strange room, then closed her eyes and turned her cheek to Sloane's chest.

She looked up at the nurse in worry. "This is totally unlike her. She's usually wide awake anywhere new. Wildly curious. Full of questions."

"She's a sick little camper. You did good to bring her in when you did."

"Any idea what she has?"

"Not yet. There has been a nasty virus going around, though. We've seen a half-dozen kids with it in the past couple of weeks."

The doctor came back in a few minutes, and Sloane laid Chloe on the bed. He did the usual doctor things—listened to her breathe, took her pulse, and looked at the chart where the nurse had written down Chloe's vitals. He looked up at Sloane. "I'd like to do a quick CT scan of Chloe's abdomen. Also, her temperature is continuing to spike, and we need to get control of that."

Sloane frowned. She knew in her gut that he wasn't telling her everything. "What do you suspect?"

"Nothing yet. I'm just eliminating various possibilities."

"Look. I'm a lawyer. I deal much better with blunt than tactful."

"Okay. Your daughter's belly is painful to the touch. But her reaction is generalized and I can't pinpoint a source of pain. Could be her spleen. Could be appendicitis. Maybe something else altogether."

"Worst case?" Sloane bit out.

The doctor shrugged, and she didn't like the evasiveness that entered his eyes. He answered, "Worst case, we admit her and watch her."

"You'd make a lousy poker player, Doctor. Wanna try that, again?"

The guy sighed. "I administered a massive dose of a broad spectrum antibiotic in that bottle you fed her. Based on what the CT shows, we may need to put her on an IV drip and throw more antibiotics at her. If her fever doesn't start responding to the meds soon, we'll have to take measures to cool her head and protect her brain from injury."

Sloane nodded stiffly, too scared to do much more. Still, she would rather know what they were up against than not. The nurse wheeled Chloe's bed out of the room, leaving Sloane to wait. And worry. And imagine the worst.

A need to *do* something overwhelmed her, and she jumped up. The room was too small and too crowded with machines for a good nervous pace, so she went out into the hall to stride back and forth.

"We have to stop meeting like this."

She looked up, startled, as she all but face-planted against Liam Kastor's chest. *Again.* "I'm so sorry."

"How's your daughter?" he asked, cutting off her apology.

"They don't know. Sick. Her fever's not coming down."

"What can I do to help?" Liam asked quietly.

"I have no idea. She's never had a bad fever before."

He smiled gently. "I was talking about you. Is there anything I can do for you?"

"Oh!" The idea of a man lifting a finger to take care of her was a completely foreign concept. "Distract me. Keep me from panicking."

"Do you want me to call Fox?"

"God, no! He wouldn't know what to do and would call Mara. And she would call everyone in the whole blessed Colton clan."

"There is that," Liam replied dryly. "When's the last time you ate?"

She frowned. She hadn't gotten around to eating because she'd been more concerned with taking care of

Chloe. And earlier, she'd left The Lodge before dinner had arrived. "Lunch, I guess."

Liam asked a nurse at the station in front of Chloe's room to call him as soon as Chloe was brought back, and then he whisked Sloane down the hallway. "Come with me. Cafeteria's this way. Food's terrible, but the coffee's outstanding."

"How do you know that?" Sloane asked. Did he work here? The nurse had clearly known who he was and had his phone number. "Are you a doctor?" she blurted.

"Me? Never."

"What brought you to the emergency room, then? Do you have a loved one here? I'm sorry to be so insensitive. I'm such a mess right now—"

He stopped just inside the door to a small lounge with linoleum-topped tables, plastic chairs and institutional fluorescent lights. Gently, he laid a fingertip on her lips. "I'm a police detective. We were shorthanded at the station tonight, so I volunteered to transport a prisoner who got sick in the drunk tank."

"You're a cop?"

He grinned and steered her over to the coffeepot.

"How was law school?" he asked over his shoulder.

How— Fox. Of course. "It was hard. But fascinating."

She scrutinized him as he studied the self-service line. She supposed some people might call him boyishly handsome, but she sensed a quiet strength in him. Mature. Reliable.

Funny, but a few years ago, she would've called Liam boring. And then she went and married an exciting man who took her straight to hell. Boring was starting to look pretty darn good these days. It was amazing how time and life changed a person's point of view.

"How do you like your coffee?" he asked.

"As black as my soul," she replied dryly.

"Do tell," he replied mildly. One corner of his mouth turned up sinfully, though, for just a moment. "Tuna salad okay with you?"

She picked up the cups of coffee and carried them to a table while he went to a vending machine and bought two sandwiches in triangular plastic packages, two bags of chips, a packet of baby carrots and a bag of apple slices.

He dumped his haul on the table and slid into the seat opposite her. "I haven't seen you around Roaring Springs since you left for college. What have you been up to since then, Sloane?"

She ripped open a sandwich package and bit into the day-old bread and nearly dry tuna. Not that she cared what anything tasted like at the moment. "After I graduated from law school at Colorado State, I moved to Denver and got a job as a criminal defense attorney at Schueller, Mangowitz and Durant."

Liam whistled under his breath. "That's a high-powered firm."

She rolled her eyes. "The women there call it Chauvinist, Misogynist and Douchebag."

"Ouch. That bad?"

"Worse," she growled.

"I sense a story."

"Don't be a detective tonight, okay?"

He threw up his hands. "No interrogations out of me." He took a cautious sip of his coffee. "Am I still allowed to ask what brings you to Roaring Springs—as a friend-slash-past-tormentor?"

She shrugged, sipping at her own coffee. "I've moved

back home with Chloe—she's my daughter—to give her a better life."

"Better than what?"

Darn it. He was being all perceptive, again. "Better than a rotten father and a failed marriage."

Liam laid his hand on top of hers briefly. Just a quick touch of his warm, calloused palm on the back of her hand. But the comfort offered was almost more than she could bear right now. She was too worried about Chloe. Her emotions—usually carefully suppressed— were too close to the surface.

She spent the next few minutes fixedly concentrating on her food and regaining her emotional equilibrium. Or trying to, at least.

As if he sensed her teetering on the edge of a breakdown, he gathered up the empty food packaging and said briskly, "Take the chips with you. Let's go see if there's any news on your daughter."

As they walked back to the emergency ward, he said quietly, "The docs here are excellent. Chloe's in good hands."

She nodded, her throat too tight for a response.

Liam's timing was perfect because, as they rounded the corner into the emergency area, the nurse who'd taken Chloe away for the CT scan came toward them.

"Where's my daughter?" Sloane demanded, her inner mama bear on full alert.

"Come with me, Mrs. Durant."

"Colton. Ms. Colton. I'm not keeping my ex-husband's name."

"Right. The doctor would like to admit your daughter overnight."

"Why?" Sloane croaked.

"The doctor will fill you in."

She wanted to scream as the nurse walked at far too leisurely a pace to an elevator. Sloane was barely aware of Liam holding the elevator door for her as it opened on the third floor, or that he kept pace beside her as she charged for the doctor standing at the far end of the hall.

Please God, let Chloe be all right. She was Sloane's entire world.

The doctor stood just outside a room with a glass window in the wall. Inside the dimly lit hospital room, Chloe was asleep in a stainless steel crib. She looked so tiny and lost among the wires and blankets.

"What's wrong?" Sloane demanded without preamble.

"She doesn't have appendicitis, or an intestinal blockage, or an enlarged spleen. But since her fever still hasn't broken, I want to keep her here for observation until we can get her temperature down to a safe level. This is probably just the virus that's been going around. But babies can get hit hard by things like this." Fixing his gaze on hers, he asked calmly, "Has your daughter been sick recently? Under unusual stress that might have compromised her immune system?"

"Oh, God." Guilt crashed in on her. "We moved from Denver recently as part of my divorce. It's been hard on Chloe, and she has been reverting to baby behaviors. I had no idea I compromised her immune system. I'm a terrible mother. I should have realized something like this would happen—" She broke off on a sobbing breath.

Arms came around her, gentle and strong. She didn't care whose they were. Her baby was seriously ill and she'd completely missed the signs until Little Bug was burning up with fever. Ivan was right. She wasn't fit to be a mother. Chloe would be better off with him and the expensive professional nanny he would hire to raise his daughter for him.

The doctor commented from somewhere beyond the circle of Liam's arms, "This virus comes on fast. You didn't miss any warning signs, Ms. Colton. The fever was likely the first symptom anyone would have noticed. And you got her here before the fever became dangerous."

Sloane lifted her head to glare at the doctor. "Don't coddle me. I suck as a parent."

Liam's voice rumbled with light humor in her ear. "You couldn't suck at anything you put your mind to."

She would have argued with him, but the doctor commented, "If you'd like to spend the night with Chloe, there's a daybed in her room by the window."

Duh. *Of course* she was staying with Chloe. Her baby would be scared to death if she woke up in a strange place and Sloane wasn't there for her.

Liam said briskly, "Give me your keys, Sloane, and I'll run by your place and pick up a few things for you. Toothbrush, a change of clothes..."

For the first time since she'd arrived at the hospital, it dawned on Sloane that she was wearing her pajamas. Thank God she'd put on her practical flannel pajamas consisting of a manly shirt and pants. Liam would think she was a total weirdo if she'd been wearing her footie onesie that matched Chloe's.

Not that she cared what Liam, or any man, thought of her, of course.

"You don't have to. I can call my brother to run by and pick up some stuff—"

"And alert the entire Colton clan that Chloe's sick? They'll descend upon you like a swarm of locusts, and you won't get a moment's rest tonight. You need your sleep, too, you know." He held out an expectant hand.

He was totally right. "Good point." She dug around in the baby bag, where she'd randomly tossed her keys earlier. It took an embarrassingly long time, but she finally came up with them. "You're sure about this?"

Liam grinned. "It's my job, ma'am. Plus, my prisoner is passed out and likely to stay that way for several hours."

She rolled her eyes at him. But truthfully, she was grateful for the help.

"I'll be back in a jiffy. Go be with your daughter and get some sleep if you can. I'll drop off your things with the nurses so I don't wake you up."

What was this? Consideration for her comfort? Huh. So that was what it looked like when a man was decent and caring. Who knew?

Liam turned and headed for the elevator, and she tiptoed into Chloe's room.

She couldn't resist brushing the hair off Chloe's forehead and dropping a featherlight kiss on Little Bug's hot cheek before she stretched out on the daybed, bunched up the lumpy feather pillow under her head, and pulled a blanket over her shoulders.

She stared at her daughter for a long time while sleep refused to come. The weight of being a single parent, for real now, not just in practical application, landed heavily on her shoulders. She prayed for wisdom to make the right decisions for her baby girl to keep her safe and healthy.

Everyone had told her she had this. That she was a great mom. That she would be better off without her spouse. How hard could it be to raise just one child by herself?

But suddenly, she wasn't so sure she had this at all.

Chapter 2

Sonofagun. Sloane Colton was back in town. And single, to boot. His boyhood prayers had finally been answered—just a decade and a half too late. The universe had one hell of a sense of humor.

If only Liam had known back then what he knew now about life and about women now. He would've gone after her with both barrels back in high school if he'd had the confidence to tell her how he'd felt about her. Instead, he'd kept his feelings hidden. But he'd learned since then to rip the lids off boxes and expose the truth, be it in solving a crime or in personal relationships. Life was too short to waste time being shy.

Sloane had only gotten more beautiful with age, which anyone could have seen coming if they bothered to take a good look at her back in high school. What he hadn't predicted, though, was the sadness lurking in her big, expressive hazel eyes. Like she'd given up on herself. What had done that to her? She'd been braver than just about anyone he knew.

A need to understand her, to find out what had happened to her, surged through him. She looked as if she could use someone to protect her. Which was quite a change from the girl he'd once known.

Ever since he'd met her at the ripe old age of seven or so, Sloan had been a firecracker, fully able to take care of herself. She raced through life like a runaway train, flattening every obstacle that dared step into her path.

Not that her fierce independence had prevented her older brother, Fox, from looking out for her just as fiercely. Of course, as Fox's best friend, it had fallen to Liam to help defend Sloane over the years. A task he'd taken on with secret relish—

Let it go, buddy.

His fantasies of Sloane Colton were just that. Fantasies. She would never see anything in a plain, ordinary, hometown guy like him. If only he could show her who he was now—

Nope. Not even then. He was a small-town cop living a small-town life. The girl he remembered wouldn't ever see any appeal in that.

Sloane had run off to the bright lights of the big city as soon as she could after high school and college. Married a rich, high-powered lawyer, and became a renowned defense attorney herself. She obviously wanted excitement out of life. Challenge. She didn't want anything to do with sleepy Roaring Springs or the people in it.

He swore under his breath. Who knew that, after all this time, he could still carry a hotly lit torch for a girl he'd grown up with? He had to find a way to douse it and get on with his life.

Liam checked in on the prisoner on the second floor, still sleeping off his alcohol binge, before heading out to his truck. It dawned on him he didn't know where Sloane lived. He could call Fox— Strike that. No Coltons. He called the police station to run her address.

Her house was only a few blocks from where he'd grown up. And where he lived now. He'd renovated and then moved into the apartment over the garage of his parents' home last year after his father died.

It was hell on his social life to be that guy who, in his early thirties, lived at home with his mom. But her health was frail and she needed help. He'd been a late-in-life only child, and there was no one else for his mother to lean on.

Sloane's street was quiet. Bucolic. Lined with trees and upscale craftsman bungalows vying to be the most authentically restored. It was well after midnight, and only sporadic imitation gas porch lights cast any glow into the dark shadows wreathing the street.

Huh. He wouldn't have pegged her for the type to live in a cozy neighborhood like this. What was up with that?

He pulled his truck into Sloane's driveway and was just reaching for the door handle when he spied something slipping around the back corner of her house.

Whatever it was looked too big for a dog or a coyote. Frowning, he climbed out of his truck and crunched up the gravel drive. He moved cautiously toward the bushes, giving a wild animal plenty of time to get away. No sense startling a bear or cougar. He turned on the flashlight function of his smartphone and shone it at the holly bush. No eyes glowed back at him. But jumbled shoe prints leaped into view in the snow. What the—?

He raced around the corner of the house, following the boot prints through the ankle-deep snow in Sloane's backyard and into the green belt behind her house. The prints led down a hill to an asphalt bike path that the snow had melted off of in the past few days. The asphalt was dry and gray and gave no clue as to which direction the person had gone. He listened carefully and heard no running footsteps.

His money was on the guy having had a bicycle parked back here. Jerk was long gone by now.

An intruder, maybe? Burglar? Peeping Tom? Or maybe he was thinking too much like a cop. It could've just been some neighborhood kid sneaking home through her yard.

Except it was too cold and too late on a school night for kids to be out fooling around. In full detective mode, he snapped photos of the footprints and called in the incident, putting it into the official police record. It was going to cause some extra paperwork for him, but whatever. Sloane might be in danger.

Before he unlocked her front door, he inspected the lock and jamb for signs of any attempt at forced entry. Nope, no scratches. Although that was a pitiful excuse for a lock. Just the original brass knob's lock protected her house. She needed a decent dead bolt at a minimum. Even an amateur thief could pick the existing lock in a matter of seconds.

Frowning, he opened the door and stepped in.

The living room was thin on furniture with only some bean bag chairs, a big recliner and a flat screen TV hanging on the wall.

The place had clearly undergone one of those open concept remodels recently that knocked out most of the walls. The living room flowed into a dining room taken up with toddler toys and no furniture and on back into a gourmet kitchen.

He headed down the hallway, and the first room he came upon was Chloe's, a princess paradise. A low bed was tucked inside a fairy castle, and a night-light cast firework patterns on the ceiling. He backed out of the room, feeling oversize and alien surrounded by so much…sparkle.

A hallway bathroom was unremarkable and he left that quickly. A utility closet held a furnace, and the door at the end of the hall revealed a bedroom much more his speed. Four-poster bed. No-frills navy comforter. A handmade-looking oak dresser and chest of drawers were crowded with framed pictures of Chloe, but other than those, the room was devoid of decoration—or any personality.

Odd. Was Sloane still unpacking, or was she that shut down emotionally?

He opened the first of two interior doors in Sloane's bedroom and found an elegant, but sterile, bathroom. It was pretty but didn't feel lived in.

Where was the real Sloane Colton hiding in this house? He hadn't found her yet.

The second door revealed a spacious walk-in closet the size of a small bedroom. A riot of color and texture assaulted his eyes as he turned on the light. Ahh. Here she was. The fiery Sloane he remembered so clearly.

He looked for something to put her clothes in and spied a duffel bag stuffed on a high shelf. He reached up, needing his full six-foot height to grab it. He turned his head to the side as he reached for the back of the shelf and happened to glance out into her bedroom. Which was probably why he spotted the tiny hole in the wall, hidden high in a shadowed corner of the room, tucked beneath the beautiful, dark oak crown molding.

Maybe if he hadn't already been suspicious of an intruder, he would've ignored the hole. But as it was, he took the duffel and moved over to the chest of drawers underneath the hole, and then took a quick peek. A tiny glass circle filled the small opening.

Alarm exploded in his gut and fury threatened to overcome reason.

For all the world, that looked like a surveillance camera.

Stop. Breathe. Think. It wasn't necessarily what it looked like.

Maybe Sloane had some sort of high-tech security system installed in her house.

Or was that camera something more sinister?

Surely, he was being paranoid. After all, he was bored to death being a police detective in a quiet little town where the occasional bicycle theft was about as exciting as police work got.

Until that murder last month out at the Crooked C ranch, of course. A high-end call girl who'd been seen up at the resort had been killed by a client. Initially, there were two possible suspects—Wyatt Colton as well as European millionaire George Stratton, who'd brought the girl in from Vegas. But upon further investigation, the sheriff's department figured out that a disturbed man who'd later killed himself had done the deed.

Liam forced himself not to look up at the camera lens as he randomly opened drawers in search of clothes for Sloane. His mind raced as he found socks, T-shirts and sweaters.

Why would anybody covertly surveil a young mother in Roaring Springs? Who had Sloane made an enemy of? A criminal she'd been involved with in her work? The ex-husband? Either way, a random stranger going to all the trouble to set up surveillance on her was not likely.

He retreated to the closet, where he spied jeans and sweatshirts folded on shelves and grabbed one of each.

He moved to the shoe rack and was bemused to discover that it rotated. How many pairs of shoes did one woman need, anyway?

He grabbed a pair of gym shoes made of a knit fabric that looked comfortable and headed for her bathroom. There had better not be a camera in there, or there would be hell to pay. He took a surreptitious look at each of the corners and spied nothing but paint. Then he did a thorough search of the walls as well to assure himself there were no hidden surveillance devices in the vicinity.

Not a sicko Peeping Tom, then. Which left something—or someone—more sinister behind that camera in her bedroom. He swore under his breath and grabbed a toothbrush and tube of toothpaste out of the cup by her sink.

Taking a moment to look at the duffel bag, he forced himself to think about what he'd forgotten to pack for her.

Goop. Fox always used to complain that Sloane was a world-class goop collector and hogged the bathroom they'd shared to smear it all over herself.

Liam warily eyed the neat rows of bottles and tubes on the counter.

Did Sloane even wear makeup? He honestly didn't remember. He'd been so shocked by the girl he'd had a giant crush on all through high school slamming into him out of the blue at the hospital that he hadn't registered any of the details he usually would as an observant detective.

What was he missing?

Of course. Underwear.

His gut jumped a little at the idea of handling Sloane Colton's unmentionables. Which was absurd. He was a decent-looking man in his thirties and had been around plenty of lingerie, and the women in it. But his very first fantasies of a skimpily clad female, all the way back in junior high, had involved Sloane Colton. He'd never admitted it to Fox and had pretended to have a crush on another girl. But it had been Sloane he'd dreamed of and woke up in hot sweats over.

He went to the dresser in her bedroom and opened a long, shallow drawer.

He inhaled sharply as a spill of brightly colored lace assaulted his eyes. Prim and proper Sloane Colton wore this sexy stuff? Wow. Uh, good to know. Of course, he was never going to look at her again without imagining which jewel-toned ensemble of silk and lace she had on under her clothes.

Swearing under his breath, he grabbed the first pair of skimpy bikinis and bra that matched—a scarlet ensemble with pert little bows strategically placed. Dammit, that was *not* sweat breaking out on his forehead.

He left the bedroom light on and headed back to the living area. Under the guise of poking around in the toy box for a stuffed animal to take to Chloe, he inspected the walls.

There. Over the front door. Tucked high in the corner under the crown molding. Another tiny, circular hole. From that vantage point, a surveillance camera would have a view of the entire living-dining-kitchen area.

Sonofa—

He ducked into Chloe's bedroom and grabbed the well-worn stuffed elephant off her bed. A telltale circular shadow lurked in the far corner of Chloe's bedroom as well. Now, why would a bad guy watch a toddler? The ex-husband climbed to the top of Liam's suspect list for being the creepo stalker.

He forced himself to keep his rampant cop suspicions in check. After all, he still wasn't positive Sloane was being watched nefariously. She could have hired a security company to monitor her, or perhaps there was some other legitimate reason for the cameras being there. But his gut was dead certain the explanation wasn't so innocent. Which was weird. He was usually the soul of logic, relying completely on facts and careful analysis. Intuitions were for amateurs. Real detectives used their minds to uncover the truth.

Assuming Sloane herself wasn't the source of the cameras, she faced a choice. Rip the cameras out of her walls and have a security firm sweep her house for any more surveillance devices. Or, she could let the cameras ride, pretend she didn't know they existed, and let him investigate who was behind the surveillance without tipping off the perpetrator.

Fury bubbled up in his gut. When he caught whoever was behind the surveillance, he was going to—

Slow down, there, buddy. He was going to hand the

bastard over to the district attorney with an ironclad file of evidence so the perpetrator got put away for a good long time. He was a law enforcement professional and didn't indulge in gratuitous violence, no matter how angry he might be.

Still. This case *was* personal. Sloane was his best friend's little sister. They'd grown up together, for crying out loud.

On his way out, Liam left on lights and turned on the TV. He doubted whoever had been lurking behind her house would come back tonight, but on the off chance that the guy was a burglar, Liam might as well make the house look occupied.

He didn't recall seeing Sloane carry a coat in the hospital, so he stopped at the cast iron coat tree just inside the front door. He grabbed a neon-pink ski jacket, pink mittens and a matching hat with a jaunty pompom. There. That should keep her warm.

He might not have noticed whether she had makeup on or not, but he'd noticed that she'd been wearing flannel pajamas without much on underneath when she'd banged into him at the hospital. Her body had been soft in all the right places with more curves than he remembered from back in the day, although she was still not much bigger than a whisper.

Of course, he'd put on about forty pounds of muscle when he took up lacrosse in college. It was the universe's karmic joke that he finally became a buff athlete type *after* having to go all the way through high school as a beanpole.

He took a hard look up and down the street as he pulled out of the driveway but didn't spot any movement. He made a mental note to ask police cruisers to roll past her house for the next few weeks.

When he got back to the hospital, he headed for the nurses' station outside Chloe's room to drop off the duffel. As he turned to leave, Sloane stepped out into the hallway.

"What are you doing awake?" he asked, startled.

"You obviously aren't a parent, or you wouldn't have to ask. I'm too worried about Chloe to sleep."

A nurse piped up from behind him, "That and we're going in and out of Chloe's room every ten minutes to check her temperature, and naturally mommy wants to know how it's doing every time we take it."

"How *is* it doing?" Liam echoed.

Sloane glanced over her shoulder toward her daughter. "High but steady at 104 degrees. They've wrapped her head in refrigerated blankets to cool her down."

That didn't sound good. But he wasn't about to voice the concern aloud. Sloane already had dark shadows under her eyes and looked on the verge of losing control. As much as he wanted to ask about the cameras in her house, that could wait until tomorrow.

"You should sleep," he suggested.

"Not happening."

"Maybe you should take a walk, then," the nurse suggested. "Movement helps burn stress. Your boyfriend brought you clothes, too."

Liam opened his mouth to correct her, but Sloane beat him to it. "I'm single. He's—"

He glanced at her, one eyebrow cocked with interest to see just how she classified him.

"—an old family friend."

He could live with that. Although handfuls of sexy red lace and her chest mashed against his flashed through his head.

Get a grip, man. She's your best friend's little sister. How much more cliché could that be? The friend code was clear on the subject: sisters were strictly off-limits. Of course, Liam didn't have any siblings, so he'd had nothing to worry about over the years. But Fox had always been fiercely protective of his sister. It probably hadn't helped matters that Fox and Sloane had lost their parents in a car accident when they were little kids. Had their aunt, Mara Colton, and her husband, Russ, not taken them in, they'd have been alone in the world.

"Would you like to finish our hospital tour from earlier?" he offered.

Sloane frowned. "It's 2:00 a.m. Surely you'd rather be home in bed."

Yeah. With her—

Strike that. Old. Family. Friend. He added for good measure, *Worried mom with sick kid.*

"I'm not tired. Do you want to get dressed or go for a walk like that?"

She glanced down at her flannel pajamas. "What? Don't you like my granny jammies?"

He grinned. "My grandmother had *much* less frumpy taste than that."

Sloane stuck her tongue out at him briefly and then whirled and disappeared into Chloe's room. She still moved like a gazelle, quick and graceful. He watched her through the window until she ducked into the bathroom and closed the door.

He was *not* thinking about that sassy red underwear. Nope. It would not look smoking hot against her pale skin and dark brown hair. Nothing to imagine there. *Move along, you old horndog.*

He turned to the nurse. "How sick is Sloane's daughter?"

"I'm not authorized to release any information to a non-family member—"

"I'm asking as a police officer. I have some news to share with the mother that may be upsetting. If the child is gravely ill, I can hold off telling it for a while."

The nurse met his gaze candidly and said grimly, "Hold off."

His stomach dropped with a sickening thud.

"How bad is it?" he murmured low.

"Children's Hospital in Denver has treated a dozen kids with this virus. Two of them didn't make it."

His jaw sagged. "As in they died?"

The nurse nodded soberly.

He whirled and stared through the window at the toddler curled up in the stainless steel crib. He hadn't been in touch with Sloane since high school, but it didn't take more than two seconds of being in the same room with her to see that she adored her daughter. If anything happened to Chloe, it would kill Sloane.

The nurse added, "It gets worse before it gets better. And she's a very young child. This little girl's got a fight ahead of her. Several dozen children have died around the country from it."

Sweet baby Jesus.

Sloane stepped out into the hallway, fully dressed, and smiled hopefully at him. Undoubtedly she didn't know how bad Chloe's illness was, or she wouldn't be able to smile at all. His belly felt like glass that had been hit by a stone and shattered into a million razor-sharp shards.

It was hard as hell to do, but he forced a fake smile for Sloane's sake and held out his forearm gallantly. "Shall we take a stroll along the promenade, madam?"

"You really don't have to do this, Liam."

"I'm working the night shift tonight."

"Then shouldn't you be out solving crimes?"

He was. He wanted to know why someone was watching her and had been lurking around her house. Were the two related?

"Tell me about where you live here in town," he said casually.

"You saw it. Pretty street. Quiet. Lots of young families. Chloe will have plenty of kids her age to play with."

"Fox was disappointed when you left the Crooked C. He liked having you and Chloe out there."

She shrugged. "It was sweet of the gang out there to let us crash with them while I got my bearings and made some decisions. But Fox is a bachelor. He didn't need Chloe and me hanging around getting in the way."

"Why did you choose not to live with your parents? Goodness knows, they've got plenty of room in that house of theirs."

"You mean the mausoleum?"

"It's not that bad."

"You didn't live there," she retorted.

"I spent a lot of time there with Fox."

"Then you know that Russ and Mara were never at home." She rolled her eyes. "I swear they had an ongoing contest going to see who could be more of a workaholic."

"What about you? Did you grow up into a workaholic like them? You were one in high school, as I recall."

"I just wanted to get into a good college so I could get away and be on my own."

"Did you escape whatever you were running from?" he asked quietly.

She glanced up at him, her big hazel eyes dark and troubled. "You must be a heck of an interrogator, Liam. You cut right to the heart of the matter. You're like a laser."

"That's me. Laser Man," he quipped. "I cut away the lies and obfuscations to expose the naked truth. It's my superpower. What's yours?"

"These days, it's making grilled cheese sandwiches and knowing the lyrics to every single princess musical ever made."

"What about before Chloe came along?"

"There was life before Chloe?" she asked wryly.

He laughed. "I don't know. You tell me."

"Don't get me wrong. She's the light of my life. I didn't know it was possible to love anyone the way I love her."

"That's obvious at a single glance. The way you look at her…" He searched for words. "It's magical."

Sloane shrugged. "I'm just a mom."

"You're a great mom."

Sloane snorted. "And yet, my baby is in a hospital room fighting some awful illness that I should have seen coming. I had to have missed something—"

"You can't control every situation every time. Sometimes life sneaks up on you."

She snorted like a prizefighter who'd just been told she couldn't use her fists in a fight.

He frowned and turned the corner into the cafeteria. "How were you supposed to know she would catch a nasty bug? Psychic powers? You're being too hard on yourself. Chloe got sick and you got her to medical care in a timely fashion. There was nothing else you could have done."

"Keep telling me that. Maybe I'll believe you someday."

He stopped and turned to face her. "I'm serious, Sloane. Cut yourself a break. Your little girl needs you to be calm and confident, not wracked by unnecessary guilt and distraction."

Sloane took a deep breath. Exhaled it slowly. "Thanks for the reminder."

"No problem. I just call it as I see it."

She glanced up at him shyly and smiled. And lit up the whole darned cafeteria. Her smile transformed her heart-shaped face from pretty to radiant. Her gorgeous hazel eyes filled with warmth and gratitude.

"There it is," he murmured. "The old Sloane Colton sparkle. Thought I'd lost you there for a while."

"I'm still plain old me. Just a little older and hopefully a little wiser."

He chuckled. "You were never plain. Do you have any idea how many guys Fox and I had to chase away from you?"

Her voice took on a stern tone. "No. I don't. Do enlighten me."

He grinned. "I'll never tell. Just trust me...none of them were worthy of you."

She planted her hands on her hips in what looked like indignation. "I thought I was a completely unattractive dork in high school because no guy would even look at me, let alone talk to me, or heaven forbid, ask me out. And you're telling me that was your and Fox's doing?"

"Guilty as charged."

"I'll kill him. Next time I see him, I'm doing him in."

Liam grinned. "Cut him a little slack. He loves you a lot. Thinks you walk on water."

"That, I definitely don't do."

Sadness overtook her entire demeanor. What had happened to leave so much pain in her soul? Just how big a jerk had the ex-husband been?

"Tell me about how you acquired wisdom en route to becoming older and wiser," Liam asked, resuming their walk down a hallway lined on one side with windows that looked out on a garden. Right now, it was bare beds of dirt covered in patches of snow. Sloane shivered a little, probably from the cold radiating off the windows.

An urge to put his arm around her shoulders, to draw her close to his side, nearly overcame him. Nope, nope, nope. Not going there with her.

"I married a charming man who turned out to be a bastard."

"How so?"

"Let's just say he was honesty-challenged."

"Example?"

She thought for a second. "Well, he said he liked kids. Wanted a family. Turned out he liked the idea of a family Christmas card in matching bad sweaters but not much more."

"That sucks."

"Oh, that's not the worst of it. Turns out he can't resist any hot female who looks at him twice, and he's a compulsive gambler. Real winner I picked, huh?"

Liam shrugged. "I'm sure he had a few redeeming qualities that drew you to him."

"You're far too optimistic about mankind in general."

It was his turn to snort. "I'm a cop. I see all the worst mankind has to offer. In fact, I find that most people harbor at least one good, ugly secret about themselves."

"Oh, yeah?" Slone asked. "What's yours?"

"I'm actually a superhero, but I can't reveal my true identity to anyone. I keep my cape hidden under my street clothes."

"Oh, that's right. You're Laser Man. I forgot."

"That's me, all right."

Sloane winced a little. "Where were you when I started dating Ivan? I was completely fooled by him."

"Sorry. I would've come to Denver and chased him off if Fox had let me know you were dating a jerk. Just like in high school."

"Is that why you tormented the boys who flirted with me?" she exclaimed. "Fox put you up to it? I'm seriously going to have to have a word with him—"

He interrupted, laughing. "I swear, we had your best interests at heart. We heard them talking in the locker room and knew they wouldn't treat you well."

"What gave you the right to be my personal dating police?"

She didn't sound angry, but he sensed danger in the lightly worded question. She wasn't a defense attorney for nothing. He answered carefully, "You were my best friend's little sister, and Fox had a bit of a temper back then. I was worried he would go too far protecting you and get himself into trouble."

"Ahh. So you didn't care about me. It was all about looking out for Fox. Got it."

That wasn't what he'd meant at all, but he wasn't sure he ought to correct the misunderstanding. This Sloane was pricklier and quicker to jump on statements he made than the Sloane of old.

"Do you like being a lawyer?" he asked her, hoping to change the subject.

"I do."

He could see how it fit her direct personality. "Are you going to hang out a shingle here in Roaring Springs?"

"I've actually just started up a nonprofit foundation with some of the proceeds of my divorce. I'm reviewing cases for prisoners who think they were wrongly convicted." She warmed to her topic. "I can work from home and do some good while I'm at it."

Her face glowed with excitement as she described having found a big mistake in a case she'd just reviewed. A wrongly convicted woman was due to be released from prison in a few days because of her discovery.

Sloane always had been softhearted. Loved to help people. Looked out for the downtrodden.

"And who looks out for you?" he mused aloud.

"I beg your pardon?"

Startled, he realized he'd voiced the thought aloud. "Nothing. Just random thoughts." Badly in need of a distraction, he commented, "Mara must love having her first grandchild back in Roaring Springs."

Sloane shrugged. "I don't know. I mean, sure, Mara loves Chloe, but she's not exactly the most maternal person I've ever met."

"True." Not like his mother, who was warm and nurturing. Fox always had preferred to hang out at the modest Kastor bungalow rather than at his own family's luxurious estate. As for him, he'd liked the Colton mansion for its elegance and proximity to the ski slopes. And to Sloane.

"So. Does a defense attorney make enemies in the course of her job?" Liam risked asking.

Sloane frowned. "That's a strange question."

He shrugged. "I figure your clients would like you because you're fighting for them."

"They do, unless they're guilty and want me to pull a miracle out of my hat and get them off. As a defense attorney, it was my job to give them the best possible legal defense, not hoodwink juries and pull television tricks to magically sway jurors to release a guilty person who's been properly tried."

He nodded ruefully. "Television gives people a distorted view of police work, too. They think I can solve any crime in forty-eight minutes between commercial breaks."

"Is there much crime in Roaring Springs these days?" she asked curiously.

"Not nearly enough."

"I beg your pardon?"

He glanced down at her. "Don't get me wrong. Low crime is great for the residents. But as a detective, it can be a bit...boring."

"What about that grisly murder a few weeks ago? I am so glad that Wyatt's name was cleared."

He nodded. "County sheriff's office investigated it. Did a good job, too."

"Poor baby," she teased him. "You didn't get to take part in any of that, did you? I can't say as I wish for another murder to keep you occupied."

Chapter 3

Dawn broke through the windows of the hospital room, and Sloane gave up trying to sleep. In the past hour, Chloe's fever had inched down slightly, but Little Bug was starting to vomit. Sloane sat by the crib with the side lowered, and Chloe curled around Sloane's hand pitifully, clinging to it tightly.

Sloane's heart broke to see her daughter suffering like this. Thankfully, the doctor came in a little before 8:00 a.m. to check on Chloe.

"She's doing worse," Sloane murmured to him.

"Actually, vomiting is the next stage of the infection, so she's progressing through the illness," the doctor replied.

"Does that mean she's getting better?" Sloane asked hopefully.

"If this progresses like it has in the other children,

the last stage will involve chest congestion, and that will actually be the most...delicate...time."

Sloane frowned. *Delicate* wasn't the word he'd been on the verge of saying. Ten to one he'd been about to say *critical*. "There has to be something more we can do for her, doctor."

"We're monitoring her closely. We're pumping fluids, nutrition and massive antibiotics into her to take the load off her immune system. All we can do in the case of a virus like this is provide palliative support, meaning we can only treat the symptoms."

"Aren't there any specific antiviral drugs you can give her?"

"Not that have had any efficacy on this particular strain of virus," he answered.

"Is this some sort of flu?"

"Although it looks like a flu, Chloe tested negative for influenza. It's something else with similar symptoms. Just be patient and let this run its course, Mrs. Durant."

"Colton. I'm not keeping my ex-husband's name."

"Sorry. A Colton, huh?"

She winced as the doctor looked at her speculatively and then beat a quick exit. An orderly brought her a tray of breakfast, and she nibbled on a piece of toast without any appetite. She downed the glass of orange juice but ignored the oatmeal. A nurse had no sooner pushed out the breakfast tray than Mara Colton swept into Chloe's room.

Rats. The doctor had betrayed her and called the matriarch of the Colton clan.

"Sloane, dear, why didn't you call me last night? We

could have had a specialist down from Denver by now to look at our sweet girl. How is she?"

Chloe, who'd recently drifted off to sleep after throwing up, stirred and whimpered. Sloane waved her mother out of the room and leaned over Chloe quickly, kissing her hot forehead, and murmuring against her daughter's skin how much she loved her and to dream about angels.

Chloe settled, and her eyes drifted closed once more. Gently, Sloane disengaged her hand from the child's grasp, placing Snuffles, Chloe's beloved plush elephant, into her daughter's arms. God. She looked so tiny and vulnerable curled up in the middle of all those wires and tubes.

Sloane hurried from the room, fighting back the tears. She had to be strong for her baby. She was a tough, independent woman. She could do this.

"How are you holding up, dear?"

Mara might not be the most maternal person in the world, but even this brief show of concern was enough to strain Sloane's steely self-control. She would *not* break down, darn it!

She took a deep breath. Lawyers never cried in court. This was just like that. She took note of the nurses and orderlies nearby, a doctor walking down the hall, a visitor looking for a room number. She was in public. She was a professional.

Her years of courtroom experience kicked in, and her emotions steadied. Receded.

Better.

She heard her own voice answer, "I'm fine, thanks, Mother. Worried, of course. But Chloe's getting excellent care. They're monitoring her closely and have seen this virus before. They know what to expect."

Liar, liar. Pants on fire. She was a wreck and to say otherwise was blatantly untrue.

"Have you eaten, dear?"

"I just had some breakfast," she replied.

"Is there anything I can do for you?"

Sloane stepped forward on impulse and gave her mother a hug. Mara stiffened in surprise for a moment, then returned the hug briefly before backing away and straightening her suit.

"I never knew being a mother was so scary. How did you survive raising five of your own kids plus Fox and me?"

"I raised seven of my own kids. You and Fox are as much mine as any of the others. And it was a trial at times."

"Weren't you scared that something awful would happen to one of us?"

Mara smiled gently, real warmth and understanding glimmering in her blue eyes. "Always. Terror is the constant state of being a mother."

"I'm so afraid I'll mess it up and that Chloe will pay the price."

"Oh, darling. No parent is perfect. You'll do your best, and you'll make mistakes. But at the end of the day, Chloe will know how very much you love her, and she'll forgive you." She sighed. "God knows, I've made my fair share of mistakes."

"Really?" Slone would've loved to hear more about what mistakes Mara thought she'd made, but Chloe let out a wail just then, and Sloane whirled and raced back to her daughter's side.

"Mommy's right here, sweetie. I would never leave you. I love you, Little Bug..."

Liam strode into the Roaring Springs Police Department first thing in the morning. The institutional metal cubicle dividers and plastic chairs were disguised with wood paneling and dark green trim paint. The place tried to be, but didn't quite achieve, a national park office. At the end of the day, it was a cold, hard police department at its core.

When he'd first gotten his badge, he'd reveled in the small town feel of this place. But recently, he'd hankered for something a little...more interesting...in his career.

He might as well do some digging into the mystery of those cameras in Sloane's house. It wasn't as if he'd gotten a wink of sleep last night, what with worrying about Sloane and her daughter, anyway.

He started by calling every security company in Roaring Springs and the surrounding towns. Not one of them had installed a security system at the address in question. He did luck out, though, when he discovered that one of the places had installed window locks at that address a few months back as part of a renovation. That company had the name of the contractor who'd remodeled the house. A quick phone call to that gentleman confirmed that no security system had been in place at Sloane's house at the time she purchased it and moved in.

Interesting.

Liam picked up his phone and placed one more call, this time to the FBI field office in Denver.

"This is Special Agent Roberts. How can I help you?"

"Detective Liam Kastor, here. Roaring Springs PD. I need some advice."

"Does this have to do with that murder at the Colton ranch? I wasn't the agent consulted on that case, but I can pass you to—"

"That's not what I'm calling about. I have a local citizen, a single mother, who appears to have someone doing high-tech surveillance in her house."

"Any idea why?"

"None. She used to be a defense attorney in Denver, but she's been down here for a little while doing the stay-at-home mom thing with her toddler. There's an ex-husband, but the divorce and settlement are finalized."

"Have you examined the cameras?" Roberts asked quickly.

"No. I haven't acknowledged that I spotted them, and the homeowner didn't stay in her house last night. Her child is sick, and they stayed at the hospital."

"Sorry to hear that, sir. Well, we've got a tech specialist I can hook you up with. He could take a look at what's installed. But you'll need a warrant to get into the house to look at the surveillance equipment."

"I have permission to enter the premises."

"That's handy. Let me give you our tech guy's number…"

In short order, Liam spoke with a man named Rahm Zogby, who agreed to drive down to Roaring Springs and take a look at what was going on in Sloane's house. But he wouldn't arrive until after lunch, so Liam had some time to kill.

An internet search of Ivan Durant proved educational. The guy was the only son of a wealthy couple and had grown up with the proverbial silver spoon in his mouth. Fancy private schools, fancier private university and law school, hired by a top law firm, fast-tracked to partner. No doubt, daddy bringing his considerable legal business to the firm hadn't hurt Ivan's career.

The guy was handsome in a squared-jawed, Nordic way. But Liam found his eyes a little too cold, the set of his shoulders a little too arrogant, the pout of his mouth a little too spoiled.

Durant had better not cause Sloane any more pain, or ol' Ivan and he were going to have a problem.

Liam used police sources to dig into Ivan's financials and discovered the guy was teetering on the edge of bankruptcy. The gambling Sloane had mentioned must be a serious problem. That, or the dude's lavish lifestyle was draining his finances. Or maybe both.

Liam did stumble across a magazine interview where Ivan railed against prenups. Durant hinted that paying his off had wiped him out financially.

Good for Sloane. At least she'd walked away from the jerk with financial security. However, it also made for a pretty decent revenge motive.

Still. She was the mother of the man's child. Surely Ivan wouldn't mess with Sloane if it meant hurting his own daughter. Or was the guy that big an ass?

"Hey, Liam!"

He glanced up at his boss, Police Chief Tegan Howard. "Yes, ma'am?" She hated being ma'amed by anyone other than very contrite teenagers, who'd *better* ma'am her or get a lecture on manners.

She rolled her eyes. "You busy?"

"Not especially."

"Any chance you could pick up that prisoner you dropped off at the hospital last night and bring him back here? He's got an arraignment this afternoon, assuming he can stand and speak coherently."

"I'm on it." Perfect. He could stop by and check in on Sloane and Chloe while he was there. Liam grabbed his coat and headed for the hospital.

The elevator door opened to the third floor of the hospital, and Liam stared at a block party in progress. Or at least, that was what it looked like. The hallway was crowded with people talking and milling around. He recognized Russ Colton with a start, then Wyatt and his fiancée, and then he spied Fox.

Aww, hell. The Colton clan had found out Chloe was here and had converged on Sloane. He waded through the crowd to his best friend. "Hey, Fox. How's Chloe doing?"

"No idea. Can't get a straight answer out of anyone around this place. What are you doing here?"

"I came to pick up a prisoner. Is Sloane around? I'd like to say hi. Give her my best."

"Yeah. She's in with Chloe. Chased everyone out of her daughter's room a few minutes ago so the kid can rest."

"With this mob out here? A dead man couldn't rest."

Fox grimaced at his family. "Yeah, you're right. Help me get rid of them?"

"Sure."

Liam strolled over to Mara Colton, whom he'd long ago identified as the real power in the family, while Fox headed for their father, Russ. "Howdy, Mrs. C. I'm sorry to hear your granddaughter is sick."

"Why, thank you, Liam. That's kind of you."

"I don't know much about these things, but do you

think all this commotion is good for Chloe? Maybe a little more...quiet...might help her rest and recover?"

Mara glanced around in fond exasperation at the crowd. "I do believe you're right. I'll go have a word with my husband."

Mission accomplished. Between the two of them, Russ and Mara would clear the place fast. Sure enough, it took about three minutes flat for the ward to go silent and deserted.

Ahh. Better.

Liam poked his head inside Chloe's room. The little girl was fiddling with the elephant he'd brought her last night, and a cartoon was playing on her television, but she looked listless.

"I hope you don't mind that I chased your family off," he murmured.

"You're why they left? Thank you from the bottom of my heart," Sloane said sincerely. She stepped away from Chloe's bed to come over to him.

"How's she doing?"

"Fever's down, but she's been throwing up, and she's starting to cough. Doc says the respiratory infection is the rough part of this virus. So we're not out of the woods yet."

"She's getting constant care and the best support available. She'll be fine," he murmured.

"From your mouth to God's ear."

"How are you holding up?" he asked softly.

"Fine."

"No. Seriously. How are you doing?"

She looked up at him candidly, and for an instant, naked fear shone in her hazel eyes.

"That's what I thought," he muttered as he gathered her into his arms for a hug.

She shuddered against him, a long, full-body shiver of terror. "I—"

Her phone buzzed, interrupting whatever she was about to say.

Frowning, she stepped out of his arms and pulled out the device. She swore quietly and moved out into the hallway, away from Chloe.

Liam followed her. "What's the matter?"

"It's Ivan. I don't want to talk to him, but I suppose I'll have to tell him Chloe is sick."

"Why? You don't owe him anything. He doesn't have custody of her."

Sloane stared up at him as the call went to voicemail. "You sound like you don't like him."

"I don't."

"But you've never met him."

"He hurt you."

Sloane's eyes widened. She opened her mouth to speak, but her phone started to ring again. "Crud. It's Ivan. He'll keep calling until I answer. Can I ask a favor of you…as a police officer?"

Startled, Liam replied, "Of course."

"Listen to the call. So you can—" her breath hitched and then she continued grimly "—so you can testify to what you heard in court, if it comes to that."

Alarmed, he took Sloane's arm and steered her into the empty hospital room next door. He pushed the door shut. "Why do you need a witness for the call? Is he threatening you?"

"Not exactly."

"What exactly?" he asked sharply. The hackles on

the back of his neck were standing up, and he realized with a bit of a start that his right hand was balled into a fist. He forcibly relaxed the fingers and focused all of his considerable observational skills on Sloane. Elevated breathing. Faint sheen of perspiration on her skin. Gaze darting around. She was *scared*.

"You'd better damned well believe I want to hear this phone call," he growled.

The phone rang for a third time, and she took a deep breath. He watched, eyes narrowed, as she put the phone on speaker and accepted the call.

"Hello, Ivan."

"Why the hell are you avoiding me?" a male voice snarled.

"I'm busy. And I don't have to answer your calls. We're not married anymore. You can speak to my lawyer if you have something to say to me. You have her phone number."

Ivan swore viciously at that suggestion, and Liam's eyebrows climbed. Temper much?

Then Ivan spat out, "I'm not kidding, Sloane. I'll expose what you did. I want Chloe back. I will take her from you."

"You don't want Chloe. You just want to punish me."

More swearing.

"Look, Ivan. Chloe's sick. She's in the hospital with a bad viral infection. If you want to come see her, I won't stop you."

"I'm busy. And besides, I don't want to catch some godawful disease."

"She's your daughter."

"I said I'm busy."

"Then get to your point. Or were you just calling to

threaten me?" Sloane asked coolly. Liam had to give her credit. She was an icicle under pressure.

"My parents wanted me to remind you that they've got a scheduled visit with Chloe next week. You have to bring her to Denver."

"I haven't forgotten. But you did just hear me say she's in the hospital, right? I don't know if she'll be well enough to go—"

Ivan cut her off. "I don't care if you have to scrape her out of her sickbed and pour her into an ambulance to get her here. I'll sue for breach of contract and overturn the custody agreement if you don't comply with the court order down to the last letter."

"She's a baby. She's very sick."

"Tough shit."

"Ivan. She's your flesh and blood. Show a little compassion—"

Ivan cut her off with another blistering round of swearing that made a muscle tick in Liam's jaw.

Then Durant snarled, "I'll drag you back into court so fast it'll make your head spin. And I'll get that effing custody order amended. I'm going to end up with Chloe if it's the last thing I do—"

Sloane cut him off, her voice hard enough to cut through glass. "I've got a police officer listening to this phone call, Ivan, so before you devolve into more threats against me, consider yourself notified that you are being monitored."

"That's a load of crap. You had no idea I was going to call you. No way did you have time to arrange for a cop to listen in. You can take your high-and-mighty attitude and choke on it, wifey dearest." His tone turned even more menacing "You're going to regret ever dragging our personal life into court. I'll make you beg for mercy before I'm done with you. You'll never see your daughter again. I ruin your life. I'll ruin you—"

Sloane had gone pale, and the hand holding her cell phone was trembling violently.

Liam lifted the phone out of her hand and disconnected the call. He was sorely tempted to give Ivan Durant a piece of his mind, but pulling a stunt like that would force him off the investigation of what was going on with Sloane's house.

Besides, she was shaken enough without him heaping any more drama on top of what Ivan had just piled onto her.

The phone rang again. Liam glanced at the caller ID and blocked the number.

"You can't block him!" Sloane exclaimed. "What if there's an emergency and—"

Liam cut her off with quietly intensity. "And what? You can always unblock him and call him, But are you really going to turn to that jerk for help with anything in your life? He didn't show even a hint of concern when you told him his own child was in the hospital. Do you really want a man like that anywhere near your daughter?"

"No. Of course not. But what if he actually does need to talk to me about something?"

"You have a lawyer. He can call him or her."

Sloane looked up at him, lost. She appeared so young and vulnerable and scared out of her mind in that moment. Liam swore silently at himself. As attracted as he was to this woman, he had no business even considering a romantic entanglement with her. She was off balance, frightened and still trying to get on her feet after what had obviously been a hideous divorce. She was in no condition to get into a relationship with any man.

God knew he didn't want to be the rebound guy. It would only end up hurting them both in the end.

"You should seriously consider installing an app on your phone that will record phone calls. If he threatens you again, it would help us to have a recording of it for evidence purposes."

"Good idea," Sloane replied woodenly.

He pressed her phone back into her hand. "You have tons of family. Friends all around you. Turn to us. You don't need Ivan Durant for anything. We've all got your back."

Sloane drew one wobbly breath. Let it out slowly. Then her spine stiffened, her chin came up and she dashed at the tears glistening on her cheeks.

Admiration unfurled in Liam's gut. What kind of strength did it take for Sloane to gather her tattered courage around herself like that, to set aside the attack Ivan had just hurled at her, and to march back to her daughter's sickbed with a brave smile on her lips? She was a hell of a woman. A warrior mom.

And the last thing she needed in her life right now was a man like him to complicate matters.

Chapter 4

Liam got rid of her family in the nick of time because over the next hour, Chloe went from bad to worse. Coughs wracked her tiny body, and each wheezing breath the little girl drew terrified Sloane a little bit more.

A new doctor came in at lunchtime and introduced herself as a pulmonologist, a lung and breathing specialist. The woman commenced listening to Chloe's chest through a stethoscope. The doctor frowned and jerked her head toward the hallway door.

Sloane's brain froze. It was bad news. A little voice somewhere in the back of her skull screamed, *nononono*.

"Ms. Colton, you daughter is very sick. We're going to do everything we can for her. We'll x-ray her chest periodically to check for fluid in her lungs, and I'm going to start support for her breathing. She'll still be breathing on her own. I just want to get a little more oxygen into her."

Sloane managed to pull her wits together enough to ask, "How long will this phase of the virus last?"

"The next twenty-four hours should tell the tale. If we can dodge pneumonia, we should be home free after that."

"What can I do for her?"

"Keep her calm. Keep the oxygen tube under her nose. If she won't tolerate it on her face, we'll have to sedate her. In fact, I may do that anyway—"

"Please hold off. I'd rather avoid sedation if we can. I'll keep her breathing the oxygen. I won't take my eyes off of her."

The doctor nodded and moved over to the nurses' station to write up the order for oxygen supplementation. Then she looked up at Sloane. "I'll check on Chloe again in a few hours. The nurses will call me if there are any significant changes between now and then."

Sloane nodded. But then she caught the grim looks that passed between the doctor and the head nurse. Crap, crap, crap.

If there was one feeling in the world she couldn't stand above all others, it was feeling helpless. And right now, there wasn't a blessed thing she could do to help her baby. This was entirely out of her hands. Which completely panicked her.

Liam had agreed to meet the FBI's tech guy at the police department and was glad he did. He would have arrested Rahm Zogby on sight if he'd seen the guy lurking around Sloane's place. The FBI technician had a chest-length beard and a ragged bandana tied around his fore-head, holding back long, lanky hair. If the man bathed, it wasn't evident, and the van, marked "Manny's HVAC Service," looked nearly as disreputable as its driver.

"Liam Kastor?" Rahm asked as Liam climbed out of his truck.

"That's me. Agent Zogby?"

"Just Zog. Or Rahm. I'm not a badge flasher."

Liam wasn't sure if that meant the guy had an FBI badge and chose not to show it, or that the guy was a civilian. Zog drove the van while Liam rode in the torn vinyl passenger seat. Liam directed him across town to Sloane's house, and the FBI man parked out front.

"What's the plan...Zog?"

"You've got the keys and permission to go in, right? That's what Stefan Roberts told me."

"Correct."

"I'm gonna go in and pretend to fix the air conditioner and heater while you put on this monkey suit and help me." The guy held out a cheap brown jumpsuit that would fit over his street clothes. "Ideally, you'd have some work boots to wear, but we'll chance it. Just pull the jumpsuit down so it covers up your shoes as much as possible."

"Got it." Liam crawled in the back of the van, sat on the hard ribbed floor, and wrestled on the uniform.

Zog eyed him critically. "Pull the baseball cap down lower. Good. Keep your face turned away from the cameras as much as you can without being obvious about it. And watch what you say. The cameras may have an audio pickup."

Liam nodded his understanding and yanked the cap down practically to the bridge of his nose.

"Here. Carry this." Zog thrust a grimy bucket full of tools at him. They climbed out and headed for the kitchen door at the back of the house.

Liam let them in, and Zog made a beeline for the thermostat on the wall in the dining room. He popped the cover off and fiddled with the electronics inside. "Gotta look at the base unit," he announced.

They piled upstairs to the slant-ceilinged office. At one end of the space was a short door that turned out to lead to a partially finished attic space.

"Perfect," Zog breathed.

Frowning, Liam watched the guy get down on his hands and knees and crawl for the corner over the front door. Flashes of light indicated that Zog was photographing something. When the guy backed up and headed for the other side of the open space, Liam estimated that Zog was on top of the camera in Chloe's room. More flashes of light.

"Hand me that zipped pouch in the bottom of the bucket," Zog muttered.

Liam passed it over and was startled when the technician went to work, quickly attaching wires to something in the corner.

"'Kay. Done," Zog announced.

Liam opened his mouth to ask what the guy had found, but Zog waved him to silence. They tromped downstairs. Zog replaced the thermostat cover while mumbling something about being glad it was just a fuse that needed replacing and chuckling over how they were gonna be able to charge for a full-service visit. Then they piled into the van and drove away from Sloane's bungalow.

"Well?" Liam demanded.

The stoner persona dropped in an instant, and Rahm spoke crisply. "State-of-the-art surveillance and transmission system. Someone's nearby monitoring the camera feed, or else there's a remote unit nearby where the data is being collected, forwarded to another location, and possibly recorded for later viewing. Either way, your stay-at-home mom has some serious hardware in her attic. Stuff's practically military grade."

"But why?" Liam blurted in frustration. "She's a *mom*."

"You sure about that? There's a good twenty grand in gear installed in that house. We're talking a top-drawer private security firm or the FBI. They're the only types who have access to that kind of tech besides the military."

Suddenly, Liam didn't know anything at all about Sloane. Who in the world would bring that kind of juice to spy on her? And *why*?

The van pulled to a stop beside his pickup truck back at the station.

"Here," Zog said, holding out a flash drive and a cigar-box-sized box with an antenna sticking out of it. "You'll need these."

"What are they?"

"Plug the antenna unit into an electrical outlet and plug that flash drive into your computer, and you'll see the exact same feed as the cameras. I cloned the whole system for you."

Liam sputtered. He didn't want to spy on Sloane! He only wanted to know who'd done it. "Is there any way we can track who's picking up the signal?"

"I planted a signal tracker at the house, but I'm gonna have to go back to the bench in my lab and catch an outbound batch burst of data before I can give you a location. Give me, say, twelve hours? I doubt the surveillance batches are going out any slower than that."

"Fair enough. Thanks for all your help, man."

Zog said soberly, "I hope you find the answers you're looking for."

So did he. It would kill him to have to take Sloane down if she was mixed up in something nefarious. And Chloe—that kid couldn't end up back in her father's hands. Could the Coltons be convinced to sue for custody—

Slow down, there, Tonto. Sloane isn't convicted of anything yet. Innocent until proven guilty, buddy.

Please God, let Sloane not be tangled up in something illegal.

Chapter 5

There was panic. And then there was *panic*. When the pulmonologist ordered Chloe moved to intensive care, Sloane learned the true meaning of the word. Her poor baby was barely conscious and hooked up to so many monitors and machines she barely looked human under all of them.

An ICU nurse introduced herself briskly and quickly walked Sloane through what all of the machines in the room did. The one that Sloane fixated on was the emergency call button. She was to hit that if Chloe quit breathing.

Oh. My. God.

The nurse finished with, "Is there a family member I can call for you? Someone should probably be with you. In case."

In case Chloe died.

Sloane's knees buckled out from under her at that point, but thankfully, a chair was behind her. "My brother," she whispered. "Fox Colton."

"Right. Have you got a phone number for him?"

Sloane couldn't remember her own name right now, let alone Fox's phone number. Numbly, she held out her phone to the woman. The nurse thumbed efficiently through her contact list and dialed the phone. Sloane listened to the call, numb.

"This is Joanne Carter down at the hospital. Your sister asked me to notify you that her daughter has been admitted to intensive care—

"Yes. Of course, I'll let her know. Yes, sir. We'll see you soon."

The nurse opened her mouth, and Sloane interrupted. "I caught the gist of it. Thank you." She didn't want to talk to anyone right now. Didn't want to think about anything so mundane as a phone call or her brother coming to be with her. She wanted a freaking act of God. A miracle. An instant fix for Chloe's lungs.

For this nightmare. To. Go. Away.

Fox looked almost as lost as she felt when he barged into the intensive care ward about ten minutes later. He hugged her hard. "What can I do, sis?"

"Pray."

"Are you gonna be okay?"

She shook her head. "If she doesn't make it…I'll…" She shrugged and her voice strengthened. "I'll go with her."

"Whoa, whoa, whoa. Let's have no talk like that."

Yup. That was it. It was simple, really. She couldn't live without Chloe. Decision made, a strange calm came over her.

Fox eyed her warily and picked his phone out of his pocket.

"Don't you call Mara," she warned him.

"I wouldn't think of landing that circus on your head." Fox muttered into his phone for a moment and then looked up at her. "But I am going to tell Mom what's going on. She'd kill us both if we didn't. But I'll make it clear you don't want company right now. Fair enough?"

Sloane nodded reluctantly. Family would have its due. Fox ended up making two phone calls, as it turned out.

Standing by Chloe's bed, hovering over the oxygen tube to make sure Chloe left it alone, she felt Liam's presence in the circular ICU ward before she saw him.

Had he been who Fox had called first? What on earth had prompted her brother to do that? Or maybe Fox had just wanted his best friend here for moral support.

It was as if a piece of the Rocky Mountains had entered the space, big and calm and solid, when Liam walked into Chloe's room. He murmured a low greeting to Fox, and the two men stepped outside to have a quick conversation.

Then only one of them returned behind her to the room.

Arms went around her, cradling her back against a rock-solid chest, and a whiff of pine and cold, clean air told her she hadn't been wrong in identifying Liam as the one who'd returned.

He didn't say anything. He seemed to know that she had no words for her terror, that she dared not give voice to the awful possibilities staring them in the face. She leaned back against him, and for just an instant, she let him carry her burden for her. The relief was staggering. She drew one full, deep, cleansing breath.

God. If only Chloe could get one breath like that.

The crushing weight of her terror and helplessness landed back upon her chest. But she'd had that moment. It had given her the strength to bear a few more minutes in this hell. Liam had given her that strength.

He stood behind her for a long time, just holding her gently, his arms wrapped comfortingly around her middle. The top of her head barely came to his chin, and his broad shoulders enveloped hers with easy strength. She stared at Chloe lying so still and small in the bed, willing each rise of Little Bug's chest to happen. Counting breaths.

When she reached a hundred, she started counting again.

Eventually, she let out a wobbly breath.

"She has your strength. She'll be fine."

"You can't know that," Sloane snapped.

She started to apologize, but Liam cut her off, saying, "I'm issuing blanket forgiveness for absolutely anything you say to me in the next twenty-four hours. You let fly with anything you need to get out of your system, okay? I get it."

"How do you know what I'm going through?" she asked curiously.

"My father died last year. Slowly and painfully. It was hard to take sometimes. Every now and then, I had to scream and yell and be completely irrational, and let the rage and grief out."

"I'm not ready to grieve yet," she ground out.

"Nor should you. Chloe's fighting. She's got a crack medical staff fighting with her, and she's got her whole family sending her prayers and good energy. And she's got you, Sloane. If mommy love counts for a damned thing in this universe, then Chloe's going to be just fine."

Sloane squeezed her eyes tightly shut as they burned with tears. She could handle just about anything in life except compassion. Go figure.

Liam finally turned her loose and stepped outside to have a quiet word with the nurse monitoring Chloe's vitals at the computer station outside the hospital room.

Sloane overheard him ask, "How long till we know anything?"

The nurse's voice drifted in through the open door. "Chloe needs to make it through the night. The kids we've seen fight this tend to claw their way back or go downhill within about twenty-four hours."

"Is there anything, anyone, anywhere can do to help Chloe that's not already being done?" Liam asked.

"No, sir. Our pulmonologist is one of the best in the country. She went to Harvard Medical School, and she specialized in pediatric infectious disease. You could not have a more qualified professional fighting for your daughter."

Liam didn't correct the nurse's mistaken impression that he was the father.

Interesting.

But then, neither did Sloane.

It was a long night. Longer than the night she'd spent in labor alone, waiting for Chloe to be born, while Ivan flew to Las Vegas to gamble and pick up women.

At least this night, she wasn't alone. Liam never left her side except to fetch her cups of water and coffee.

Other members of her family came and went in carefully orchestrated shifts that smacked of Mara's organizational skills. But Liam was the constant.

That and the labored, rasping sound of Chloe's breaths, each one a monumental effort for her little body.

The pulmonologist came by every hour, then every half hour. As the infection reached a crisis point, the doctor stayed in Chloe's room, sitting on a stool on the other side of the bed from Liam and Sloane, her gaze locked on the monitors reporting Chloe's oxygen levels and respiration rate.

Liam didn't say much. He suggested she splash water on her face. Take a walk around the ICU bay outside Chloe's room to revive the circulation in her legs. He might have fed her some food, but Sloane had no memory of eating.

She wanted to scream and hit things, to fight and rage against what was happening to her child. But there wasn't a single damned thing she could do to make it better.

At one point, Liam dragged her into one of the family respite rooms.

"What are you doing?" she protested. "I need to get back to Chloe."

"Do you need to punch me? Go ahead. I'm big and tough. You won't hurt me."

Even though that was exactly her impulse at the moment, Liam saying it aloud shocked her into stillness.

"Go ahead. Make a fist and bury it in my gut. I dare you."

She gasped instead as if he'd punched her in the gut. She managed to choke out, "What am I going to do?"

"You're going to do what you always do. You're going to charge full-steam ahead and do everything you

can for your daughter. You're going to be her rock tonight, and you're going to will her to fight this off. She's
your child. She has your will to live. Believe in that."

It helped to hear those words spoken aloud. Leave it
to Liam to cut right to the core of the matter. Tonight's
fight was a simple one. Life or death.

And she would be damned if she let her daughter
succumb without putting up the mother of all fights.

Steadied by Liam's clarity, she took a deep breath,
donned her emotional armor, picked up her mommy
sword and marched back into battle for her baby's life.

She sat down beside Chloe's bed and very carefully
took Chloe's hand in hers. The tiny fingers wrapped
around her index finger and hung on. Weakly. But by
God, Chloe hung on to her.

She willed strength into her child. Willed stubborn-
ness and fight into her. And she sent all the love in her
heart into that tiny hand clutching hers.

Sloane's entire world narrowed down to just those
tiny, labored breaths.

In. Gasp. Out. Rattle.

Pause.

Please God, let her draw one more breath.

Another gasp. Another rattle.

Thank God.

Please God. Just one more.

Don't take my baby from me.

The universe narrowed down even more.

In.

Out.

One breath.

Two.

Three.

If time had ever existed, Sloane forgot what its passage was. The long hours of this night were never going to end.

On the one hand, she begged the clock to run faster. For Chloe to reach the end of this nightmare. To be released from her suffering. But on the other hand, she begged the clock to stop. In this second, Chloe was still alive. Sloane would be all right with living in this one second, suspended here forever, knowing her baby was still in the world.

But then the second hand ticked.

And time moved on.

Toward what fate for her baby, she didn't know.

Liam had experienced some difficult situations in his career—fatal car crashes, making death notifications to family members. But nothing had prepared him for the nightmare of waiting helplessly for a tiny child to live or die. How Sloane wasn't collapsing into a heap on the floor, he had no idea.

Fox left to go tell Russ and Mara what was happening, and at Sloane's request, to insist they not descend upon the ICU. That was why he went in person to talk with them. It was the only way to assure they didn't barge in here and stress out Sloane even more.

The only thing he could do was stand vigil with her, offering silent support. Although she seemed barely aware that he was there, so intently was she concentrating on her daughter and the epic battle the two of them were waging against the virus.

Every time he stepped out and came back with a cup of water or some coffee for her, Sloane clutched his hand convulsively for a second with her free hand before taking the drink. It was the only outward sign of her agony.

The hours crawled by.

Finally, around daybreak, Chloe did something new. She coughed.

It was a bare breath of sound, a tiny puff of exhaled air. But the pulmonologist leaped to her feet and listened intently to Chloe's chest through a stethoscope. Liam realized he was holding his breath and forced himself to exhale.

"She's breathing a little more deeply," the doctor announced.

Sloane reached for his hand without looking away from Chloe and squeezed his fingers so hard he could barely stand the discomfort.

"Is that good news, Doc?" Liam asked, voicing the words Sloane clearly could not.

"If she can continue to cough and to start clearing her lungs, she'll be headed in the right direction."

Sloane did collapse then. Her legs just went out from under her, and she went down to the floor. Liam bent down quickly and lifted her up, looping a strong arm around her waist. "Lean on me," he murmured.

She did. Although she was such a tiny thing, he barely noticed her weight in the crook of his arm.

The next hour passed more quickly, and it became clear even to him that Chloe had turned a corner for the better. The labored quality to her breathing started to ease a bit, and the ICU staff even seemed more relaxed.

By midmorning, the pulmonologist declared Chloe out of the woods. They were going to keep her in the ICU for a little longer just to be safe, however. But Chloe's immune system had kicked in strongly enough and in time to combat the dangerous infection. So far, no fluid was accumulating in her lungs. Another good sign.

At noon, Liam ducked his head out of the room to ask if it was safe for Sloane to take a breather. When the nurse answered affirmatively, he returned to the child's bedside.

"Sloane, I'll stay with Chloe. Why don't you go grab a shower and a nap? You were up all night."

"So were you."

"Yeah, but I'm used to pulling long stakeouts. And you were down on sleep going into last night." He didn't mention aloud that he could physically see the strain last night had been for her. Dark smudges rested under her eyes, and her fair skin had taken on a transparent quality. The crisis had stretched her right to the breaking point.

"Wake me in a half hour?"

"An hour. And make the shower fast so most of the hour is sleep."

Thankfully, she didn't put up a fight at that and shuffled tiredly from the room.

He actually let an hour and ten minutes pass in hopes that she would get a full hour of rest. He ducked into the small respite room and Sloane was curled up in the middle of the bed, clutching Snuffles as tightly as if the stuffed toy was Chloe herself. Smiling a little, he sat down on the edge of the bed beside her and stroked his hand gently down her narrow back.

"Hey, Sleeping Beauty," he murmured as she woke groggily.

She blinked up at him in confusion.

"Hospital," he supplied. "Chloe's getting better, but I sent you in here to get a shower and a nap."

Her hand reached up to touch the damp strings of

her hair. "Right," she mumbled. "I feel like I've been run over by a truck."

"I can imagine. You had a rough night."

"So did you."

He shrugged. "I'm glad I could be there for you."

She looked up at him. "Me, too. For real. I don't know if I'd have made it through the night without you."

"You'd have done fine—"

She cut him off. "Don't underestimate how much you helped me, Liam. When I panicked and couldn't see my way forward, you showed me the path."

He frowned. "I just told you the truth."

"And I needed to hear it."

He smiled gently. "God help you as a parent if Chloe turns out to be half as strong-willed as you."

"I'm just glad to have that problem."

"Want me to remind you that you said that in about a dozen years, when she's sneaking out of the house and demanding her freedom and driving you crazy?"

"Yes. Absolutely."

Their gazes met, and he was stunned to see her looking as startled as he felt. Was it possible? Did Sloane see him as someone who might be in her life in a decade? Surely she thought of him as no more than an extension of her brother.

Except he could swear that was awareness in her eyes…of him…as a man.

Something warm unfolded in his heart. It was intimate and personal, a connection between them, forged in last night's crisis.

A cell phone rang, and he jumped as hard as Sloane did. She fumbled on the bedside table for her phone and frowned at it. "I don't recognize the number. It might be a family member, though."

She put the phone to her ear. "Hello?"

Dismay broke across her face, and Liam didn't even have to ask who was on the other end of the line. "Put him on speaker," he bit out.

Sloane fumbled at the phone, poking at several icons, and then Ivan's angry voice filled the room. "How dare you block me? I had to get a burner phone just to speak to you."

Liam made a chopping motion across his throat at Sloane, and mouthed, "Hang up."

She rolled her eyes at him and said instead, "Chloe spent the night in intensive care."

"What? Why?"

Liam's eyebrow arched in surprise. Huh. Was that a shred of parental concern from the bastard?

"I told you, she has a serious viral infection. It's like the flu but not quite the same. She seems to have turned the corner, though. They're hoping to move her back to a regular room this evening."

"And how much is a night in intensive care going to cost me?" Ivan snapped.

Liam's mouth actually fell open. The guy's daughter had nearly died!

"*My* health insurance covers Chloe. Thanks so much for your concern," Sloane snapped.

"Don't get snippy with me, missy."

"Ivan. Don't ever call me that again. In fact, I'll thank you never to take that tone of voice with me again."

Liam nodded encouragingly to her. It was about damned time she stood up to her ex-husband.

Ivan, however, took a dim view of the idea and exploded. Liam couldn't think of another word to describe the spate of cursing and threats that erupted from the phone. It was protracted enough that Liam was able to pull out a small notepad and actually take notes of some of the more colorful threats the bastard leveled at Sloane.

Ivan finally wound down and abruptly hung up on Sloane. It sounded like the guy had smashed the burner phone by way of disconnecting the call.

"If you insist on interacting with Ivan, please tell me you at least installed a call recording app on your phone."

Sloane smiled a little. "I did, actually."

"In that case, I'd love to have that little display of temper as evidence"

"Fine by me."

"Would you mind if I take your phone down to the police station, pull the recording and put it into evidence against your ex?"

"Not in the least, Detective."

Liam reached for her phone but then frowned at it. "I don't want to leave you without a phone in case you need to get in touch with me—" he corrected himself fast "—or with your family, of course."

He pulled his own phone out of his pants pocket and handed it to her. "Take mine." He gave her the password to unlock it and pocketed hers.

"Go home and get a shower and a nap yourself, Liam. You've gone above and beyond the call of duty for Chloe…and me."

He smiled at her. "It was my pleasure. Well, not a pleasure to go through last night. But I'm glad I could be there for you both."

Their gazes met, and that moment of connection was back. They'd been to hell and back together last night, but the three of them had come through the fire mostly unscathed. Sloane reached out and laid her hand on his cheek.

"What would I have done without you?" she whispered.

"You'd have survived and been there for your daughter."

"I don't know. Your strength and support were all that got me through a few of those hours."

"Any time you need me, you call me."

She leaned forward, her chin tilting up and her lips parting slightly.

He didn't hesitate. He took the invitation she was offering, tilted his head slightly to one side and kissed the girl of his dreams.

Sloane's mouth was soft and sweet and welcoming. All the things he'd ever imagined and more. She tasted faintly of toothpaste, which was kind of perfect, too. It was clean and fresh, a throwback to his longing for her going all the way back to junior high.

Twenty years of wanting this moment rushed over him in a wave of wonderment and…relief. He'd desired this woman forever. And here she was, at long last. It was like coming home after a sojourn of thousands of miles and many long years.

Reverently, he kept on kissing her. It was sweet and gentle and tentative, and he felt no pressure to make more of it than that. It was a beginning. A promise of more to come.

She drew away first and rested her forehead against his.

"I'm sorry," she breathed.

"Don't be. I'm not." He should be—he had no intention of being the rebound guy—but he wasn't sorry. Not at all.

"Okay, then. No regrets," she replied slowly.

"Promise?"

"I promise."

"Great. I'll bring you supper here at the hospital at six. I need you to promise to take another nap this afternoon when your mom or one of your siblings is here to give you a break."

"Okay." A pause. "And thanks for looking out for me."

"Thanks for letting me." He dropped one last light kiss on her mouth, loving the fullness of her lips and the way they parted a little in surprise beneath his, the little gasp of indrawn breath she took when he smiled down at her. As second kisses went, it was pretty damned near perfect, too.

He had big plans for their third kiss. Soon. When Chloe was back on her feet and Sloane had the mental energy to give her undivided attention to the epic kiss he was going to coax her to share.

He wasn't sure his feet actually touched the ground as he exited the hospital and drove back to the station to download the recording of that phone call and put another nail in Ivan Durant's coffin.

Chapter 6

Chloe was finally moved out of intensive care in the late afternoon. Little Bug seemed nearly as exhausted as Sloane after last night's fight for her life and was mainly interested in sleeping.

A nurse murmured to Sloane that Chloe would be out like a light for the next few hours, and if Sloane wanted to sneak away to go home, shower, eat and nap, now would be the perfect time. Mara, whose shift it was to keep Sloane company, promised not to leave Chloe's side until Sloane returned.

She looked doubtfully back and forth between the nurse and her mother.

"Go on, darling. Go take care of yourself. Chloe needs you to be strong and healthy for her."

"Okay, Mom. I won't be long."

"Take your time. I've got a good book with me, and Chloe looks wiped out."

It felt strange to leave her daughter's side after the crisis they'd just been through together. She lectured herself all the way out to the parking lot that she couldn't be so overprotective of Chloe going forward. She had to let her be a normal kid. Although how she wasn't going to turn into a total overprotective germophobe after this scare, she had no idea.

She'd just climbed into her car when Liam's phone rang. She probably shouldn't answer it. Except he was a police officer. What if it was some emergency and someone really needed to get a hold of him? She would just answer it and tell the person to call him on her cell phone number.

"Hello. This is Sloane Colton on Liam Kastor's phone."

A man's voice said, "Oh. Uh. Great. I have the results from the surveillance cameras in your house, Ms. Colton. If you could pass that on to Liam, I'd be grateful. They're all operational. The images are being sent to an address on the east side of Denver. I can text you the address."

Surveillance cameras? In her house?

"Umm, yeah. Sure," she mumbled. What the hell was Liam up to? Was he *spying* on her?

All thoughts of a shower fled her mind as she pointed her car toward the Roaring Springs Police Department, rehearsing the blistering tirade she was going to level at him. Anyone who saw her stopped at a traffic light, ranting to herself in the car, would no doubt think she'd lost her mind. Tough. Liam was going to lose a few body parts before she was done with him.

She stormed into the police department and spotted Liam sitting in a cubicle on the far side of a large room housing a dozen desks. Razor-sharp speech on the tip of her tongue, she plowed through the maze of cubicles toward him.

A woman of middle age was sitting in a chair beside Liam's desk, speaking quietly. Liam typed on a computer and then paused to ask a question. As Sloane neared, she overheard the woman.

"And I was worried when she didn't return any of my calls. I texted and texted her and she never answered. It has been so long without a word from her. Then I saw a picture on TV of that girl who was murdered last month and my heart dropped to my feet. My April looks so much like her—slender, with big dark eyes, fair skin, long, dark hair…"

The woman stopped speaking as if unable to go on and held out a five-by-seven photograph of a lovely young woman, who did, indeed, bear a striking resemblance to Bianca Rouge, the girl who'd been found dead on Wyatt's ranch.

Sloane's tirade derailed abruptly as Liam said quietly, "Mrs. Thomas, of course I'll look into your daughter's disappearance. You said she told you she was coming to Roaring Springs for a job interview. You're sure she didn't say who with?"

"I'm positive," the woman answered in obvious frustration and desperation.

"And this was…" he glanced at his computer screen "…a year ago?"

"Almost to the day. I reported her missing to the Denver police, and they called someone down here. But the local police said there'd been no sightings of her in Roaring Springs. They didn't think she ever came here."

"Do you know if the Denver PD spoke to the Roaring Springs Police Department or the county sheriff's office?" Liam asked.

"I have no idea."

Tears spilled over onto the woman's cheeks, and Sloane's heart broke for her. She knew exactly how she would feel as a parent if Chloe disappeared without a trace. She would want to die.

Determination lined Liam's face, but his voice was gentle. "I can't promise to find your daughter, but I can promise to turn over every rock in Roaring Springs and see if we can find out if she was ever here."

"Thank you for not calling me crazy," Mrs. Thomas mumbled.

Liam pressed his business card into her hand. "You're clearly not crazy, ma'am. You're a worried parent. I'll do my utmost to help you. Here's my phone number if you remember any more details that might help, or if you want an update on my investigation. Call me anytime."

That was generous of him. She would think twice before inviting her clients to call her anytime. The woman stood up and Liam rose as well. Mrs. Thomas threw her arms around Liam impulsively, and although he threw Sloane a wry look, he hugged the woman warmly.

He even walked her to the front door, and Sloane heard him say, "Thank you for coming in, Mrs. Thomas. We'll do our best to solve this mystery."

He came back to his desk, where Sloane still stood. "To what do I owe this pleasant surprise visit?"

Right. Cameras in her house.

"I got an interesting phone call. On your phone," she started acidly.

Obviously alarmed by her tone, he steered her into

the conference room behind his desk. Smart man. She was going to rip him a new one.

Liam closed the door and turned to face her. He crossed his arms over his chest, muscles bulging beneath the oxford cotton. Sometimes she forgot how big and strong he was now, but as he towered over her, frowning heavily, she was reminded of her relative puniness in comparison to this man.

"Who called my phone?" he asked evenly.

"Some guy. Weird name. Ziggy. Zigby."

"Aww, hell." He sighed as if sensing where this conversation was about to go. "Zogby. Rahm Zogby," Liam supplied. A muscle rippled in his jaw like he was clenching his teeth. Hard. Bracing himself.

Yeah, buddy. Go ahead. Brace yourself. This was going to hurt him a lot worse than it was going to hurt her. Highly trained courtroom lawyer that she was, though, she remained silent and let Liam's anxiety build before she moved in for the kill.

When he appeared unable to stand the suspense any longer, Liam blurted, "What did Zog have to say?"

Her brows snapped together as her restraint broke all at once. She spoke crisply, enunciating each word like a sharpened blade. "He told me your surveillance cameras are all operational, and that the signal is being sent to an address in Denver."

"Did he give you the address?" Liam asked quickly.

"He said he would text it to you."

"Perfect."

"Perfect?" Her voice rose perilously close to a screech. "You're spying on me in my own home and all you have to say is, 'Perfect'?"

"Whoa, whoa, whoa." Liam threw up his hands in

surrender, or maybe supplication. "I swear I'm not spying on you, Sloane. But someone is. I'm trying to figure out who."

"What do you mean, you're not spying on me?" she demanded. Dammit, why did he keep knocking her off balance?

He spoke quickly. "Two nights ago, when I went to your house to pick up clothes for you, I spotted what I thought might be a surveillance camera in your bedroom. I covertly searched your house and found two more cameras…one in Chloe's room, and one in the living room. On the assumption that you didn't install them—"

"I didn't!" she interjected sharply.

Liam nodded as if that was what he'd expected, and then continued, "I called the FBI and had them send down one of their technicians to check your house. That was Zog. He verified that surveillance cameras were, indeed, installed in your home and sending a wireless signal somewhere. He tracked that signal to Denver, apparently."

Her mouth opened and closed several times without words coming out. Who on earth would put surveillance cameras in her house?

The answer was obvious, of course. It was totally the sort of thing Ivan would do. The guy simply could not stand to lose. He didn't actually want custody of Chloe, but he would be damned if she got to have her beloved daughter. He'd played dirty in the custody hearing, but thankfully, she was so squeaky clean he hadn't had much to work with against her. Personally, she thought Ivan would be much happier without the responsibility of a child, so he could resume his gambling and womanizing unhindered. But covert surveillance against his ex-wife? That was vintage Ivan.

Sloane paced the length of the conference room, turned and came back to stare up at Liam. "Darn it. I had a fantastic tongue-lashing all prepared for you. I was going to nuke you until you glowed."

Liam's mouth twitched once, but he had the good sense to keep his voice grave when he replied, "I would have told you about the cameras immediately, but Chloe was so sick. I thought that took precedence."

"Well, hell. I was really looking forward to laying that speech on you. It was epic."

"You can still do it if you want the practice at delivering blistering rhetoric," he offered gallantly.

"No. It loses its punch if there's no actual righteous anger behind it."

He nodded in commiseration. "As soon as Zog sends me that address in Denver, I assume you'll want to know who lives there?"

"Oh, hell to the yes."

"Listen, Sloane. This is an active police investigation. You're a lawyer, so you know what that means. I need you to stay out of it and not get anywhere near the investigation, lest you taint the evidence."

She scowled. "I know the drill. But that doesn't mean I have to like it."

He grimaced. "You do have a decision to make. Do you want me to have Zog pull the cameras out, or are you willing to let them ride for a little while so the Roaring Springs police can figure out who installed them in your house?"

"Will you show me where they are?"

"I will, but you have to promise not to walk right up

to them and stare at them. You can't do anything to tip off whoever's watching you."

She stared at Liam in indecision. She hated the idea of anyone spying on her and Chloe. It made her skin crawl, honestly. It was such an invasion of privacy.

Liam added, "There are no cameras in the bathrooms. I thoroughly checked both of those. You don't have to worry about that."

"How long do you need these cameras in place?"

"Only as long as it takes us to figure out who planted them. We'll grab that joker and squeeze him until he tells us why the cameras were installed."

She added grimly, "I'm betting someone hired a Peeping Tom to spy on me."

"Any guesses as to who?"

She looked up at him soberly. "Ivan's the most obvious candidate, but his parents could be pushing him to do it. Which technically would make them co-conspirators."

"If they're helping him in any way, they're accomplices to his crime."

"But you don't know for sure yet that it's Ivan. There's a chance it's someone else."

"You tell me. Do you have any other enemies?"

She shrugged. "I mostly succeeded in defending my clients. I got the innocent ones acquitted, and the cases I lost were due to guilty clients. But even they knew I fought for the fairest sentences I could get for them. Maybe a disgruntled family member of a client who expected me to free their loved one?"

"It's a stretch."

"It doesn't feel right to me, either. I haven't been in court since Chloe was born. I confined myself to research and reviewing cases for other lawyers in the firm after she came along. Anyone I've ticked off in court has had over two years to get even with me, so it makes no sense why they would have waited so long to exact their revenge."

Liam nodded. "I've done a little digging into your ex-husband already. He doesn't exactly come across as a lily-pure, all-American boy."

"He's a real piece of work, isn't he?"

"He's something."

Liam didn't know the half of it. She filled him in. "When we divorced, Ivan paid a psychologist to testify that I wasn't a fit mother because I continued to work as an attorney after Chloe was born. Never mind that I dropped my hours from sixty to twenty a week, employed a part-time nanny and spent several hours with Chloe every day." She added bitterly, "Unlike him. He barely touched Chloe and never spent more than a few minutes in the same room with her. He resented her and made no secret of it. But that didn't stop him from pulling strings to maneuver our custody case onto the docket of a notoriously pro-father, anti-working-mother judge, too."

She paced the conference room, worked up even thinking about the custody fight. "When it became clear that the judge, who is known for ruling against mothers in custody cases, was actually considering giving custody of Chloe to Ivan, I showed Ivan the evidence a private investigator had gathered for me of Ivan's extracurricular activities."

Liam frowned. "How angry was he?"

"Apoplectic. Mind you, I never showed any of it to the judge. Just to Ivan. I reminded him that if I entered the pictures and receipts into evidence, they would become a matter of public record, and his parents and the partners in his law firm would see them, too."

"Is that when he withdrew his demand for custody?" Liam asked.

Sloane nodded. "I didn't like blackmailing him like that. But it's Chloe. And he has the parental instincts of a spoon. I couldn't risk playing fair."

"You didn't play unfair. Legally, you were well within your rights to produce evidence proving his lack of character and unfitness to be a parent. You showed admirable restraint in not ruining him."

Sloane smiled a little as if, for the first time, the weight of her guilt at blackmailing Ivan lifted a little. "Let's just say Ivan doesn't see it that way."

Liam snorted. "I'm sure he doesn't."

"He did accuse me of not ruining his job so he can continue to pay fat child support checks to Chloe."

Liam rolled his eyes. "He wanted to have his cake and eat it, too. He wanted a great wife and an adorable kid…and he wanted his sidepiece women and gambling and partying." A muscle ticked in his jaw. "But that's not how life works. A guy earns a great family, and a guy lucky enough to have one damned well works at taking care of it."

"Huh. I never thought of it like that."

"You undervalue yourself, Sloane. You always have."

She frowned up at Liam, and he drove the point home. "You're an amazing woman, and any guy would be lucky to have you. Trust me, you deserve a whole lot better than what Ivan Durant dished out to you."

A flush rose to her cheeks. "Thanks," she mumbled.

"So. About those cameras. What's your preference?"

"My *preference* is for them to be gone. But I can live with them for a little while if it helps your investigation."

Liam nodded. "Good for you. If you get crazy living in a fishbowl, give me a shout. I'll come rescue you."

It seemed like every time she turned around these days, Liam Kastor was rescuing her from one predicament or another. If she wasn't careful, she was going to drive him away. He so wasn't a drama kind of guy. If only her life could be the same.

Liam watched Sloane's slender back retreat across the police station and sank into his chair in relief when she disappeared outside. Whoa. That had been a close call. If she hadn't listened to him, hadn't let him explain about the cameras, that could've been a big-time mess. Thank God she'd proven to be reasonable.

But then, she'd always been a reasonable person. She wasn't quick to leap to conclusions, and she was thoughtful before forming opinions. But once she made up her mind, she didn't hesitate to pull the trigger.

He glanced down at the picture lying on his desk of Ruth Thomas's daughter, April. The young woman not only looked a lot like the recent murder victim, but she also looked a bit like Sloane.

Slender, fair, dark-haired, doe-eyed, attractive—

He swore under his breath. What if there was a connection between Bianca Rouge's murder and this girl's disappearance? Did that mean Sloane was in danger, too?

As a hum of panic started low in his gut, he tamped it down. Hard. He was a cop. He dealt in facts. If there was a connection, he would find it and follow it back to the killer.

April Thomas had been missing for a year. Which made for a cold, difficult trail to follow. It also didn't bode well for a happy outcome to this search. Too many young, beautiful women were snatched into the sex trafficking trade, or into the drug world, and never heard from again. He hoped against hope that April's story wouldn't end tragically. But his gut told him to prepare for the worst case scenario.

He picked up the phone and called Deputy Sheriff Daria Bloom. "Hey, Daria. It's Liam Kastor. Any chance I could interest you in a cup of coffee?"

"Is this business or a date?"

He grinned. "Sorry. It's work."

"Then I'll leave my dancing shoes in my closet. I'll meet you at the No Doze Café in, say, a half hour?"

"Perfect. See you then."

The No Doze was just down the street, so Liam spent the time compiling a quick missing person's report on April Thomas. She was already in the national database of missing persons, but he put together a quick dossier with her picture in it to distribute to local law enforcement officials.

He still had a few minutes before the meeting, so he typed in the address that Zog had texted him of where the surveillances images were being sent. It was in the eastern suburbs of Denver. A property rental company was listed as owning the place. Liam dialed the company's phone number.

"This is Detective Kastor with the Roaring Springs Police Department. Can you tell me who's renting the

Daria swore quietly as she stared down at the picture. "I have to make a call."

Liam waited while she quickly filled in her boss, Sheriff Trey Colton.

Daria ended the call and then leaned forward, speaking very quietly for his ears alone. "I've never been entirely convinced that Nolan Sharpe strangled Bianca Rouge."

"Why not?" Liam asked, startled. "I thought Sharpe left a note taking credit for the murder."

"He did. Except it's too pat having some low-level thug, who's never done anything close to murder, up and claim responsibility for a crime like that in a suicide note."

"Then why do you think Sharpe confessed?" Liam asked.

Daria shrugged. "Maybe he wanted some postmortem notoriety. Or maybe someone paid him to confess. Or maybe he didn't write the note at all. I was never able to make a handwriting match between the note and any other known samples of his writing. At this point, I'm not even certain he committed suicide. There's just not enough evidence to lock down anything in the Rouge murder or the Sharpe suicide."

"But the cases were declared closed."

"Russ Colton declared the cases closed and was public enough in doing it that Trey couldn't exactly come out and openly disagree with him."

Trey was one of the Colton cousins and had recused himself from the Bianca Rouge murder investigation because the body had been found on his cousin's ranch. Tough call, but the right one to make. Liam mentally winced a little. He was treading perilously close to the edge of an ethics problem himself by investigating Sloane's ex-husband, given his personal feelings for her.

The café door opened, and a tall figure in uniform filled the doorway. Trey Colton, in the flesh.

"That was fast," Daria commented.

"I happened to be in the area," Trey commented, sliding into the chair beside his deputy. "I hear you've got some information for us on the Rouge murder."

"I've picked up a missing persons case that may be linked," Liam replied.

"That would make it my department's case, then," Trey responded.

"No, it wouldn't. Your department shut down the Rouge murder investigation. I had a mother walk in my door today asking me to help find her daughter. My case."

Trey glared at Liam, who glared back. They'd known each other long enough that they didn't stand on professional ceremony.

Liam finally broke the stalemate by murmuring, "Look at it this way. If you let the Roaring Springs PD handle the Thomas disappearance, it diffuses the heat Russ Colton can lay on you. He'll have to come after us, too. Besides, our two agencies can pool resources and cover more ground this way. I'll have an excuse to poke around at the Rouge murder, and you guys can poke around at the Thomas disappearance."

Trey hesitated a moment more and then nodded. "Deal. But Daria keeps the lead on the Rouge murder."

"Absolutely," Liam answered firmly.

"Is that April Thomas?" Trey asked, gesturing at the photograph lying between them.

"Yup. Looks like Bianca, doesn't she?" Liam answered grimly.

"Yeah," Trey replied equally grimly. "I think I interrupted you when I sat down. What were you saying?"

Liam circled back to the earlier discussion with Daria. "If someone killed Sharpe and left a note fingering him for Bianca's murder, that person could be Bianca's actual killer. We could be looking at a perpetrator of multiple homicides."

"Worse than that," Daria murmured. "We could be looking at a serial killer."

All of their gazes snapped down to the picture of young, pretty April Thomas lying between them. The resemblance between her and the murdered girl found on Wyatt's ranch really was striking.

Daria added, "And we may have just figured out what our serial killer's preferred victims look like."

Liam's gut felt heavy. This was exactly the kind of case he'd spent his whole career preparing for, but now that it was here, all he felt was dread. Not dread that he wasn't up to the challenge. Rather, dread that more pretty brunette girls were going to die before they could catch this killer. There was nothing at all exciting in that knowledge. This case was going to be a grim race against time and death. None of his crime investigations books had talked about that.

Worse, Sloane was a slender, pretty brunette with big dark eyes and long brown hair. And *that* panicked him outright.

He reminded himself hastily that so were a half-dozen other women he could think of in Roaring Springs off the top of his head. They were all in danger. Not just Sloane.

He muttered, "Should we put out some kind of warning for young women who match the general description of Bianca and April to be cautious?"

Daria looked at Trey, who told her, "I recused myself from this case. That's your call."

Daria bit her lip, thinking. She looked at Liam reluctantly, her dark eyes even darker than usual. "Before we go public, we're going to need more evidence than a missing girl who happens to look like a victim of a supposedly solved murder. The Coltons would have a fit if we made some big announcement about a serial killer being on the loose and chased off all the tourists at the height of the ski season."

Trey responded quickly, "It's not about money. It's about safety."

"I know that," Daria snapped. She exhaled hard and continued more calmly, "But politics matter in this town. And when the Coltons are involved, it's political."

Liam winced. She was not wrong.

Daria continued, "Tell you what. I'll put the word out in the sheriff's office to be on high alert, if you'll put the same word out—quietly—in the RSPD. If you guys need extra manpower to beef up your patrols, maybe add drive-bys of the homes of single women in town who fit the possible MO, let me know."

"Will do," Liam answered.

He stopped speaking as a waitress set down a cup of black coffee in front of him. He took a long pull of the cup of rich, roasted brew.

When the waitress had moved out of earshot, Liam continued, "I have to go to Denver on other business. I thought I'd stop by the Denver PD and ask them to share their file on April Thomas with us. I'll ask if there's anything *not* in the file that we should be aware of."

Daria winced. "Like whether or not she might have gotten into the high-end escort business like Bianca did?"

He sighed. "Yeah. That." He didn't begrudge women a living as sex workers if that was the only or best way they could make ends meet. However, even in the best of circumstances, it could still be a dangerous and violent business.

"You'll let me know what you find out?" Daria asked.

"Of course."

"Thanks for the heads up, Liam."

"No problem. Coffee's on me, this time."

Daria lifted her chin. "Next cup's on me."

"Let's hope you have better news for me next time."

They traded grim looks. Both of their guts were clearly screaming the exact same warning at them. A serial killer had come to Roaring Springs.

Chapter 7

Sloane wasn't sure who was happiest to be home, her or Chloe. Little Bug was exhausted and weak from her ordeal but still ran into her bedroom and flopped on her bed, laughing with joy to be back with all her stuffed toy friends. Sloane smiled as her child said hello to each and every one and asked how they were doing and if they had missed her.

Liam had said the camera in Chloe's room was in the corner over the doorway. Sloane almost glanced up at it as she tucked Chloe in for a nap, but at the last second forced herself to look out the door into the hallway.

As she headed into her own bedroom, she ordered herself in advance not to look up into the corner over her dresser. She ducked into her closet to grab clean clothes and then went into her bathroom for a much needed soak in her big, old-fashioned tub. Even knowing there were no cameras in here, she felt nervous and exposed as she stripped down and climbed into the tub.

She poured in a big glob of bubble bath and ran the water until the bubbles piled up around her neck, concealing all of her. Ugh. This business of living under surveillance was harder than she'd realized it would be.

She let the hot water soothe her tired muscles and frayed nerves, lingering until the water was tepid, dreading having to face the cameras once more.

Finally, when she was shivering in the cold water, she forced herself out of the tub and quickly wrapped herself in a big towel. She had to get control of this paranoia. She was safe in here and had nothing to hide from. She could do this. And if it would help Liam nail Ivan once and for all, she would parade through her house stark naked.

The next few days passed quietly. Chloe got progressively more antsy being housebound, and Sloane became progressively more aware that she was smothering her child. Part of it was fear over a relapse of Chloe's illness, but part of it was knowing those blasted cameras were watching her baby girl's every move.

Finally, she called Wyatt's fiancée, Bailey, to ask if Chloe could come out and spend the night at the Crooked C. Chloe dearly loved playing outside there and visiting the horses. Bailey, eager to get some parenting practice in, agreed readily.

Sloane and Chloe drove out to the Crooked C on a mild, sunny day that hinted of the springtime still some months away. Sloane walked through the barn with the toddler, who insisted on feeding a piece of carrot to every single horse down the aisle, scratching their fuzzy necks and petting their velvet noses.

For dinner, Bailey baked a big casserole of home-made macaroni and cheese, a Little Bug favorite. Then the three of them settled in to watch a princess movie.

Chloe dozed off, but when the adults tried to stop the movie, she woke up and demanded to see the ending. Sloane and Bailey smiled over her head at each other and indulged her. Sloane was just glad Chloe was here to insist on torturing the adults with a movie they'd all seen a hundred times.

She smoothed Chloe's hair affectionately. She simply couldn't imagine life without her. Not now, and not fifty years from now. That poor woman in Liam's office yesterday whose daughter went missing—Sloane shuddered to even imagine that kind of pain and heartache.

"You okay?" Bailey murmured over Chloe's droopy head and half-closed eyes.

"Yeah. I was just thinking about how much I love this munchkin."

Bailey's hand landed on her own belly, where a baby of her own was growing at long last. "I already love this kiddo, and I haven't even met him or her, yet."

Sloane smiled knowingly. "In a few more months, your baby will start to show its personality, even in there. This little extrovert used to love to jump up and down on my bladder, and the noisier an environment I was in, the more active she became. It was clear from the get-go she was going to be the life of the party."

Bailey smiled gently. "I can't wait." Then, "Have you considered having another child?"

Sloane wrinkled her nose. "Another child would be fine. But not the man who'd come with it."

"You don't have to be in a relationship to have a baby, you know."

"Yeah? Then why did you go back to Wyatt to ask him to help you have a baby?"

Bailey's cheeks pinkened. "It was complicated."

"Apparently!" Sloane grinned over at her friend. "But you're happy now?"

"Blissfully. I can't imagine life being any better than it is now."

Sloane laughed quietly. "Wait till your baby is born. There's a whole next level of love you haven't even discovered yet."

"Wyatt and I are looking forward to that. He's really excited about this baby."

Sloane's smile slipped. What would it have been like to share the thrill of her pregnancy with Ivan? Well, not with Ivan. He wasn't capable of loving anyone but himself. But with a man who actually loved her and loved the child they made together? "I'm so happy for you two."

"You need to find a decent guy, Sloane. One who will treat you right and take care of you."

"I don't need anyone to take care of me."

Bailey shrugged. "I don't *need* anyone to take care of me, either, but it's sure nice to have someone who wants to, and who will let me take care of him, sometimes."

Yes. That. But her first priority was to Chloe. Besides…finding a good man would involve actually trusting one again. Which was not likely anytime soon.

Liam's face flashed into her mind in counterpoint to that mental assertion. It wasn't that she didn't trust Liam, but he didn't count. He was an old friend from well before she'd learned that men could have treacherous hearts under their charming smiles.

Correction: Liam was an old friend who'd kissed her.

And she'd kissed him back.

Did that mean he wasn't just a friend anymore? Or would they settle into some friends-with-benefits limbo because she was incapable of committing to another relationship that might destroy her the next time around?

Liam was a great guy. He deserved better than that.

In the cold light of day, with the crisis of Chloe's health off the table, she saw things more clearly. She genuinely liked Liam. Found him attractive, even. The guy was smoking hot, after all. And he was, indeed, a good man. She loved his directness and the way he cut through to the heart of a matter and laid it bare.

If she really cared for him, she would cut him loose. Let him have a chance at finding love with a woman who could fully return his feelings.

Truth was, she was too broken inside for love. The only love she had left inside was for Chloe, and she'd decided to pour her entire self and soul into that.

Bailey picked up Chloe, and immediately, the toddler woke up, interested and alert. Sloane and Bailey smiled and shook their heads at each other.

"How about a bubble bath, Squirt?" Bailey asked.

"Dubbuh bubbuhs?" Chloe asked eagerly.

"Sure. Double bubbles."

Chloe squealed with excitement. Sloane had seen the results of a bubble bath with Auntie Bailey, and it involved mountains of bubbles and the entire bathroom and everyone in it becoming sopping wet.

"That's my cue to flee the scene of the crime before I'm implicated," Sloane laughed.

Bailey and Chloe laughingly declared Sloane no longer needed, and Bailey jogged down the hall toward the bathroom, bouncing Chloe up and down while Little Bug giggled in delight.

Smiling, Sloane headed home. She had big plans for her first night home alone since she'd moved into the new house. She was taking a bath of her own, but with bath salts, candles and soothing music. And then she was going to bed. If she didn't soak too long, she could be in bed by nine o'clock. Which sounded like pure heaven after the week she'd just had.

She stepped through the front door, and the weight of being watched landed on her shoulders like a truckload of bricks. Lord, she would be happy when the police figured out who'd planted those cameras and could remove them.

The Denver police were doing surveillance on the house where the signals were going. Liam reported that no one had been seen entering the house since they'd started watching it. Whoever was watching the feed was either forwarding it remotely to some other location or only checked the video occasionally. Liam was working on a search warrant for the Denver house, and that should come through any day now.

Sloane smiled fondly at the mess in the living room and picked up toys, put away games and folded blankets. She was just closing the lid of the big toy chest when a slight movement made her look up at the side window about six feet away to her left.

A man was staring in at her.

Sloane screamed and started so hard that she knocked herself flat onto her behind. Scrambling in panic, she leaped to her feet.

The man's face was gone.

Oh, God. Was he coming in?

She was so freaked out she couldn't draw a full breath.

But there was no doubt whatsoever that she'd seen a face in the shadows. She yanked out her cell phone, her hands shaking so bad she could hardly dial 911.

"What's the nature of your emergency?"

"There's a...man looking in...in my window. I'm at 217 Maple Street..."

"The police are on their way, ma'am. A cruiser should be there in approximately ten minutes. Go into your bathroom and lock the door."

No way! There was a window in the bathroom! "I'm leaving," she gasped.

Sloane's need to flee was so overpowering that she'd actually been running around her house collecting her car keys from the kitchen counter, and her coat off the rack, as she'd been trying to speak to the emergency operator.

"Ma'am. The person may still be outside—"

Panic won out over reason. She was not staying in this house one minute more. Her hip banged painfully into the kitchen counter and she bounced off of it and kept going. *Must get out of here!*

She bolted into her garage. She opened her SUV's door and frantically examined the back seat and cargo area to make sure no one was in her car before she climbed in. Then she jumped inside and locked the doors.

Okay. That felt a little better.

She simultaneously started the car and hit the garage door opener. As soon as the door was far enough up to clear, she gunned her SUV out of the garage, roared backward down her driveway and sped away.

Her heart was pounding so hard it hurt, and she was so panicked her brain couldn't seem to form coherent thoughts. She turned the corner hard. She took another corner a few blocks later without warning, slamming her vehicle into the turn without signaling and hardly braking.

She realized which street she was on with a start. Peering at mailboxes in the dark, while driving, was a challenge, but she spotted Liam's address.

She pulled into the driveway of a modest but neat white bungalow with a porch at least as wide and welcoming as hers. Liam had said something about living in the apartment over the garage.

She spied a big detached garage behind the house, and she drove right up to it. On one side of the structure was an exterior staircase, and she raced up that, pounding frantically on the door.

Be home. Be home. Be home—

The door opened and she flew into Liam's arms, knocking him back a step as he caught her weight against his body in surprise.

"What's wrong?" he bit out. "Is it Chloe?"

"No. She's at the ranch. There was a man looking in my window—"

He started to disengage from her. "I have to call the police—"

"I already called 911. But I couldn't stay and wait for that man to come inside and kill me. Oh, God. It was awful. I looked up and there he was in my window in the dark. He looked so sinister..."

She shuddered and buried her head against Liam's chest.

And then it dawned on her that said chest was bare.

And muscular. And warm. And chest hairs tickled her nose. He smelled clean and slightly damp like he'd just taken a shower.

The arms wrapped around her were strong. Really strong. With big, bulging biceps only a few inches from her face. She knew he'd filled out, but she had no idea he'd filled out *this* much. Dang. He was serious eye candy.

"What did the 911 operator say?" Liam asked.

"She said a cruiser would be there in ten minutes."

"Did you leave the house unlocked?"

"Of course not!" Sloane exclaimed.

Liam bent down slightly, taking her with him, and then a strong arm swept behind her knees and lifted her off her feet. With swift strides, he carried her across the one-room studio and deposited her on a sofa. He pulled a thick plaid wool blanket off the back of the couch and draped it over her, then set the television remote beside her on the armrest.

"Stay here where you'll be safe. I'm going over to your place to help the uniforms look around. Do you have your house keys, and will you give us permission to enter and search the premises?"

"Yes, and yes." Sloane held up her car's key fob with a loop of keys attached to it. "That brass one is the house key."

"I'll come back as soon as I can. But it may take a while. There may be paperwork to file. And if we catch the bastard, there will be a lot of paperwork."

She nodded, shivering even under the heavy blanket as he yanked a shirt out of his closet and threw it on, buttoning it fast.

"Help yourself to anything in the kitchen if you get hungry or thirsty."

And then Liam was gone, locking the door behind him, and silence settled around her.

His place was about like she'd expected. Neat. Utilitarian. No wasted space.

On the opposite wall from the sofa was a large flat screen TV. To her right, just inside the front door, was a tiny kitchenette that would have been at home on a nice yacht. To her immediate left was a door that led to a bathroom, no doubt. In the far corner was a big bed, with a closet beyond it along the far wall. To the right of the front door was a small desk, and in the corner beyond it, two pairs of skis and poles leaned against the wall.

So. He still skied. He'd been a champion racer in high school but had elected to pursue college and an education instead of the uncertain and injury-prone life of a professional downhill skier.

The apartment's floor was a beautiful hardwood, stained a light, smoky brown. The furnishings were cream with touches of blue here and there. The entire apartment felt spacious and comfortable, even though it was quite small. Maybe the high-pitched ceiling had something to do with that.

Leave it to Liam to turn an old attic into a nice place to live. He seemed to bring order and rightness to everything he touched.

Surrounded by his comforting presence in every square inch of his place, her breathing finally slowed. And at long last, her brain reengaged.

She recalled the face of the man in her window, and she focused hard on it, memorizing it as best she could.

Then, throwing back the blanket, Sloan went over to the tiny desk under the front window. She opened a few drawers and rummaged around until she found what she was looking for. Grabbing several sheets of plain paper, along with a pencil, she headed back to the sofa and went to work sketching the face of the man in her window. He'd worn a black watch cap, but she was pretty sure she'd seen dark sideburns. His brows had been flat and on the thick side. She struggled to capture his nose and had to erase her efforts and restart the nose a half-dozen times before she was satisfied with it. The mouth, she got on the first try.

The eyes—

She had another panic attack at the memory of those eyes staring at her. They'd looked dark and sinister. But then, she could be imagining that given how badly he'd scared her. Or maybe she wasn't imagining it at all.

Oh, God. There went her breathing again, breaking into choppy little gasps that didn't send nearly enough oxygen to her brain. She began to feel light-headed.

Who was doing this to her? Surely it was Ivan trying to terrorize her. A thread of fury wove its way into the fabric of fear draped over her. Jerk.

She'd be damned if she ever let him anywhere near her daughter again. If only Liam and the cops were able to catch the Peeping Tom, maybe he would name Ivan as his employer. That would make getting a restraining order against her ex a piece of cake, and it would finally put the kibosh on his plans to steal Chloe away from her like some spoil of war.

She went back to work on the sketch, adding shadows and making small changes until she was satisfied she'd captured the face exactly. She laid down the sketch, and it stared back up at her with a flat, cruel expression.

And...she panicked anew. She'd done too good a job on the sketch and freaked herself out. It was as if the guy was staring at her again, this time from Liam's coffee table. She darted out her hand from under the blanket and flipped the picture over, facedown.

Better.

But tears still leaked out of her eyes as her entire body trembled with fear.

And of course, that was exactly when Liam walked in on her. When she was boo-hooing like some sissy who couldn't take care of herself. Ivan had always sneered at these kinds of outward displays of emotional vulnerability.

Liam took one step inside, spied her crying and strode over to her. She braced herself for his contempt.

Without saying a word, he picked her up, turned around and sat down on the sofa with her cradled in his lap.

Startled, she sat very still. Why was he doing this?

Liam merely tucked the blanket around her, lightly urged her head down to his shoulder and held her gently, saying nothing. Apparently, he planned to let her cry out her fear and stress.

Which opened the floodgates. Except it wasn't fear and stress making her cry now. It was gratitude that he hadn't made fun of her. That he hadn't ridiculed her when he'd seen her crying. That he'd silently given her permission to feel scared and stressed and didn't seem interested in judging her. Which was just as well. She was judging herself enough for both of them. She'd barged into his house and dragged him into her mess without even asking him if he cared to be involved.

When her sobs finally wound down, he reached over to the small end table and came back with a tissue in hand. He held it out to her, and she took it, mopping at her face.

"I'm—" she hiccuped "—I'm sorry."

"For what?"

She peeked up at him. He sounded genuinely surprised. "For banging on your door in the middle of the night and forcing you to run around chasing some guy."

"Sloane. Stop."

"Stop what?" she blurted, truly alarmed that she'd overstepped some boundary she hadn't been aware of.

"Stop apologizing for including me in your life. I'm honored that you trust me and are willing to turn to me for help."

She frowned, struggling to process the meaning behind his words. *C'mon, Sloane. You're an intelligent, highly educated attorney. Surely the obvious interpretation is the correct one. He likes you.*

Her stomach fluttered nervously. It had been so long since she'd dated or since she'd flirted with anyone. Since she'd even considered the idea of a relationship with someone besides Ivan. Did she dare go there with Liam? Or would she ruin the friendship growing between them?

At a loss over how to proceed next, she mumbled, "I must look like a wreck. My skin blotches when I cry and my nose turns red."

"You look cute. And lucky for you, I'm a huge fan of Rudolph the Red-Nosed Reindeer."

She scrubbed her red nose with the tissue.

"You've had a hell of a week, sweetheart," he murmured. "First the scare with Chloe, and now this."

"I guess so."

"I'm glad you came to me tonight when you were scared."

She smiled up at him, feeling more waterworks threatening. "I really am sorry I barged in on you like that. I was totally panicked, and I didn't think about where I was going. All of a sudden, I just found myself pulling into your driveway."

Liam smiled back, and his light green eyes sparkled like gemstones. She'd forgotten how beautiful his eyes really were. His lashes were dark and thick, too, and the combination was devastating.

Up close like this, his jawline was more rugged than she'd ever noticed before. His cheekbones were more chiseled than she remembered, too. The softness of youth in his face had given way to a devastatingly handsome man who would only get better with age.

While the tan might have faded from his arms, his face was still bronzed, and strands of honey gold wound through his brown hair. His job probably put him outdoors a lot. And apparently, he still skied.

Speaking of which, it dawned on her that his thighs were powerful and hard beneath her legs. Liam Kastor had grown up and become a man's man.

Huh. He'd always been attractive in a boyish, charming sort of way. But now that he'd matured, he was stronger. More confident. Sexier. He wore the hard edge of being a police detective very well, indeed. The flutter in her belly intensified, and it had nothing to do with panic. But it did startle her into even sharper awareness of the man holding her.

"You okay?" he asked, his voice a low, comforting rumble.

"Why do you ask?"

"Your breathing accelerated."

Busted. No way was she admitting to him that she was breathing hard because she was sitting on this hot guy's freaking lap. Oh, no. She was definitely not confessing that. She still remembered his capacity to tease her mercilessly from junior high school—

Although maybe that had changed about him as well.

"I—" she started. "You—" She stopped again. "Thank you."

A little wrinkle formed between his eyebrows. "For what?"

"For letting me charge into your place and practically knock you off your feet. And for letting me fall apart on your sofa. And for going over to my place to check it out while I cowered here. Speaking of which, did you find anything?"

"More footprints. Similar to the ones I found before. Men's boots. About the same size as the first set. Whoever's hanging around your place is coming up from the park behind your house and leaving that way, too. I'm going to stake out the woods and that bike path for a while and see if I can catch the bastard who's scaring you."

"You don't have to do that," she replied quickly. "I don't want to be that much trouble to you."

His expression turned a tiny bit withering. "Since when do you say stupid things, Sloane Colton? You always were the smartest girl in the whole school."

She laughed without humor. "I was until I met Ivan. He was a colossal mistake. The man totally wrecked my faith in my own good judgment and ability to make intelligent decisions."

"If you don't mind my asking, what did you see in him?"

She replied reflectively, "I paid a therapist a ton of money to answer that very question."

"Did you get an answer?"

She looked down at her hands, her fingers twining together fretfully. "Yes. I did."

Gentleman that he was, Liam didn't pry. Didn't ask what the answer was, even though he had to be curious. She volunteered the information anyway. After all, he'd let her into his house and was showing extreme kindness to her. Not to mention, she did actually trust him. "Apparently, I have deep-seated abandonment issues from losing my parents when I was so young. There was nothing particularly special about Ivan except that he was the first person who offered to marry me, which represents safety in my mind. I apparently craved permanence."

"Marriage is supposed to be permanent," Liam murmured.

"You would think, wouldn't you?" she responded ruefully. "My therapist thought I was so desperate for someone in my life who wouldn't abandon me that I leaped at the first guy to come along who promised to stick around. Truth be told, I'm not sure I ever loved Ivan. I just loved the idea of a home and a family of my own."

"And now you've got those for yourself without him. Are you happy?"

She rolled her eyes. "You don't have to be Laser Man *all* the time, you know."

"Sorry," he murmured. "But I'm still curious. Are you happy here in Roaring Springs? It seems…small for you."

"After the mess with Ivan, I realized it represents home to me. Family. I might have been running away from the loss of my parents, but I guess it finally dawned on me that I already have a family."

He smiled without much humor. "You have an enormous family."

"For better or worse," she muttered.

For all their flaws, the Coltons did stick together like glue.

Liam spoke up. "You still haven't answered my question. Are you happy now that you have a home and a family of your own?"

"My home has been invaded, and I almost lost my child a week ago. I can't say that I'm feeling particularly secure in my life at the moment, no."

"Are you happy to be here or not?" he pressed.

After one last hesitation, she finally gave him a straight answer. "I'm happier to be here than I thought I would be." His eyes lit up with fierce pleasure. He rightly surmised that he had something to do with her answer.

But then a shadow entered his eyes, and his arms tightened around her in obvious preparation to rise and dump her off his lap.

She threw her arms around his neck. "Don't move," she pleaded.

"Sloane, I refuse to take advantage of your recent troubles and emotional vulnerability."

"I got the noble, decent guy memo from you already.

You're not taking advantage of me if I want to be with you."

He subsided beneath her. "You're sure?" he asked quietly.

"Yes. I feel safe sitting here like this with you."

"Safe. Right." His voice was dry, and she thought she sensed disappointment in his voice. Was he real attracted to her in *that* way? The fluttering in her be grew decidedly more pronounced. She laid her head on his shoulder, considering what she wanted from him. The possibilities were staggering.

Finally, she murmured against his neck, "Liam?"

"Hmm?"

"Would you mind kissing me?"

He reared back hard to stare down at her. "Are you sure that wouldn't be a mistake? Don't get me wrong. I'd love to kiss you again. But I don't want you to regret it later."

"What if I promised not to have any regrets?" she responded.

"Come again?"

"Kiss me. *Please.*"

His head bent down to hers, and he paused, his mouth no more than an inch from hers. "Sloane?"

"Yes?" she whispered breathlessly.

"You don't ever have to say please to get me to kiss you. For that matter, you don't ever have to ask. You can kiss me anytime you'd like."

Well, in that case…

She tilted her chin up and captured his mouth with hers. It was as warm and wonderful as she remembered from the hospital. Except this time, he surrounded her

Chapter 8

For once in her life she didn't care if this was a mistake or not. She'd had a rotten week, and the only bright spot in it—besides Chloe pulling through and recovering—was this man. She'd been so damned responsible for so damned long that she was more than ready, eager even, to make a big, fat, feel-good mistake.

"We're not stopping," she murmured.

She plunged her fingers into his thick, short hair, loving how silky it was against her palms. Then, tilting her head to fit their mouths together better, she kissed him the way she'd been imagining doing for the past week, like when she soaked in her bathtub or late at night when she lay in her bed before sleep came. She'd been imagining kissing him at other times, too. Like when she cooked dinner or vacuumed or dusted or shopped or…well, pretty much all the time.

completely, and she relished being engulfed by his size and strength and muscular physique.

She deepened the kiss, and he opened his mouth for her. She touched the tip of her tongue to his and then jerked back, startled. Was that a chuckle making his chest shake like that?

"Chickening out, are you?" he murmured humorously against her lips.

"Me? Hah! Challenge accepted, buster."

She pushed off of his formidable chest and shifted position, throwing one of her thighs across his lap and straddling his hips. The position put her more on his level, and she was really able to kiss him now.

He grinned back at her, the dare glinting in his eyes, which had darkened to the color of wet grass.

Their gazes met, and the humor drained from his eyes, leaving behind a fire that would be intimidating as heck if this weren't Liam, whom she'd known for most of her life. Whom she'd grown up beside. Who was practically family already.

"Seriously, Sloane," he growled. "If you're going to think this was a mistake tomorrow, we need to stop now."

His mouth was just the right combination of firm and smooth, yielding and warm, and she relished the feel and taste of him as if he were a perfect bite of her favorite food.

For his part, he sat frozen beneath her as if he knew not to move too abruptly and scare her. But desire abruptly rolled off of him, and the muscles in his thighs and arms suddenly felt tightly coiled around her. She tensed, and immediately his mouth stilled.

"Second thoughts?" he muttered against her lips.

"No. Not at all."

"Glad to hear it." His hand slid around under the weight of her hair to cup the back of her head, and he drew her back into the kiss this time. But he took it easy and didn't try to dominate her. For which she was imminently grateful. She needed to take this slow for now.

As he continued to let her set the pace, she relaxed and remembered why she'd been fantasizing about kissing him. The man was *hawt*.

Not to mention, this was Liam. Unfailingly kind, considerate, honorable Liam. Fox's best friend in the whole world, and her brother was a great judge of character. Her hands slid down his corded neck and across his broad shoulders. Bulging muscles proclaimed his physical power. And yet, for once, she wasn't freaked out by a man being much bigger and much stronger than she was.

Her fingertips encountered the buttons of his oxford shirt, and a desire to feel the skin underneath had her undoing them and pushing the starched cotton aside. His chest was as warm and hard as before. All those acres of yummy muscles hadn't been her imagination.

A desire to taste his skin came over her. She hesitated, then remembered he'd said she never needed to ask to kiss him. She ducked her chin down and touched her lips to the hollow at the base of his throat. Tendons grew taut, muscles jerked and his pulse leaped beneath her lips.

She kissed her way across his collarbone and his entire body went tense, waiting, beneath her. She pushed back on his lap and kissed lower, tracing down his breastbone in the hollow between bulging pectoral muscles. She moved to her right and heard his sharp intake of breath.

A surge of power roared through her. How weird was this? She was making him respond in all these visceral ways just by kissing him. Yet another first for her, compliments of Liam.

She continued exploring his chest, pushing his shirt open. She paused long enough to sit up and stare down at him, sprawled on the sofa beneath her, his eyes glittering with intensity, but his body casual. Lionlike.

His jeans were tight across his crotch, but she could still see he was reacting to her. Strongly. *Well, hello, sailor.*

"Like what you see?" One side of his mouth quirked up.

The question rocked her to her core. Since when had the self-effacing, insecure teen become this daring, dangerous man, challenging her to do more and go further with him? He'd become a force of nature somewhere along the way.

"Yes. I do like what I see," she purred, something hungry within her reacting to the gauntlet he'd thrown down before her. "A lot. You've grown up very nicely, Detective Kastor."

"So have you, Counselor."

She shook her head. "Where did the years go? It seems like yesterday we were awkward teenagers, and here we are, all grown up."

"Thank God. I hated being a teenager."

"Why?" she asked curiously.

"Besides the fact that I wanted to screw pretty much anything that moved, all the time, I had no social skills and no idea how to go about talking to girls."

"Are you kidding? You were super outgoing, and you had all kinds of female friends."

"Yeah. But not the one I wanted." He stared at her significantly.

Her brows twitched into a frown. "Seriously? You didn't know how to talk to me? We talked all the time."

"Yeah. About stupid stuff. I had no idea how to tell you how I really felt about you."

Her eyes widened. "You had feelings for me?"

He huffed. "See? This is exactly what I'm talking about. I was crazy about you, and I had no words to tell you so. It was awful."

"You have the words now," she said softly.

He reached up to push a lock of her hair off her cheek. His fingertip traced the shell of her ear lightly as he tucked the hair behind it. A shiver passed through her.

"Thing is, I don't know what you do or don't want to hear, now."

She considered him soberly. "I honestly don't know. I...wasn't expecting you."

He smiled a little at that. "I wasn't expecting you, either."

She planted her palms on his chest and leaned in a

little. "But I'm glad I ran into you…and that you weren't scared off by the craziness in my life." She closed the remaining gap between them, feeling the heat radiating off his torso, her mouth a breath away from his. "I want to hear whatever you've got to say to me, Liam. If I don't need permission to kiss you, then you don't need permission to say whatever you want. Deal?"

"Deal."

He captured her mouth with his, significantly more intensely than before. His head tilted to one side and his tongue tangled with hers as he kissed her passionately. Shocked, she opened her mouth beneath his. She couldn't remember the last time a man, any man, had really kissed her. Maybe one never had.

But as Liam's arms swept around her, dragging her up his body to better fuse their mouths together, and arching her backward over his arm just enough to make the peaks of her breasts rub through her shirt against his bare chest, the man really *kissed* her.

And she liked it.

She amended her assessment. Liam didn't just kiss her; he made love to her with his mouth. He kissed her cheeks and jaw. He nibbled her earlobe, then swept his tongue along the column of her throat, sending shivers through her whole body. She realized his hands were gently kneading up and down her spine, dissolving tension she hadn't even realized she was holding there.

This man melted all her defenses. And any need to push the situation, to control the outcome, to drive this moment to some end goal, evaporated.

She felt warm and soft and boneless in his arms, and a strange, liquid heat began to form low in her belly. Whoa. She hadn't actually been attracted to a man in that way since before she'd gotten pregnant with Chloe, something like three years ago. That was a *long* dry spell. But hoo baby, the drought was apparently over.

Tentatively, she kissed him back, and his mouth curved into a smile against hers.

"Welcome to the party, Sloane," he rasped.

She smiled back against his sexy lips. "I may be slow on the uptake, but once I get there, I'm the life of the party."

"Oh, yeah? This I have to see, Miss Save-the-world-but-don't-take-care-of-myself."

She started indignantly, "I don't—" She stopped. "Okay. Fine. I do take care of everyone but me. But that doesn't make me a bad person."

"Far from it. But it does mean that every now and then, you should let someone else take care of you."

He kissed away the frown that wrinkled her brow as she realized she had no idea what that meant or how to do it.

As if he'd read her mind, he murmured, "Like tonight, for example. Let me take care of you."

She pulled back far enough to look at him. At this range, his eyes were a blend of light green and gray, shot through with silver flecks. His gaze was intent. Waiting.

Waiting? For what?

Oh.

He wasn't going to proceed any further without permission from her. Huh. So that was what adult consent looked like. Ivan had never bothered to ask. She'd been married to him, and he figured he could take whatever sexual favors he wanted from her as his conjugal right whether she wanted it or not. More often than not she hadn't wanted it, but it hadn't been worth fighting over.

Better to just close her eyes, think of England and get it over with.

She realized she'd squeezed her eyes shut like she used to in bed with Ivan. Startled, she opened her eyes to find Liam studying her quizzically.

"Sorry," she mumbled.

"There's nothing to apologize for. Where'd you go just then?"

She sighed. "I was thinking how strange it was to actually be asked for permission to continue doing... whatever we're doing."

"A, just how big an ass was your ex? And B, why on earth would I want to do anything to you or with you that you don't enjoy? The whole point is to give each other pleasure."

"Duly noted."

Except he didn't do anything. He just sat there, staring at her.

"What?" she finally asked.

"I've been waiting twenty years for you, but this is brand-new to you. Plus, you're the one with the complicated life and who had the big scare earlier." Reaching out, he gently cupped her chin in one hand. "I'm not making any assumptions about what you do or don't want to do tonight. If you want me to take you home, I will. If you want me to hold you so you can sleep, that's fine. If you want more than that, you're going to have to tell me."

She gulped. She might be a bold woman in her professional life, but she couldn't say the same when it came to romance. She'd seriously dated one man in her life and had married him. Which had, of course, been a colossal mistake. She should have dated around.

Learned that there were better men out there than Ivan Durant. She should never have jumped into marriage with the first guy who came along.

"To be honest, I'm scared to death," she finally confessed.

"Of me?" Liam exclaimed. He tensed, clearly planning to put her off his lap.

"No!" she answered hastily. "Stay where you are," she added. "I like having you hold me like this."

Liam stilled beneath her, but the tension didn't leave him as he waited for her to say more.

She appreciated that he didn't take the idea of sleeping with her lightly. And it meant so much that he didn't want to take advantage of her vulnerability after her big scare tonight. But…

She took a deep breath. "I want to be with you tonight, Liam. In *that* way."

"You're still getting over your divorce. You've had a lousy week. You were terrified earlier. I seriously don't want to be the rebound guy you use and lose. If you're not ready for a real relationship, I would rather wait."

"I'm not sure I even know what a real relationship is," she admitted.

"All the more reason to take things slow."

"Or," she replied, "it's all the more reason for you to show me what a real relationship is like." She added slowly, "I think I'd like to know."

Liam frowned. "Are you sure? Relationships are messy and come with feelings and decisions and possible commitments."

She knew plenty about messy. And she knew about hurt feelings and hard decisions, too. Problem was, that deep-seated need for home and family and safety and belonging that she'd always had, the same void that had driven her into marriage with Ivan, still yawned inside her.

And she had a sneaking suspicion Liam might just be the kind of man to fill it.

Did she dare try again?

A few times in her life, moments had loomed in front of Sloane that she knew would shape much of her future to come. Getting her acceptance to law school. Saying yes to Ivan's marriage proposal. Holding her baby girl in her arms for the first time.

And now. Straddling Liam's lap, staring into his gorgeous, honest eyes.

If she went for it with him, there would be no going back. Her life would be forever changed.

That soul-deep yearning tugging within her whispered that life would not only be different. It could be better. Richer. This man might just be the answer to all her unfulfilled dreams.

Of course, if she was wrong, the disappointment would be crushing.

Did she have the courage to find out?

Liam's gaze was steady. Unwavering. He saw her so clearly. He stripped away the extraneous details and went straight to the core of her dilemma. There would be no casual sex between them, no halfway relationship, no friends with benefits arrangement. Being with him would be an all-or-nothing proposition.

She reached inside her heart, deep into that dark, empty void. In its stillness, she asked herself the question one last time. Did she dare risk everything to find love?

Chapter 9

The answer came to her gently, flowing into her heart on a tide of warmth.

Of all the men in the world she could have chosen to take the leap of faith with, Liam was the one man she would choose.

"Yes," she breathed.

"Yes, what?" Liam asked carefully.

"Yes, I want to be with you. Yes, I understand that this can't and won't be a casual fling. Yes, I'm willing to take a chance on a real relationship with you."

Liam stared hard at her, clearly measuring the sincerity of her words. At length, he asked, "You're sure?"

"Positive."

A smile broke across his handsome face and enveloped his whole being. His eyes lit with shock and exultation and joy that warmed her through.

He wrapped her in a giant hug and buried his face against her neck for so long that she began to worry that *he* was having second thoughts about his offer. But then he lifted his head and peppered her face with kisses, murmuring sweet words of praise and adoration all the while.

Being…worshipped…like this was strange and new. But nice. More than nice. It was awesome.

Funny thing, she kind of wanted to worship him back. She met him halfway, kissing him in turn, her hands roaming across his chest and shoulders, slipping behind his neck, her fingers sliding into his silky hair.

"I can't get enough of you," she whispered, shocked at the truth of her words.

"Glad to hear it, baby. The feeling's mutual, I assure you."

She met his gaze shyly, unsure of what to do next. Ivan had always taken the lead between them and dictated what would happen, when and how. He'd been a selfish lover, not interested in her in the least. But Liam seemed to be waiting for her to tell or show him what she wanted.

"I—"

Lord. For a lawyer known for her gifted arguments in court, she was having a hard time expressing what she wanted. "I, uh—"

Liam took pity on her. "You're cute when you're at a loss for words."

She stuck her tongue out at him, and he laughed aloud.

"Let me guess," Liam teased. "You want more, but you're embarrassed to say so aloud. What you actually want is for me to carry you over to my bed, kiss you some more, and see where things go."

"When did you get so smart about women?" she blurted.

"What do you think I did with my college years when I wasn't pining for you? I got to know girls and learned how they think."

"A ladies' man, huh?"

"Oh, I wasn't sleeping around. I was talking with them. If you want to know a woman, you have to listen to her."

"Wow. You may be the first male of the human species to discover that."

He dropped a light kiss on the end of her nose. "Aww, c'mon. We're not all that bad."

Sloane rolled her eyes at him. "You have no idea." Her heart raced as his lips quirked up into a self-deprecating smile. Where had this guy been all her life? Not only did he listen to women, but he knew how to put them at ease, too. He knew when to tease, when to be serious, when to wait and when to act.

Speaking of which, his body suddenly tensed beneath her.

"C'mon Sloane. Let's go where we can both be more comfortable."

He stood up, taking her with him as if he didn't even have to strain to lift her.

"What do you do to get so strong?" she breathed as he strode across the small room to his bed.

"I lift weights. Box a little. Run when the weather's decent. And at this time of year, I try to ski at least once a week."

"Well, clearly it's all paid off."

Liam laughed a little as he bent down so she could yank back the comforter. "If I had known I would one day get to use my strength to carry you to my bed, I would be a world-class body builder by now."

He laid her down on soft flannel sheets.

He'd really been carrying a torch for her all these years? That was so sweet. If only she'd known...

He stretched out beside her, apparently in no hurry to get her naked. For which she was eternally grateful. Ivan had scorned her postbaby body, and she was self-conscious about the stretch marks and more womanly curves. Not that she would trade either one for her precious baby girl.

Liam propped himself up on his elbow beside her and stared down at her as if he was memorizing the sight of her lying back against his fluffy pillows.

Desperate to distract him, she asked, "Have you really had a crush on me ever since high school?"

"Nope. Since fourth grade. When you showed up for the first day of school, third grade it would have been for you, wearing that white lace dress with a pink satin bow in the back, and a matching ribbon in your hair, I was a goner. You looked like some kind of fairy princess. I was sure you were the most beautiful creature I'd ever seen."

She recalled the outfit now that he mentioned it, but she was stunned that *he* remembered it.

He added huskily, "You still are the most beautiful creature I've ever seen."

"Liam. I hate to disappoint you, but I'm really a rather regular person. I can't possibly live up to the inflated image you seem to have built of me in your mind."

He wrinkled his nose at her. "I'm a cop. I deal in facts and see what's directly in front of me, no judgment, no opinions. I *see* you, Sloane."

"And you still want me?" she blurted.

"Yes." His answer was firm. No hesitation.

How was a girl supposed to resist that? He saw her clearly for who she was, and he hadn't run screaming. Well, then.

"Come here, Liam. I think I need you to kiss me some more. And maybe you ought to get rid of some of your clothes."

He loomed over her, grinning. "I do know how the mechanics of this goes, thank you."

"I wasn't sure. You were taking so long getting around to it, you know."

"I didn't want to scare you. You've had enough of a fright for one evening."

"You're the one who may end up getting a fright," she retorted.

He lurched back. "Why do you say that?"

"I'm not some twenty-two-year-old ski bunny. I've had a baby." She added hesitantly, "And I haven't done... this...for, well, a really long time."

He frowned. "For real?"

Embarrassment bloomed on her cheeks with fiery heat.

Liam swore. "I knew your ex was a jerk, but I had no idea just how gigantic a jerk." He leaned down and kissed her tenderly. "Any man—" another kiss "—who managed to gain your love and who didn't worship you for the rest of his life—" a more lingering kiss this time "—and who didn't make love to you morning, noon and night—" another very long kiss that left her breathless and more turned on than she could believe "—doesn't deserve to live, let alone to have you."

Even though he delivered them quietly, his words were intense. One hundred percent sincere.

Something unfurled in her heart, like a bud opening into a flower beneath a layer of melting snow. Who knew a heart could actually thaw? Had she really been that completely frozen inside? Apparently so, because the warmth coursing through her was totally unfamiliar.

She reached for Liam's zipper, determined to see this strange, wondrous sensation through, possible gigantic mistake or not.

What would it be like to make love to a man who genuinely wanted her? Who respected her and found her attractive in spite of her many flaws?

His hands slipped under her sweatshirt and he pushed it over her head, kissing her soundly when her face popped free of the neckline. He laughed at how her hair stood up every which way and took his time smoothing it down with long, languid strokes.

She arched into him, eager to get rid of the rest of her clothes, but he murmured, "We're going to take this slow. If, at any time, you don't like something or change your mind, just let me know. Okay?"

She placed her palms on either side of his face and gazed deep into his beautiful eyes, letting her gratitude show. "Okay."

"Stop that."

Startled, she replied, "Stop what?"

"The gratitude thing. I'm the one on my metaphorical knees here, overwhelmed with thankfulness that you would choose to be with me."

"I guess we're going to have to agree to have a mutual gratitude society, then. You're a good man, Liam."

He grimaced. "I'm not sure that's a compliment coming from you."

She pulled back to stare up at him. That was a genuinely insightful observation from him. Not many people saw the risk-taker within her. She kept that side of herself carefully hidden beneath everyone else's expectations of her. She'd been a dutiful daughter, a diligent student, and a devoted wife. Until Ivan had utterly rejected her and the home she'd desperately tried to build for the two of them.

"I meant it as a compliment." And she was a little surprised herself to realize she meant that. She said more emphatically, "You are a good man. And I'm coming to realize how rare those are."

He smiled broadly. "You don't know how good I am...yet. But I'm planning to show you."

She snickered at him, and commenced kicking off her jeans while he kicked off his. They fell into each other and got hopelessly tangled up, and ended up laughing together while they awkwardly stripped their remaining clothes off each other, bumping knees, and dodging elbows in eye sockets.

It was exactly what she needed to break the tension of her nerves. Sweet, funny, charming Liam. He'd always been her Liam: she just hadn't realized it until now. In the same way she hadn't realized how wonderful—and sexy—a nice guy could be.

She'd always gone for the dark-souled, dangerous types, and look where that had gotten her. Her life had imploded and she and Chloe had barely made it out. Apparently, she'd needed to grow up before she realized that kind, good men had it all over on selfish, immature bad boys. Emphasis on men, and emphasis on boys.

As the revelation washed over her, Liam opened his arms to her, and she went to him willingly, joyfully, her heart wide open.

Liam felt the emotional shift when Sloane came to some final decision about him. He didn't know exactly what she'd figured out, but the last vestiges of her reticence fell away all at once, and suddenly, he had a warm, eager, happy woman in his arms.

Mind. Blown.

Sloane Colton wanted him. Really wanted him. And she was in his bed, naked and soft and all woman, her thigh thrown across his legs, her small, beautifully formed breasts pressed against his chest, a smile on her lips as she burrowed close.

"What's your pleasure?" he managed to ask.

"I don't actually know," she confessed.

God almighty. Her ex-husband really was a monster. And a fool. He hadn't even bothered to pleasure his own wife properly? For real, what an idiot. And what a waste of an extraordinary woman. It was *not* a mistake he planned to make.

"Let's find out what you like, together." He rolled her onto her back and commenced kissing his way across her body. He kept an eagle eye out for when her hands fluttered up self-consciously, and he duly avoided her hips and sides, although he had no earthly idea why she was worried. The faint stretch marks on her skin were badges of motherhood, and beautiful to him. Her skin was fair anyway, and the marks were barely visible.

He moved instead to kissing her stomach and swirled his tongue in her belly button until she was giggling helplessly. She always had been ticklish. He and Fox used to ambush her and tickle her until she screamed with laughter.

"Are your ribs still your Achilles' heel?" he rasped against her stomach, his hands sliding up her sides.

"Don't you dare!"

He grinned devilishly as he slid his fingertips across her ribs and felt her squirm. Instead of tickling her, though, he cupped her breasts in his hands and rubbed the pads of his thumbs lightly across her nipples. She gasped and her back arched up off the mattress. He leaned down to capture one rosy peak in his mouth, rolling his tongue lazily around the excited bud. Another gasp, and he smiled against her velvet skin.

So responsive. Honest. Direct. So very…Sloane.

"Better than rib tickling?" he murmured.

"*So* much better."

She tugged at the short hair tumbling across his forehead, pulling him up her body to kiss his mouth deeply. Her legs wrapped around his hips, and her heels dug into his glutes, urging him to get on with business.

Her impatience was contagious, and all the careful restraint he'd been exercising evaporated. He needed to be inside her, part of her, joined with her, now. So long he'd waited for this. He fumbled in the drawer of his nightstand for a condom and quickly took care of protecting them both.

And then he reached down between their bodies, cognizant that she hadn't done this for a very long time. He definitely didn't want to hurt her. Thankfully, she was wet and ready, and his body reacted hard to the evidence of just how badly she really wanted him.

He couldn't remember how long he'd yearned for this exact moment, and he sternly reminded himself to savor it and make a memory of it.

He positioned himself carefully. Leaning on one elbow, he looked down at Sloane, who stared back up at him, wide-eyed and breathless. She looked like a fey creature, too beautiful to be of this world. He didn't understand what she saw in him, but he damned well wasn't going to question it.

"You're sure about this?" he murmured one last time.

"Positive."

Talk about feeling like a conquering hero. Sloane Colton was positive she wanted him. Praise the Lord. Joy overflowed his heart and broke across his face.

Determined to get it right, he pressed into her as gently as he could possibly manage.

It was torture. Her body was tight and slick and so hot around him that he felt as if he was burning to ashes inside her. Inch by glorious inch, he eased deeper. It was bar none, the best eternity in his entire life.

Swear-to-God fireworks actually detonated inside his brain as triumph exploded in his soul. After all these years, he'd finally found his way to Sloane. And somehow, miraculously, she wanted him back.

She moved impatiently against him, wiggling a little, and inadvertently driving him even deeper inside her. He'd thought he was all the way home, but apparently not. It was a struggle to keep his eyes from rolling back into his head as pleasure engulfed him.

Experimentally, he rocked his hips a little.

"Do that again!" Sloane exclaimed breathlessly.

"Liked that, did you?" he ground out from between clenched teeth.

"Yes. Again." This time she was more demanding. She undulated against him, and the feel of her coaxing him to pick up the intensity just about did him in.

Grateful beyond belief to be able to let go of the reins of control a little, he complied. The groan his increased pace wrung from her was so sexy he could barely hold it together. *Must. Take. It. Slow.*

"Don't take it slow," she panted.

"You're killing me, Sloane. I'm trying not to hurt you."

"I won't break. And I want you. Now."

Ahh, sweet, impatient Sloane. The woman was simply perfect. He moved easily within her, setting up a slow, steady rhythm that was surely going to drive him out of his mind. He watched her closely, praying it would do the same for her.

Her eyes widened and then drifted closed as a beatific smile spread across her face.

Thank goodness.

Sloane gasped, then moaned, then cried out as she surged against him and he met her thrust for thrust. He stared down at her, and she stared up at him, their gazes locked in wonder, then awe, then in eyes-glazed-over pleasure so intense he could hardly see through it.

But always on the other side of the pleasure, Sloane was there, her lovely, heart-shaped face lit with ecstasy that exactly mirrored his own.

The sex was great. But the lovemaking was unbelievable. The connection between them was intense as they shared everything they were feeling with each other.

He held nothing back, and he didn't see any evidence of Sloane holding back, either. Not that it would be her style. She threw herself into life with a passion.

As exquisite as her inner core felt, tight and hot, clenching around him, it wasn't just about physical pleasure. It was about finding in her the home he'd always been searching for. And finally, it was about gratitude. Soul-deep, humbling gratitude that they'd found each other at long last.

As they reached smashing climaxes together and collapsed back against the mattress, breathing hard, tears actually traced down Sloane's cheeks. He kissed them away gently, silently thanking her for the gift of her body and the piece of her heart he sensed she'd just shared with him.

He hoped she knew that she had all of his heart in return. Of course, it was way too soon to say something like that aloud. He might have the words now to express his feelings, but he'd also learned to guard his heart and not scare off women by oversharing.

He rolled onto his back, and Sloane followed him of her own volition, her ear plastered to his chest, one slender arm thrown lazily across his stomach. His hand rested naturally between her shoulder blades, and he reveled in the satiny softness of her skin. Her dark, thick hair spilled across the back of his hand, mink-like, as warm and silky as she was.

Sloane, never at a loss for words, rested drowsily on his chest, seemingly content just to lie there and listen to his heartbeat. A deep calm seeped into his soul as they lay there quietly, enjoying being together. For once in their lives, there was no need to say anything.

The moment was perfect. Being here with her like this was exactly right. Why in the world it had taken them all these years to get here, he had no idea. But he was damned glad they'd finally made it.

He jerked awake sometime later to the sound of his cell phone jangling on the floor beside the bed. His bedside clock said it was after 2:00 a.m. Crap. That had to be work.

His jeans lay in a tangled pile, and he dug frantically, looking for the right opening to the right pocket. Finally, he yanked out his phone and slammed it to his ear.

"Detective Kastor," he bit out.

"Stan Palichek here. Denver PD. Your guy has shown up at the house you've had us watching. We ran the license plates and have an ID on him."

Liam swung his bare feet to the floor and sat on the side of the bed, naked. A warm, female body wrapped around his hips from behind, and he smiled down at Sloane in the faint moonlight coming in the window. She still looked like a fairy princess, a seductive one these days, her eyes dark and mysterious, her smile inviting. Lord, it was tempting to hang up the phone and crawl back into her arms.

"Who is it?" he managed to collect his thoughts enough to ask the cop on the other end of the line.

"Private investigator. Name's William Gunther. Works solo. Does cheating spouse cases mostly. Strictly a follow 'em and film 'em guy."

"Thanks for the call. I'll head up to Denver in the

morning and try to push through the search warrant on the house, now that we know who we're dealing with."

"See ya then." Palichek hung up and Liam laid down his phone thoughtfully.

Gunther sounded like exactly the kind of man Ivan Durant would hire to stalk his ex-wife. Now, if only the PI would roll over on Durant and give up the guy as his employer. Then he and Sloane could pin a restraining order on Ivan's sorry ass and be rid of him once and for all.

Chapter 10

Sloane woke up languorously to the smell of frying bacon and the sight of Liam standing in front of the stove, barefoot, wearing only a pair of jeans slung low on his hips and cupping his tight behind just right. The muscles of his back flexed as he flipped over the bacon in a fascinating play of changing shapes. Now *that* was a sight for sore eyes.

Never in her life had she woken up feeling this content. She stretched lazily.

Liam glanced over his shoulder and smiled at her. "Good morning, beautiful. Can I interest you in some breakfast?"

"Absolutely."

"How do you like your eggs?" he asked.

"Over easy if fried. With cheese if scrambled. Loaded with veggies if an omelet. Soft-boiled if you're feeling European. And any way at all if I'm not cooking them for myself."

Liam laughed. "Are you always this easy to please?"

She grinned back. "I don't know. You tell me."

He slid two fried eggs onto a plate, loaded it with bacon and toast and carried it over to her.

She would never get tired of watching his long, muscular legs and the easy, confident way he walked. How on earth had she ever missed what a total hunk this guy was?

"Seriously, Liam. How did you manage not to have girls crawling all over you in high school?"

"I was only interested in one girl, and she barely knew I existed."

"Oh, I totally knew you existed." She winked at him coyly. "You were my big brother's best friend who tortured me all the time."

"Yeah. About that." He sat down on the edge of the bed and waited to hand her the plate of food until she'd put a couple pillows behind her back. "I'm sorry about chasing off the other boys and making your life miserable."

"You and Fox were just looking out for me. I can't be mad about that. You probably saved me a lot of heartache and my grade point average posthumously thanks to you."

He leaned over to kiss her before handing her a glass of orange juice. "What are your plans today?"

She sighed. "I have to pick up Chloe from the Crooked C and take her to Denver. She has a court-ordered overnight visit with her grandparents scheduled for this evening."

Liam glanced out the window above the headboard

and then back at her in concern. "I thought you didn't like driving in bad weather."

"I don't," she replied in alarm. "What's the forecast for today?"

"Snow's moving in. It's supposed to get bad tonight and tomorrow."

She swore under her breath. In any normal, reasonable world, she would call Ivan's parents and reschedule the visit for another time. But the Durants were neither normal nor reasonable.

"Why the exasperation?" Liam asked.

"Ivan threatened to take me back to court and challenge the custody agreement if I don't obey the court-ordered visitation schedule exactly."

"Can he do that?"

"Technically, yes. He managed to get our divorce heard by the biggest troll of a judge in all of Colorado. I wouldn't be surprised if he or his parents had this judge in their pocket. I really don't want to end up in court again. Anytime a custody case goes to court, there's a certain roll of the dice involved. I just can't take that kind of chance with Chloe."

Liam nodded sympathetically. Then he surprised her by announcing, "I have to go to Denver on business today, too. Do you want me to drive you and Chloe up there in my truck? It handles bad roads beautifully."

"Are you sure you want to be trapped in a vehicle for hours with an impatient toddler?" she responded doubtfully.

"Why not?"

"She has quite a set of lungs when she's frustrated."

"She's a baby. She's supposed to scream when she's unhappy."

Sloane laughed a little. "You don't know what you're getting yourself into."

"I'm game to find out."

"You are either insanely brave or insanely ignorant of two-year-olds."

He grinned and kissed her, tasting of bacon and orange juice. Yum.

"When does Chloe have to be at the Durants' house?"

"Just sometime today. The court documents don't specify a time."

"Feel free to use the shower. I'm going to run down to the police station to pick up some paperwork I'll need. Then I'll swing by here, take you over to your house to get whatever you need, and we'll head out to the Crooked C to get the munchkin."

She couldn't remember the last time she and Ivan had seamlessly coordinated on anything. But then, it had always been about him. She'd been expected to fit her life in around the edges of his.

As she showered and dressed, she tried to remember anything at all good about her marriage. Had it really been as consistently awful as she recalled? Surely not. But for the life of her, she couldn't summon any memory of her four years with him in which she'd been truly happy or even at ease.

Yet here she was, after one night with Liam, relaxed and comfortable with him, smiling for no reason at all, and impatient to see him again, even though he'd been gone less than an hour. Weird.

When he pulled into the driveway of her house, he glanced over at her grimly and said, "I'm going to stay out here in the truck while you go in and pack whatever you and Chloe need for the trip to Denver. There's no reason for me to show up on the surveillance feeds any more than necessary. We wouldn't want to make your stalker suspicious of me."

He made sense. She went into the house, packed an overnight bag for herself and then did the same for Chloe, being sure to include Chloe's favorite blanket, pajamas and a few toys that tended to occupy her for long periods of time. She even packed the *Winnie the Pooh* book in case the Durants wanted to read her a bedtime story.

It felt strange helping her ex-in-laws bond with Chloe. But there was no reason to make Little Bug miserable in her stay with her grandparents. And Niall and Carol were, in fact, Chloe's blood relatives. They had a right to a decent relationship with their grandchild without Sloane poisoning it.

Liam had already moved Chloe's car seat into his truck and installed it in the back seat of the big crew cab when she joined him outside.

As she climbed into the passenger seat, she commented, "A baby seat looks pretty incongruous in your big, manly truck."

He grinned over at her. "I like it, personally."

"Really?"

"Yes, Sloane. Really. I knew going into this that you and Chloe were a package deal."

Wow. She hadn't even thought about that aspect of their relationship. She'd been so gobsmacked by her own reaction to him that she hadn't factored Chloe into the equation, yet.

"You're sure you like kids?"

"Love 'em. I want a big house full of them someday. How about you?"

She laughed. "Chloe is the center of my universe. I would die for her."

He nodded. "I get that. So would I."

"But she's not your child."

"She's part of you, and that's enough for me."

Sloane stared, and he added lightly, "Not to mention, she's a cutie pie. She has her mommy's ginormous eyes and fairy princess features."

Sloane looked out the window quickly lest she spot the tears welling up in her eyes. Chloe's own father had never said anything remotely that nice about her.

When they arrived at the Crooked C, Fox looked back and forth keenly between her and Liam. Sloane did her best to keep her expression bland. She wasn't ready to share her newfound relationship with Liam yet, and she prayed he would catch the hint and play it cool, too.

He did.

"Hey Fox," Liam announced. "I'm driving your sister up to Denver with me. Snow's forecast for later and you know how she hates to drive on bad roads."

Sloane recognized the shadow that passed across her brother's features. Their parents had died in a car crash, and both of them shared a raw nerve when it came to potentially dangerous driving conditions.

"Thanks, bro," Fox replied.

Chloe blasted out the front door just then, swathed in a powder-blue ski suit Sloane had never seen before.

"Hey, Bug! Where'd you get this fancy ski suit?"

"Bay-wee."

Sloane looked up at her future sister-in-law, who'd appeared in the doorway behind Chloe. "You didn't have to," she chided.

"Oh, but I did," Bailey replied, smiling. "I'm told all

Coltons are avid skiers, and no self-respecting princess can ski without a proper outfit."

"Wanna go zoom!" Chloe shouted.

"You've created a monster," Sloane groaned.

Liam piped up. "Hey, if Chloe wants to learn how to ski, I'd be glad to teach her. I taught kiddie ski classes over my winter breaks all through college. My parents probably still have my first skis and boots, too. I bet they'd be about the right size for a two-year-old."

Chloe squealed in delight and clapped her hands. "Cwo-ee ski!"

Liam picked her up in the air and swung her around, and the squeals turned into screams of laughter. Liam lifted her nose to nose with him and spoke solemnly to her. "It's a date, kid. You and me. We're going skiing as soon as we get back from your grandma and grandpa's house."

Chloe threw her arms around Liam's neck and hugged him tightly.

It was all Sloane could do not to tear up again. But she dared not. Not in front of her all-too-perceptive brother nor in front of her well-meaning future sister-in-law who wouldn't think twice about spilling the beans to Fox and Wyatt that Sloane had feelings for Liam.

Liam popped Chloe into her car seat and Sloane buckled her in. She set up a princess movie on a tablet in a stand attached to the arm of the toddler's car seat, and they were on their way.

For once, Chloe was an angel in the truck. She finished the movie, ate a snack and then fell asleep, not waking up until they pulled up in front of the Durant mansion in an exclusive Denver suburb.

"Nice house," Liam commented.

She replied under her breath, "Don't be impressed. If you think Russ and Mara's house is cold, this place is Antarctica. I'll take your apartment any day of the week and twice on Sunday compared to this place."

"Twice on Sunday, huh?" he murmured back. "That can be arranged."

Laughing at his innuendo, she unbuckled Chloe and carried her up to the porch while he waited in the truck.

She leaned over to let Chloe push the doorbell. Little Bug crowed when she heard chimes echo inside the house.

The Durants' housekeeper, Anna, opened the front door. "Mrs. Durant. It's good to see you again. Hi there, Miss Chloe."

She didn't correct the woman over her last name. No sense causing friction as she was about to hand her child over to these people.

Carol Durant strolled into the grand foyer, looking as elegant and frigid as ever. "There you are, Sloane. You're late. I've missed an appointment with my manicurist while I waited for you." She reached out for Chloe, who recoiled in Sloane's arms.

Sloane clenched her teeth. She *hated* handing over her daughter to Ivan's mother. And she wasn't about to apologize for causing this woman to miss a manicure.

She spoke as politely as she could manage. "I don't know if Ivan told you, but Chloe was very sick about ten days ago. She was in the hospital for two days. She's still recovering and needs not to get overtired or overstimulated. I packed a bunch of movies she likes and some quiet toys for her to play with. But please don't do too much with her."

Carol shot her a withering look. "I am a mother, too, you know. I do know how to raise a child."

Sloane bit back a snort. If Ivan was any indication of the woman's parenting skills, Carol shouldn't be bragging.

Carol reached for Chloe again, and Little Bug shouted, "No way!"

Sloane bit back a smile. Good for Chloe. She said diplomatically to her daughter, "Would you like to go with Anna and feed the fish in the pond?" The Durants had a heated koi pond in their formal garden, and Chloe was fascinated by the big, colorful fish.

"Feed fishies!" she exclaimed, wiggling eagerly in Sloane's arms.

She set Chloe down, and the toddler raced past Carol to the housekeeper, who'd retreated to the back of the foyer. Anna met Sloane's gaze of entreaty at her employer's back and nodded at Sloane in silent promise to take care of Chloe.

Sloane trusted Anna. The woman had a slew of children and grandchildren, and handled Chloe beautifully with just the right combination of indulgence, firmness and humor.

As the pair disappeared into the bowels of the mansion, Sloane passed Chloe's baby bag to Carol, who set it down on the antique Louis XV fainting couch with distaste.

"Okay, then. I'll see you tomorrow," Sloane said. She turned and retreated quickly toward the truck. She had no desire whatsoever to get into a sparring match with her ex-mother-in-law. Their relationship had been chilly when she'd been married to Ivan, and she had no reason to believe Carol would thaw toward her now.

She climbed back into the warmth of the truck, and Liam pulled away immediately.

"You okay?" he asked quietly.

She reached out blindly with her hand, unable to see through her tears, and he took it, squeezing it sympathetically.

"It's just one night, sweetheart," he murmured.

She nodded. He was right. And she had work to do today. She had petitions to file with various courts in Denver, and she had a pile of files to pick up for clients who'd asked her to review their cases.

Liam parked and after a quick kiss goodbye, she headed for one court clerk while he headed for another to work on the search warrant for the home of whoever was watching her surveillance cameras.

They agreed he would pick her up at the courthouse at five o'clock.

For once, she felt as if she had her life together. Chloe was occupied, she got to be a lawyer for a few hours and at long last, she had a great guy in her life. Happiness bubbled up inside her, filling the hollow place deep within her and comforting her inner lost child, still wailing after all these years for her dead parents.

Chloe's birth might have quieted that inner howl of loneliness, but Liam was the first ever to completely silence it.

Things couldn't get much better than this.

A little voice in her head warned her against getting too comfortable, but she dismissed it impatiently. After all, what could go wrong?

Chapter 11

Liam headed for the police station that had handled the April Thomas disappearance. He'd made an appointment with the detective in charge of the investigation, and the cop, a gray-haired veteran, walked Liam through everything they'd done to try to find the young woman.

The detective's work had been meticulous. It took Liam an hour and the help of two cops and a secretary to make copies of all the documents, interviews and statements surrounding the search for the missing young woman.

But eventually, he carried a big cardboard file box out to his truck. The snow was really coming down hard now, accumulating fast. He had to push a good three inches of the stuff off the door handle to open it. He stowed the box of files and was just climbing into his truck when a cop called out from the doorway of the precinct.

"Hey! Are you Detective Kastor of the Roaring Springs PD?"

"Yeah, that's me."

"Just got a call from the front desk. A search warrant has arrived for you."

Liam jogged back inside, pausing to shake snow off his shoulders. He followed the cop through the big building and signed for the sealed courier pouch that held his warrant.

Perfect. If he caught a lucky break, he could nail Ivan Durant, today. He pocketed the search warrant and hurried from the station, antsy to get to the house in east Denver before the occupant left and he had to wait another week for the guy to show up.

While he drove, Liam called a police operator and had himself patched through to the undercover cops staking out Gunther's house. The officers verified to him that the occupant was still inside.

He parked in the next city block and slipped between houses to approach the stakeout vehicle from the passenger's side, across the street from the house under observation. Snow was falling in big, fat flakes that blanketed the ground in several inches of white fluff.

Liam slid into the back seat of the stakeout car and introduced himself, and the pair of cops in the front seat did the same. The driver said, "When you execute the search warrant, we'll back you up."

No time like the present to find out who this dude was, and more importantly, who he worked for. Liam hopped out and jogged across the street.

The residence in question was a haggard brick ranch

house that would have been chic in about 1960. The silver aluminum screen door sagged on its hinges, and the front door behind it desperately needed painting. Liam peered in the little diamond window at face height and saw a dark hallway and a narrow living room to the left. No sign of anyone inside.

He knocked on the door and heard movement beyond the living room. Probably a kitchen back that way. No one was forthcoming to answer the front door, however.

He knocked again.

This time he heard a sound that made him swear. A door opening and closing at the back of the house.

One of the cops standing behind him yelled, "We've got a runner!"

Liam tore around the side of the house, slipping and sliding in the snow. He quickly outdistanced the other cops. He hadn't been a champion skier for nothing.

Spying a figure cutting across a backyard and ducking around the corner of a house, Liam pounded after the fleeing man. The guy's footprints were clear as day in the snow. Truth be told, Liam could have walked after the guy and just followed the tracks. But on the off chance that this dude had a getaway car stashed somewhere nearby, Liam kept running.

He caught up quickly and took note of the balding head, beer gut and awkward stride. Rather than tackle the man, he got close enough to call, "Don't make me knock you down. I don't want to hurt you. I just want to talk."

The runner stumbled to a halt, sagging against someone's garage wall, panting like a dying dog.

"Are you okay, buddy?" Liam asked. "Do you need to sit down?"

The older man swore colorfully. "Ain't as young as I once was. Probably ought to cut back a pack or two a day on the cigarettes, too."

Liam grimaced. "Take your time, sir. Catch your breath."

"Don't patronize me. I used to be a cop."

Liam's eyebrows shot up. Really? How did a cop become a cheap gumshoe? Did he mess up a case? A personal problem maybe? A bad shooting?

"You gonna arrest me?" the guy asked truculently.

"Not unless you try to flee again. I really do just want to talk. Are you William Gunther?"

The man eyed him warily. "I'm gonna need to see a badge before I answer any questions."

Liam pulled his out.

"Roaring Springs? Well, shit. I guess I know why you want to talk with me, then. You better come back to the house with me, Detective Kastor. Bill Gunther. Pleased to meet you."

Liam kept pace beside the man as they retraced their steps to the home. They caught up with the two Denver cops and all four of them trudged back to the house through the snow.

One of them held the back door open for Gunther, who led them into a family room at the back of the home. Three computer monitors sat side by side on a table, and Liam's jaw tightened at the live views of Sloane's house showing on them.

"Did you install those surveillance cameras yourself?" Liam asked casually, trying to sound impressed.

"Yeah. I was a tech guy in my former life."

"That's nice gear," he threw out to see what kind of response he would get.

"Client told me to get the best money could buy. His dime, so I spent it." Gunther chuckled a little, and Liam smirked along with him. If the FBI tech Zog was right, this surveillance setup had cost Ivan Durant thousands of dollars.

Liam jumped on the opening Gunther had given him. "Who's your client?"

"Can't say."

"Can't or won't?"

"Can't. I honestly don't know who it is. The person pays for this house and my fees out of an offshore bank account and communicates by encrypted email."

"Can you give me the account number? I can track it down."

"You think I don't have the resources to run down a bank account?" Gunther retorted scornfully. "I was a cop. I've got connections."

"Yeah? What did your connections tell you?"

"That whoever owns the account buried his or her identity behind an unbreakable shell corporation."

"Any guesses as to who the client might be?" Liam threw out.

"The ex-husband, maybe. He and the dame have had a couple pretty nasty phone calls that I caught on tape. But that's just a guess. I've got no evidence to support it."

Liam asked, "What were your instructions specifically, regarding Ms. Colton?"

"I'm supposed to get dirt on her. Anything that can be used to smear her good name and ruin her reputation."

"Did the client tell you why he or she wants to destroy Ms. Colton?"

"Nope. Just to look for dirt and send along anything I find."

"Have you found any?"

"Nah. This chick's one of the most boring people I've ever watched. Her kid's cute, though."

Liam's jaw muscles rippled in irritation, but he tamped down the emotion. He had to keep things light and friendly. He gestured at Gunther's monitor array. "So how does this setup work? How do the cameras send a signal to you? By cell phone tower? Wireless over the internet?" Zog had already explained it to him, but Liam wanted to keep this guy talking.

"Nah," Gunther replied. "The cameras shoot a short-range radio signal to a receiver and signal booster I installed in the woods behind the lady's house. I attached them to a telephone pole and spliced the receiver into a phone line. I call a phone number, and stored images dump through a modem to this computer."

"That sounds complicated."

"It's old school, but it leaves a small digital footprint. Hard to track. Speaking of which, how did you find me?"

Liam shrugged. "Once I spotted your cameras in the lady's house—"

Gunther interrupted. "Hey! Ain't you that guy who came into her house late at night a few weeks back and took some of her clothes? What was up with that? Are you some kind of creepo yourself?"

Liam answered stiffly as the Denver cops perked up with interest. "Her daughter was in the hospital, and I volunteered to go to her home and get her a change of clothing and a toothbrush."

"Is the kid okay?"

"I believe so," Liam answered carefully. "At any rate, once I spotted your cameras, I called the FBI. They cloned your equipment, followed the signal and tracked you down."

"FBI, huh? Okay, then. I don't feel so bad if it took the big boys to find me."

"Since you were a cop, Mr. Gunther, you do understand that I can charge you with a bunch of crimes, right? Breaking and entering, illegal surveillance, invasion of privacy, evading arrest. You know the drill."

"Yeah. I do know the drill." Gunther threw him a sly look. "Whaddiya want from me in order to look the other way?"

"Would you mind coming down to the police station and making a formal statement for us? Tell us everything you can about your client and give us the bank routing number and email address the client uses?"

"Yeah, sure. But let me get this deal straight. I tell you everything I know and you guys don't charge me with anything. I walk, and my private investigator's license isn't touched."

The Denver cops bristled at that, obviously not thrilled. But Liam didn't care if they'd been trying to nail this guy or not. He wanted all the information he could get on who had hired Gunther. "Correct. That's the deal."

While he drove the PI to the police station, Liam kept up the casual banter, eventually circling back to who might have hired Gunther and why.

Gunther was more at ease without multiple cops hovering and waxed chatty. "In one of the emails the client sent me, he griped about it taking so long to find dirt on the dame. He said if I could get pictures or video of her with any man, they could be photoshopped to look worse than they were. Even if the guy was fully dressed and they weren't doing anything out of line, I should forward the images to the contact email."

Liam gripped the steering wheel until his hands ached. "And did you?"

"Nah. She's never with anyone. Lives like a hermit."

"Did the client give you any idea what he or she wants to do with this dirt on Ms. Colton?"

"Oh, he told me what he plans to do. He's showing it to a judge. Wants to get her disbarred and make her lose her kid. He's out to ruin her but good."

A need to hurt this nameless client surged through Liam. "How do you know it's a man?" he asked tightly.

Gunther shrugged. "I don't know for sure. But it seems like a guy thing to ruin a person's career and get their kid taken away. Women tend to go for the personal kill. They want to humiliate the husband or boyfriend by confronting them with pictures, catching them in a lie and kicking them to the curb dramatically."

Liam thought that was a wildly sexist observation, but he wasn't here to argue with Gunther. He was here to get the guy's cooperation.

"Have you ever asked the client for more money?"

"I'm getting free housing and three grand a month plus expenses to monitor the dame. Why would I rock that boat?"

"Would you be willing to send an email to the client and demand more money just to see what kind of a response you get?"

Gunther shrugged. "Might as well. You're gonna be yanking out those cameras now that you know who I am, aren't you?"

"Oh, yeah." Liam added, "And thanks for helping me out with this, Bill. I really appreciate it."

"Maybe you'll owe me one before this is over with."

"I already owe you one, man. You quit running when I yelled at you to stop."

Gunther laughed. "You ain't a half-bad guy. For a cop, that is."

The PI took his sweet time writing out a statement by hand. He seemed to be getting a kick out of the police needing his help and was milking the attention, chatting up cops in the precinct and joking over how bad the coffee was and how much he'd missed it.

Liam watched the time anxiously and finally was forced to pull out his cell phone and give Sloane a quick call.

She answered cheerfully, "Hey, Liam. I'm just winding up here at the courthouse. I'll be ready to go to dinner in a few minutes."

"I'm running a bit late here. I should be done in the next half hour or so. Would you mind grabbing a taxi and meeting me at the restaurant? I'm really sorry."

"Of course not," Sloane answered. "What's the name again?"

"The Enchanted Plate. It's a dozen blocks west of the hotel on the same street."

"Perfect. I'll drop off these boxes of files in my room and freshen up a little, and then I'll meet you there."

Liam realized he was smiling at his cell phone as he disconnected the call and pocketed the device.

"Hot date?" Gunther asked shrewdly.

Liam shrugged. "Dinner. With a colleague who happens to be female." And with whom he'd slept and hoped to do so again soon. No way was he dishing on

Sloane Colton with this man who'd been watching her every move for the past several weeks.

"Gotta say, kid. I'm glad you caught me. I was gonna have to head over to Roaring Springs in person before long to tail the dame the old-fashioned way. And I eff-ing hate snow."

Liam laughed a little to cover up his horror. "Then why do you live in Colorado, Bill?"

A shrug. "Maybe I'll head for the West Coast after this. Or maybe go to Florida. Whaddiya think? Do more folks cheat on their SOs in California or Florida?"

"Hell if I know," Liam retorted. "Are you about done with that statement?"

Chapter 12

Sloane wished she'd packed a slinky little black dress, but alas, she had only conservative business suits in her bag. Oh, well. If Liam didn't think she was sexy after the smoking hot night they'd shared together, he was probably a lost cause anyway.

She realized she was smiling at herself in the mirror as she carefully applied makeup and let down her hair from the severe French twist she usually wore in court. Liam had that effect on her. He relaxed her. Made her feel at home in her own skin for a change.

Honestly, she couldn't remember the last time she'd felt like this. It was more than happiness. She was hopeful for the future, and that she and Chloe would be happy in their new home. That things would work out with Liam.

Huh. She hadn't seen that last one coming. But

darned if he didn't make her think about a long-term relationship. She'd seriously thought she was done with those, but he'd shown her she still had the capacity to love in that way.

The restaurant Liam had chosen for their dinner was one she'd never been to before. It had a funky Western vibe and casual decor, but the linen tablecloths were perfectly starched, the seasonal menu was gourmet and the waitstaff was impeccably trained.

She arrived first and was led to a table for two in a secluded corner overshadowed by a hanging Navaho blanket. The waiter had just poured her a complimentary glass of the house red wine when Liam strode in.

Every female head in the room turned to note his entrance.

Appreciating the view as well, Sloane took in the way his jeans clung to his thighs and how his tweed sports jacket outlined his big, brawny shoulders. Yes, indeed. Liam Kastor had grown up very nicely.

She sighed dreamily. If she were to make a list of all the things she was looking for in a man at this time in her life, he would tick off just about every box.

Liam slipped into the seat across from her, and the first thing she noticed was how his gaze darted around the room guardedly, taking in everyone cautiously. Should she be worried about something or someone? She looked around herself but saw only patrons eating their dinners and talking.

"You look lovely tonight. How did your day go, Sloane?"

Her gaze snapped back to him, and she smiled warmly. "Thanks. And my day was productive. Yours?"

"Very productive."

"Does that mean you identified the man who's been watching me?"

"I did better than that. I spoke with him. At length. He even gave the Denver PD a formal written statement."

"Really? Do tell." Anticipation exploded inside her chest. If they could nail Ivan once and for all—

Liam interrupted her thoughts. "The guy's name is Bill Gunther. Private investigator. Unfortunately, he has no idea who hired him to spy on you."

"Then we're back to square one?" she asked in dismay.

"Not entirely. Bill gave us a bank account number in the Cayman Islands and an encrypted email address belonging to his employer. The FBI's working on penetrating the identity of their owner."

"How long will that take?" she asked.

Interestingly, Liam's gaze went even darker and more closed than before. "I don't know."

She started to ask him what was wrong, but he forestalled her by declaring himself starving and occupying the next few minutes chatting with the waiter about the menu. Her internal alarm bells started to ring a little. What was he hiding from her? He'd been nothing but an open book in the past. What had changed?

Liam ended up ordering the prime rib, and she ordered a cassoulet of marinated pork, white beans and root vegetables. A fancy French stew, in other words.

She tried to ask Liam what was wrong over dinner, but every time she cleverly maneuvered the conversation in that direction, another sumptuous course of food was served and she ended up totally distracted by it. Not to mention, she got the distinct impression from

Liam that he was avoiding talking about whatever was bothering him.

Sometimes, having the finely honed instincts and people-reading skills of a courtroom attorney sucked.

Was it her? Had she done something to put him off? He'd been perfectly pleasant and relaxed on the ride into Denver. Surely this had to do with his work and not with her. But years of living with Ivan had made her prone to self-blame. Her ex had always found a way to make her responsible for his bad days.

Unable to stand the suspense any longer, she leaned in closer to Liam and blurted, "Have I done something to upset you?"

"Why on earth would ask something like that?"

Oh, God. Whatever was bugging him did have to do with her. "Look, Liam. I'm no good at this whole dating thing. I didn't do it much in college, and I met Ivan the first day of law school. If I've done something to tick you off, please just tell me."

"You haven't done anything wrong."

He was lying. His shoulders were up around his ears, and he was all but shouting defensiveness. That was when the panic hit. Her breathing accelerated, and her gaze darted across the room, seeking the exit. A feeling of being trapped in here, of needing to run away surged through her. He was dumping her. She'd already blown it somehow. Crud. What had she done? Her mind raced in futile circles in search of the answer.

Which was when it dawned on her she'd already fallen a lot harder for him than she'd realized. She shouldn't beg, but she couldn't help herself.

"Liam, you're amazing. I never thought I could have any feelings for another man, but you've shown me I can. I never thought I would feel like a woman again, and yet I do."

Stop begging, Sloane. But I can't lose him!

She continued, "I only hope I make you feel half as good as you make me feel. I really think we have something special between us."

Lame, lame, lame. Shut. Up.

She heard more words fall out of her mouth. "I want you to get to know Chloe if you're willing, and I want you in our lives. I trust you like I never thought I'd trust anyone again. I'm so grateful to you for everything you've done for me. For us."

He opened his mouth to say something, but the waiter arrived just then with dessert.

Damn! What had he been about to say?

Frustrated, she waited in silent terror for Liam's response to her grand declaration. It was a huge risk to let her feelings all hang out like this. In fact, what had she been thinking to blurt out all of that? He must think she was the most desperate woman on earth.

A deep and powerful need to slide off her chair and crawl under the table all but overcame her.

Frozen in dread, she stared at the gigantic slice of dark chocolate cake before her.

Liam dug into his crème brûlée and didn't seem to notice her bizarre behavior.

Sloane picked up her fork. Stabbed the slice of cake.

Liam probably didn't time it intentionally, but he spoke up exactly as she wrapped her mouth around a forkful of creamy frosting and moist, sumptuous cake. "We've got a problem," he announced grimly.

She could only raise her eyebrows in question above

the mouthful of chocolate sin. Which was just as well. Way too many words would have spilled out otherwise.

"Bill Gunther may not know who his client is, but he did share the instructions he received from the client. His job was to gather dirt on you that could be used to ruin your reputation and take Chloe away from you."

She choked in the act of swallowing the cake and had to cough, then had to rinse the rest of the cake down with a swig of water before she could belatedly squawk, "What? Why?"

Liam sighed. "Whoever hired Bill is out to destroy you."

"The good news is I haven't done anything that could ruin me. So there's nothing for anyone to see."

Liam laid down his spoon and said soberly, "You spent the night with me at my place last night."

"I'm not married. I can sleep with whomever I like."

He responded heavily, "In the context of sullying your reputation and painting you as an irresponsible adult not fit to be a parent, sleeping around could cause you trouble in front of the wrong judge."

"You're one guy. That doesn't constitute sleeping around. And I have no intention of sleeping with any other guys."

"Thanks for that. I'm glad to hear it. But if evidence of us having an extramarital affair was put in front of the wrong judge, it could still be a problem."

"This is the twenty-first century, Liam. No way would sleeping with you cost me Chloe."

"Are you willing to take that chance?" he asked quietly.

She stared back at him. Were they really having this insane conversation? She'd been awarded full custody of her daughter. She was allowed to have a life of her own now. Ivan was no longer part of her life or Chloe's life. Right?

Breaking into her thoughts, Liam said, "Bill Gunther can't continue to watch you. He got pulled in by the cops and spent the afternoon at the police station running his mouth about the rich client who hired him to spy on a well-known Denver attorney. If the client is half as rich and connected as I think he is, he'll find out soon enough that we've shut down Bill and his cameras."

He released a breath. "And then the client will hire someone else to spy on you. The next guy may not be as lazy as Bill and could decide to tail you in person. Your every move could end up being watched."

"Why?" she wailed under her breath. "What does this mystery client want with me?"

"You tell me."

Liam was in full detective mode, biting out the question quickly and sharply enough to startle her into blurting, "I'm not important to anyone. I don't have any enemies that I'm aware of."

"What about your ex? Surely he considers you his enemy."

"Ivan? I can't imagine him having enough money to hire a private investigator and set him up with a house and expensive surveillance gear."

Liam shrugged. "Maybe he got lucky gambling."

"Ivan doesn't get that lucky. He's a compulsive gambler. When he hits a hot streak, he can't quit. He keeps going until he loses it all. Trust me. I've seen the receipts from the casinos."

Liam looked skeptical.

"I honestly have no idea who else it could be."

"Regardless, you and I shouldn't be seen together until we find out who's after you and why. We shouldn't be together at all."

She looked up at him quickly, devastated. The words stuck in her throat before lurching out. "You want us to break things off?"

"No, I don't want to," he replied sharply. "But I won't be the person who costs you your daughter. I would never come between you two."

He might as well have kicked her in the solar plexus. It wasn't that she'd forgotten about Chloe for a second. But she'd started to get used to the idea that she might be able to pull off being both a mom and a woman. An adult woman in a relationship with a great guy. A great guy who was making a certain sick kind of sense at the moment.

When would this nightmare of trying to get away from Ivan ever end?

"You're right, of course—" Her voice broke and she couldn't continue. Suddenly, the rest of the cake loomed on her plate like a dry mountain of sawdust and glue. She laid her fork down with careful precision, lest it— or she—shatter into a million pieces.

"I'm so sorry, Sloane. If there were any other way… believe me. I would do whatever it takes to be with you right now. But we just can't risk it. This is Chloe we're talking about. Lord knows, you wouldn't want her to end up in Ivan's tender loving care."

"He doesn't even like children," she burst out. Nonetheless, if whoever was trying to wreck her life succeeded, Ivan would be next in line for custody of their daughter.

Silence fell between her and Liam, heavier than the cake and darker than the night outside.

She felt her eyes filling with tears and stared down at her hands, clenched in her lap, until the threatening moisture subsided. She looked up in anguish at Liam and caught him staring at her like his heart had been ripped out of his chest. He looked away quickly.

"What are we going to do?" she whispered.

"We're going to stay away from each other. No calls, no texts, no dates, no nights together. We're not going to do a single thing to threaten your custody of Chloe."

"For how long?" she managed.

"Until I catch whoever's stalking you."

"Catch him fast."

Liam's eyes glittered harder than emeralds when she looked up at him again. "Count on it. I'll be working on this every waking moment until I nail the bastard."

Neither of them felt like finishing their desserts or lingering in the restaurant, and Liam settled the bill quickly.

There wasn't a cab to be found when they stepped outside a few minutes later. Liam called for one and was told it would be at least an hour before one could come for her. Perfect.

"I'll give you a ride back to the hotel," he offered.

She'd hoped he would share her room with her tonight. But that obviously wasn't happening now. "A ride would be great," she replied dejectedly.

"I parked a few blocks away. You stay here and I'll go get the truck."

"I'd rather walk," she announced. Not only did she not want to stand alone on a dark, deserted street for ten minutes, she could use the exercise. Her stress levels were off the charts and she needed to walk off a little of the toxic chemical soup coursing through her blood.

"Will you be okay in those shoes?" he asked doubtfully.

She was wearing heels and nylons completely unsuited to walking of any kind, let alone hiking through snow. "If you let me hold your arm, I'll be fine."

He promptly held out his shearling-clad forearm. It felt old-fashioned to wrap her hand around his muscular arm and lean against his height and steady strength as they stepped outside and stopped in surprise.

As if the universe was determined to heap misery on top of melancholy, the snow had turned into ugly sleet during supper and had already coated the deep snow with a layer of gray ice.

"We can wait for a cab—" Liam started.

"No," she interrupted. "We can't. I'm not going to make it another hour before I fall apart, and I'd like to be back in the privacy of my hotel room before I embarrass myself in that way. After all, my entire life is apparently on *Candid Camera* these days."

"Do you at least have gloves?" Liam asked.

"My coat has good pockets, and your arm is warm." To that end, she jammed her free hand into a pocket and nodded stubbornly at him.

Liam sighed. "I'm so sorry about this—"

"Don't." She couldn't handle any more emotions right now. The slightest hint of kindness or compassion could undo her completely.

She shivered and just wanted off the street where prying eyes might be watching her.

They'd gone not even a block when a pair of blindingly bright headlights roared at them without warning. The vehicle had jumped the curb and bore down on them. Fast. There was nowhere to go.

No space. No time. They were going to die.

A flash of Chloe's face was all she had time for before Liam slammed into her, driving her hard into a recessed doorway, covering her body with his.

A big, dark SUV roared past, missing them by inches and throwing up a rooster tail of sleet that smacked into both of them like a thousand icy daggers.

The SUV swerved back out into the street without even slowing down, let alone stopping to check on them, and sped away.

"Sloane! Are you okay?" Liam asked urgently. His big body pressed against hers from chest to knee, solid. Warm. Safe.

She clung to him tightly while terror tore through her. Her life didn't exactly flash before her eyes, but an image did come to her of Chloe crying, juxtaposed with an image of herself as a little girl at her parents' funeral. She'd clung to her older brother's hand as her entire world had come crashing down around her head.

She'd known then things would never be right again, and she hadn't been wrong. Her entire life had been an exercise in searching for normal. And to date, she'd failed.

She simply couldn't do that to Chloe.

"I'm okay. You?" she gasped.

"It missed me by a hair. You sure you're okay? I tackled you pretty hard."

How were they still alive? That car had come straight for them. Almost as if it had targeted them.

She took a more detailed physical inventory. "I hit

the back of my head, and I twisted my ankle. But considering the alternative of being flattened, I'm fine."

Liam gently set her back on her feet.

"Did you get a license plate?" she asked.

"I got a partial."

She said breathlessly, "That poor driver probably lost control and scared himself silly. He or she might not have even seen us jump out of the way."

"Or..." he hesitated and then said in a rush, "the vehicle was waiting for us to leave the restaurant and intentionally tried to run us down."

"Paranoid much?"

He shrugged. "It's not paranoia if someone's really trying to kill you."

"We've established that my stalker only wants to wreck my life and make me suffer. If someone actually tried to kill us, that would make you the target. Who wants to kill you?" she challenged him.

Liam stared at her for a long time. Long enough for the cutting cold to freeze snowflakes against her cheeks. "I did ask around at the Denver Police Department today about. April Thomas. She's the missing girl whose mother visited me. She might be tied to the murder at your brother's ranch."

"How publicly did you ask around?"

"The division I visited was set up as an open bay of desks. I made no secret of what information I was looking for. Anyone could have overheard me."

"Maybe you were the target of that driver, then. But still. I think the odds are much better that the driver just skidded on the snow and lost control."

Liam shook his head. "That SUV had big new snow tires and chains on them. Plus, it was traveling toward us on the other side of the street. It had to swerve across three lanes of traffic to get to us. If it were out of control, the vehicle would have gone ahead and crashed into the building. But the driver had enough control to steer back out into the street and drive away without any problem."

She stared at Liam in dismay. "So it really was intentional?"

"I don't think we can interpret it any other way."

Chapter 13

Liam was by turns livid and scared stiff. Someone had nearly succeeded in killing him and Sloane. Question was: Which one of them had been the target?

He didn't much like the answer either way.

If he was the target, he'd obviously kicked a bigger hornet's nest than he'd realized when he started asking around about the disappearance of April Thomas. He didn't like the implications of that.

And if Sloane was the target, was this payback for him taking Bill Gunther out of the picture? If so, it was awfully swift payback. It meant the client had an employee ready and waiting to attempt murder on very short notice. He *really* didn't like the implications of that.

If the client was this dangerous, what were the odds Bill Gunther hadn't been entirely forthcoming with him earlier? Hell, had that been Gunther driving the SUV that nearly mowed them down?

Liam knew one way to find out. He'd dropped Gunther off at the east Denver house the client had rented for the surveillance operation on Sloane.

"Can you walk?" Liam asked Sloane grimly.

"I don't think my ankle's seriously injured. The pain's already subsiding."

That could also be shock setting in and dulling any pain she felt. But it wasn't as if they had any choice. They had to get off the street. There was nothing to keep that SUV from turning around and coming back to finish them off. He said, "Take my arm and lean on me. We have to move."

Sloane looked behind them and lurched against him in alarm. "That SUV isn't coming back to kill us, is it?"

"I doubt it. But I have someplace to go."

"Are we going to the police station to report a near hit-and-run? No crime was actually committed, but assuming we can find the driver, we can press charges for intent to cause grave bodily harm—"

"No. We're going to visit Bill Gunther."

"The guy who has been watching me?"

"One and the same," Liam bit out.

Sloane's limp gradually diminished as she moved and put weight on her ankle, but it was still an interminable walk to reach his truck a few blocks ahead. Every loud vehicle approaching from behind them made him and Sloane both whip their heads around in alarm, and he caught himself reaching for his sidearm each time.

Finally, they arrived at his truck. He helped Sloane climb inside, and she sighed in relief to sit down and get off her ankle. She wasn't being honest with him about how hurt she was, dammit.

He climbed into the driver's seat and made a phone call on the vehicle's Bluetooth system as he pulled out onto the street.

"Denver PD Dispatch," a brisk voice said.

"Liam Kastor. Roaring Springs PD. I need a partial license plate compared to a name."

"Go ahead."

Liam rattled off the digits he'd seen and then said, "I need to know if a William Gunther is associated with those letters."

"Standby one."

Liam drove in grim silence as the heater fought back the storm to warm the interior and defrost his windows.

The dispatcher's voice filled the truck cab. "Negative. Nobody named Gunther is associated with any license plate in the state of Colorado with that combination of numbers and letters."

"Thanks." Liam disconnected the call, frowning. If the would-be hit-and-run driver wasn't Gunther trying to take out Sloane, did that mean the driver had been targeting him?

Surely not.

Gunther and his mystery client had to be involved, somehow.

Even if Gunther hadn't used his own vehicle in the hit-and-run attempt, it still had to be the PI who'd tried to run them down. After all, who else would have known where to find them? He could believe Sloane had one enemy, but multiple enemies trying to come after her at the same time? No way.

How much had the client offered to pay Gunther for killing Sloane outright?

Liam's jaw tightened in outrage that was quickly building toward fury. By the time he pulled into the driveway of the dingy house, Liam was having to resort to anger management techniques he'd learned as a cop.

Good. Lights were on in Gunther's place.

"Stay in the car," he told Sloane tightly.

"Not a chance. I want to meet this guy who's been making my life hell."

"Not a good idea. And I'm sure he won't be watching you anymore, now that we've made him."

"All the more reason for me to meet him," Sloane insisted. "I've got demons of my own to put to bed, thank you very much."

He was tempted to ask what demons she was carrying around, but right now, he needed to have a small conversation with Gunther about trying to kill the woman he planned to—

—he planned to what?

Shock rolled through him, abruptly derailing his fury. He carefully set aside the thought for later consideration. Now was not the time for such things.

But when would it be the time? How many years had he spent secretly wanting this woman? Fifteen? Twenty? All of his adult life, for sure.

Wow. He had it worse for Sloane than he'd realized. And he already realized he had it for her *bad*.

Mentally, he shook his head. *Must. Focus.*

"I'm serious, Sloane. Stay in the truck. If this goes down ugly, I don't want you caught in the crossfire."

"All the more reason for me to be with you," she retorted. "You'll know where I am and can keep me safe. You know you would worry about me if something bad were to happen and you didn't know if I was okay. I would be more of a distraction apart from you than right behind you."

She was right, dammit. "Fine. But stay behind me and do whatever I tell you to without question."

She nodded, her eyes even wider and rounder than usual.

Well, hell. He didn't like dragging her along with him, but what other choice did he have? Liam climbed out of his truck and stomped up the front steps to Gunther's door with Sloane on his heels.

He banged hard and insistently on Gunther's door. On the other side of it, a male voice yelled out for him to hold his horses. When the door finally opened, Gunther stood there in a long, sloppy bathrobe and socks.

"Oh! Hey, Detective. What brings you to my door at this time of night?"

"Have you been out this evening?" Liam asked without preamble.

"Do I look like I've been out tonight?" Gunther retorted.

"Appearances can be deceiving."

"What's got a burr up your ass, kid?" Gunther asked. "Man, it's cold out there. Come inside so I can close the flipping door."

Gunther moved to one side for Liam to enter, and that was when Bill spotted Sloane. "As I live and breathe. If it ain't Sloane Durant. You're even prettier in person if I do say so myself, ma'am."

Liam didn't have to look over his shoulder to feel Sloane's scowl behind him. He *knew* it had been a bad idea to bring her along on this interview.

"That's not him," Sloane blurted.

Liam half turned to face her without losing sight of Gunther. "Come again?"

"That's not the man who was looking in my window in Roaring Springs."

"I never looked in your window!" Gunther exclaimed. "Hell. I never went to Roaring Springs except for that one time when I installed the cameras in your house. And I'm sorry about that, Ms. Durant."

"Colton. I dropped my ex-husband's last name," Sloane corrected him, still staring at Gunther.

"You're sure Bill's not the same guy?" Liam asked.

"Positive."

"Let's all step inside so you can look at him in good light."

"I don't need good light. It was shadowed and dark outside where I saw the Peeping Tom. I'm telling you. This man looks nothing like the one I saw," Sloane insisted.

Liam moved into Bill's small house and loomed in front of the PI. "Tell me, Bill. Did your client hire a second investigator to tail Sl—Ms. Colton?"

"Not that I'm aware of. But it's possible, I suppose. Seems like it would be overkill if you ask me."

"Is it possible this second, hypothetical PI would have orders to take out Ms. Colton in the event that you didn't find enough dirt on her?" Liam asked.

"Yeah, I guess. I mean I've never been in the business of roughing anyone up. I was a cop too long to be comfortable using strong-arm tactics like that. I don't do loan collections for that exact reason. Believe me. The money's a hell of a lot better working for a loan shark than it is chasing down cheating spouses—"

"I never cheated on Ivan!" Sloane exclaimed. "He cheated on me!"

Bill shrugged. "That's what I told my client this afternoon after I got back from the police station. I sent an email to whoever it is saying I never found a shred of evidence that you're anything but a good mom living a quiet life with your kid."

"That's exactly the kind of message that could have triggered a hit man," Liam ground out.

"A *hit man*?" Sloane exclaimed.

"Where's your kid?" Gunther asked, startling Liam out of his train of thought.

"I beg your pardon?" Liam asked the older man.

"I'm just sayin'. If a hit man went after Ms. Dur— Colton, a hit man could go after her kid, too."

"Ohmigod," Sloane gasped. "Chloe. We have to get to her before someone hurts her!"

Liam whirled to follow Sloane, who was already flying down the steps toward his truck. "Come *on*!" she cried out over her shoulder at him.

"Sorry to bother you," Liam tossed hastily at Bill before chasing after Sloane.

"Good luck!" Gunther called after him.

Cripes. Not Chloe. Poor kid had already been through so much—

If he'd driven fast to Gunther's place, he drove like a bat out of hell to the Durant home. Before he'd barely come to a full stop in the Durant's circular driveway, Sloane was out of the truck and racing toward the home. The front sidewalk of the Durant mansion was black with ice, and Sloane eschewed the concrete to run up to the front door through the snow-covered grass. Liam winced as he charged after her. Sloane's feet were going to be soaking wet and half-frozen by the time she hit the front porch.

He reached the porch just as the front door opened. The sound of a child screaming was the first thing he registered. The second thing was the utterly shocked expression on the woman's face at the door. A woman he recognized from his research into Ivan Durant as Carol Durant, Ivan's mother.

"What are *you* doing here?" Carol blurted rudely.

"There's an emergency, and I need to take Chloe home, tonight. I'll be happy to reschedule another visit at your convenience, Mrs. Durant—"

"We have legal rights, and just because you're an attorney doesn't mean you get to trample all over them," Carol snapped.

"This isn't about trampling your rights," Sloane said with barely contained patience. "Someone may have tried to hurt me earlier, and we have reason to believe that person may target Chloe, too. My daughter's in danger and I need to get her to a secure location."

"Chloe most certainly is not in danger! She's my grandchild, for goodness' sake—" Carol broke off abruptly, as if suddenly realizing what she was saying and thinking better of it.

Liam's detective radar fired off a hard alert. What had the woman been about to say before suddenly clamming up? And why was Carol so sure Chloe wasn't in danger? Sloane had just announced that someone had tried to harm her, and Carol hadn't batted an eyelash.

More screams pealed through the house, and a male voice bellowed from another room, "Will someone get that brat to quit caterwauling? She's giving me a damned headache."

"Anna!" Carol called out loudly.

The housekeeper appeared immediately, as if she'd been hovering nearby.

"Please close Chloe's bedroom door so we don't have to listen to her cry anymore."

Sloane stared in openmouthed shock, and Liam did the same. He didn't know much about kids, but it couldn't be good for Chloe to be as upset as she sounded so soon after such a serious illness.

"Give me my daughter," Sloane declared.

"I beg your pardon?" Carol replied, sounding huffy.

"Right now. Give me Chloe."

"I most certainly will not. She's here to spend the night. You can pick her up tomorrow."

"She's my child, and you're not rendering proper care to her. Don't make a fight out of this, Carol. You will lose. I'm her parent, and I have legal custody of her."

Liam thought he heard Carol mutter something along the lines of, "We'll see about that."

The woman reached for the big door beside her, and sensing what she was about to do, he stepped forward fast and put his police boot in the doorjamb. "I wouldn't try that if I were you, ma'am."

"Get out of my house!" Carol screeched. "And take that woman with you!"

"That woman is the mother of your grandchild," Liam said evenly. "And she does have custody of Chloe. I'm going to have to insist you surrender the child to her legal parent."

"Who are you? The police?" Carol snapped.

Liam reached inside his coat and pulled out his badge. "That would be correct, ma'am. Detective Liam Kastor."

Carol physically took a step back at that, and he took advantage of her shock to push the front door fully open once more. He spied a woman in a uniform wringing her hands in the shadows. "Are you Anna?" he asked.

The woman nodded.

"Please bring Chloe and her things to Ms. Colton."

The housekeeper hurried up the curving staircase and disappeared from sight as Carol Durant shouted "Niall! Get out here!"

A gray-haired gentleman Liam recognized as Ivan's father stepped into the foyer, the expression on his face irritated. The second Niall spied Sloane, however, his entire demeanor changed radically. The man actually came to a halt to stare at her. He might as well have seen a ghost.

What on earth? It wasn't as if Sloane wasn't well known to the man. And given that her child was here at the house, it wasn't entirely unreasonable that she should be here. Sloane wasn't supposed to come until tomorrow to get Chloe. But still. That didn't justify the man's utter, horrified shock.

Liam glanced back and forth between Niall and Carol and caught the loaded look they exchanged with each other. What was up with that? Both of them had reacted out of all proportion to Sloane's appearance at their front door.

His train of thought was derailed by the arrival of Chloe, sobbing uncontrollably. The toddler caught sight of Sloane and all but fell out of Anna's arms, she leaned so hard toward her mommy.

Both arms outstretched, she screamed, *"Mommy!"* as if someone were tearing her limbs off and she was in desperate need of rescue.

Chloe's face was blotchy and swollen, her eyes red. She'd been crying for a while if he was reading her correctly.

Sloane reached out and snatched Chloe from Anna's arms. She hugged her daughter tightly, making soothing sounds. Chloe quieted immediately but continued to hiccup and draw sobbing breaths as she wrapped her little arms tightly around Sloane's neck.

Liam caught sight of Sloane's expression and took a quick step toward her to restrain her. She was a mama bear on the warpath.

Sloane's voice was deadly calm as she turned toward Anna and enunciated carefully, "How long has Chloe been crying?"

"Several hours, ma'am."

"Hours?" Sloane echoed ominously, turning a murderous glare on Carol.

The older woman waved a dismissive hand. "You always did spoil the child too much. You have to let them cry it out and learn to take care of themselves."

"That explains quite a bit about my ex-husband," Sloane replied acidly. "What part of 'she nearly died last week and is still recovering from a life-threatening illness' didn't you understand, Carol?"

Ivan's mother had the good sense to take a step back from Sloane. Liam balanced on the balls of his feet, ready to intervene and block Sloane from whatever violence she intended. Thankfully, the fact that she was holding Chloe tightly in her arms seemed to deter Sloane from doing anything ill-advised.

Chloe looked absolutely wrung out by her crying jag, and neither of the Durants seemed to have the least remorse for having put their granddaughter through the trauma.

Rather than risk Sloane attacking her ex in-laws and potentially jeopardizing her custody of Chloe, Liam stepped in front of her and said to the Durants, "I'll be filing a statement with the court on the condition the child was in when recovered by the custodial parent. I imagine you'll be hearing from Ms. Colton's attorney shortly. Until then, the child stays with the mother. Is that understood?"

Carol and Niall both nodded quickly. Too quickly. Carol had been truculent when they arrived, but now she was folding up and swallowing any protests far too easily. What in the world was going on with those two? They acted guilty as sin. But of what? Did *they* have something to do with that SUV jumping the curb and nearly killing him and Sloane?

His suspicion meter was climbing fast. What the hell was going on with the entire Durant family? He followed Sloane outside and gripped her elbow firmly to help her down the slippery sidewalk. She climbed into the truck, still holding Chloe.

"Don't you want to put her in her seat?" he murmured, surprised.

"Just get us out of here," she replied under her breath.

He complied, and when they were several blocks away from the Durant estate, well out of sight of Carol and Niall, Sloane murmured, "Okay, you can stop now, so I can pop Little Bug into her car seat."

Ahh. Sloane didn't want the Durants to know that Chloe's car seat was installed in his truck, which would indicate that he and Sloane knew each other personally and had traveled up to Denver together. Cautious, but probably a good call. At a minimum, the Durants weren't nice people. At worst, they were somehow involved with the danger swirling around Sloane.

She climbed in the back seat with her daughter, whom she quickly strapped into her safety seat. "I'm going to stay with her back here. She's had a rough night and doesn't want to let go of me."

"I don't blame her," Liam answered grimly. "Where to? We can spend the night here in Denver, or I can drive you home and have the hotel send your stuff back to Roaring Springs for you."

"Home, please," Sloane replied. She sounded nearly as exhausted as her daughter. But then, confronting the Durants had to have been stressful for her, too.

Both Colton women fell asleep quickly in the back seat of his truck, and Liam drove carefully, vividly aware of the precious cargo on board.

He pointed his truck toward the front range of the Rockies, and the roads went from bad to terrible. After about an hour of crawling along at a snail's pace, he pulled into a rest stop to get chains out of the storage box in his truck bed and put them on his tires.

When he climbed back into the cab of his truck, he was surprised to see Sloane awake and sitting in the front seat. "Hi, Sleeping Beauty," he murmured.

She smiled sleepily at him, and his insides tightened almost painfully. With her hair messy and her eyes warm and soft, she was almost too much for even his formidable self-control. A need to pull her into his arms, kiss her senseless, have Liam straddle his hips again... maybe in less clothing for both of them...

Nope, nope, nope. He had to banish such thoughts from his mind before they turned into action. They had to stay apart until her stalker was caught. He needed to get on the road again and furthermore, he needed all of his attention on driving.

"How's Chloe doing?" he asked.

Sloane's expression hardened. "Wiped out. She'll sleep like the dead after getting so worked up."

"Poor kid."

"I have half a mind to sue to revoke their visitation rights," she muttered.

"Do it. I meant it when I said I would be filing a police report on the incident."

"Thanks. But don't expose yourself to ethics inquiries by going to bat for me."

"Hence the need for us to cool it until this mess is sorted out once and for all." It was thoughtful of her to worry about his career. But he was determined to get Ivan Durant and his crazy-ass parents out of her life once and for all. He started the engine and eased back out onto the snow-covered highway.

"I thought Ivan and I *were* sorted out for good," Sloane muttered as he merged onto the mostly deserted roadway. "Will this nightmare never end?"

"Be patient. Things will work out for the best," Liam said encouragingly. He reached over and squeezed her ice-cold hand briefly before putting his hand back on the steering wheel.

They'd only driven a few moments before she said nervously, "Are you sure we should be driving in this weather?"

"I just put chains on the tires. I can't go fast in them, but I've got plenty of traction now."

"I don't know. When we get up into the higher elevations the snow and the visibility are going to get worse. Maybe we should just find a place to stop for the night."

He glanced over at her in surprise. "It's okay, Sloane. You don't have to be afraid—"

He broke off, swearing under his breath. Of course. Her parents had died in a car crash in a blizzard. She had to be scared stiff. "I'm sorry. I forgot. I'm an insensitive bastard. I'll pull over at the next town and find us a room."

"I'm sorry I'm such a wimp," Sloane confessed.

He snorted. "You're a lot of things, but a wimp is not one of them."

She shook her head in disagreement, and soft waves of dark hair drifted around her face. She looked like a fey creature, perched nervously on the seat beside him, peering out into the swath of snow in his headlights.

It took about a half hour, but an exit sign loomed abruptly out of the dark, announcing a small town coming up in a mile. Liam eased off the highway onto the exponentially worse exit ramp and slid all the way down it, in spite of his chains, which meant he was driving on sheet ice. He barely skidded to a stop before the intersection at the bottom.

Sloane gasped beside him, gripping the center armrest like she thought the passenger door was going to fly open and the blizzard would suck her out. He let out a breath of his own and then told her, "We're okay. You can breathe."

"That skid... I thought we were going to go off the road. Maybe off a cliff. Die..."

"There are no cliffs, sweetheart. We've descended into a valley, and everything around us goes up, not down. We're safe, okay? You can relax. I've got this. I've got you."

She didn't relax, but she did nod once at him. At least she seemed to be breathing again. He eased forward toward a small town laid out along a single narrow road at the bottom of the steep valley.

He found a motel and pulled into the parking lot, praying there was a room at the inn for the night. "Stay here with Chloe while I check this place out."

Sloane nodded and he stepped out into nearly knee-deep snow and slogged inside the office. Liam rang the bell on the counter and a white-haired man came out of the back, blinking in the sudden light.

"Can I help you?" the man asked.

"I'm hoping you have some rooms for the night. Two, ideally."

"I've only got one room left."

"Any chance you have a baby's crib we could use?"

"That I do have."

Liam debated quickly. Sharing a room with Sloane promised all kinds of dangerous temptation. But no way was he taking her back out on the highway given how terrified she was of dying in a car crash. Liam handed over a credit card, and in a few moments, the gentleman passed over a key attached to a plastic paddle.

"I'll have that crib at your room in a jiffy. If you've got a little one, you must be exhausted traveling at this time of night."

"That's no lie."

Liam walked in his own footprints back to the truck and drove down to the room on the end. He helped the proprietor carry a folded crib through the snow and set it up inside the small, plain, but spotless room. A quick towel-off to dry the snow from it, and Sloane was able to lay Chloe down gently. She secured blankets around the munchkin and tucked Snuffles into the toddler's arms.

Silence fell around them, the deep silence of a snowy night, with no cars moving outside, just the quiet hum of the heater and the wind blowing through the pine trees beyond the motel.

It was cozy, just the three of them in this quiet oasis from the storm. If he used a tiny bit of imagination, Liam could imagine them as a family. It was a seductive illusion: the woman of his dreams, the child he'd always dreamed of having—

Careful, Liam. None of this is real.

But God, he wished it was.

"I don't have any pajamas," Sloane observed in dismay.

"My luggage is still in the back of the truck." He jogged outside and carried in his bag, opening it briskly. "Here. Borrow one of my T-shirts. On you, it'll make a decent nightshirt."

Shyly, Sloane took the white cotton shirt and disappeared into the bathroom. When she emerged, he gulped, and suddenly the room felt overly warm. Her legs—correction, her sexy, smooth, bare legs—looked fantastic emerging from the bottom of his T-shirt.

As for her chest… He gulped again. The soft cotton clung to the curves of her breasts, revealing almost more than it concealed. A need to cup that tender flesh, to rub his thumbs across the nipples he knew to be so responsive to his touch, very nearly overcame him.

Dare he succumb to temptation?

After all, nobody could have possibly followed them here. There had been no headlights on the highway behind them after they'd left Denver and climbed into the mountains. The occasional snowplow and only a handful of other vehicles had been on the roads. No one had followed them down the exit ramp, and no one could possibly perform surveillance on them at this random, isolated, out-of-the-way motel.

For tonight, they were safe.

Sloane crawled into bed while he kicked off his boots and stripped off his jacket, tie and dress shirt, left over from their dinner date. He grabbed the back of the neck seam and yanked his T-shirt over his head. As his face popped clear, he caught Sloane taking in his chest and flexing muscles appreciatively.

"Keep looking at me like that," he warned, "and it won't be sleeping we're doing tonight."

Her mouth curved up into the sexiest smile he'd ever seen because it was aimed at him. Sweet baby Jesus. She didn't have sleeping on her mind, either.

Suddenly, his fingers were clumsy as he unzipped his fly, pushed his jeans down to his ankles and impatiently yanked his feet clear of the denim. As he reached for the waistband of his boxers, Sloane leaned over and turned off the lamp beside the bed. Darkness cloaked the room. Only a faint slit of diffused light came in between the curtains, a distant streetlight reflecting off the bright white of the snow outside.

Naked, he slipped between the cold sheets and encountered Sloane's warm, welcoming arms.

"We shouldn't do this—" he started.

She rolled against him, plastering her body against his from chest to toes, her mouth capturing his and stopping his half-hearted protest. "We'll have to be quiet so we don't wake Chloe," she whispered against his lips.

So much for his grand declaration of staying away from her until everything was resolved with whomever was stalking her. He could probably have predicted that they wouldn't be able to keep their hands off each other. Which was actually kind of awesome…as long as they didn't get caught.

"I think I can manage to be quiet. Can you?" he challenged her.

"You'd be amazed what I can do in the name of having you," she replied in a bare breath of sound.

He gathered her in his arms, his hands roving across her back until he found the hem of his T-shirt and tugged it up, exposing the satin flesh and feminine curve of her back. His hands cupped her rear end, and she groaned into his mouth.

"Hush," he breathed.

"Tease," she breathed back.

"Oh, you have no idea." All of a sudden, the idea of seeing just how far he could push Sloane without her making any noise turned him on harder than he could believe.

One hand resting lightly over her mouth, he commenced kissing his way down her neck, tracing the V-neckline of the T-shirt, tugging the fabric until one of her breasts popped free. He sucked at the exposed nipple, pebbled with cold and maybe desire between his lips. He swirled his tongue around the nub, loving how Sloane lurched, shoving her breast up into his mouth even more deeply.

He pushed the T-shirt up until it bunched around her collarbones, and then proceeded to kiss his way down her warm, velvety-smooth body. The shudder when he licked across the other excited peak of her breast, the stretch of her stomach muscles, the goose bumps that rose on her skin tasted sweet and sexy, innocent and hot, pure Sloane.

The tip of her tongue touched his palm over her mouth, and he jumped. It swirled erotically across his hand, licking delicately between his fingers. The thought of her tongue doing that to other parts of him caused the most remarkable reaction. His male flesh hardened until he could practically drill solid rock with it.

Fueled by the need to be inside her, to make her moan, to capture her moans in his mouth, he kissed his way back up her body, across the gentle swell of her belly, pausing for a moment to tickle her belly button until she squirmed impatiently beneath him, and then up the delicious valley of her breasts. Her skin smelled like bergamot and orange blossoms, and he inhaled deeply of her essence.

She tugged at his wrist, moving his hand away from her mouth, and then she pulled his head to hers, kissing him deeply, communicating without words how much she wanted him. The first time shyness was gone, leaving behind raw passion for him that he didn't think he would ever get enough of.

He positioned himself between her legs and then paused, swearing under his breath.

"What's wrong?" she whispered.

"My wallet's in the back pocket of my jeans. Which are on the floor."

She surprised him by pushing on his shoulders. He gave way, rolling onto his back as she rolled with him, sprawling across his body luxuriously. He grinned and fondled her behind as she hung half off the bed, groping on the floor for condoms.

"Ah-ha!" she crowed in a whisper. She pushed up

against his chest, kneeling beside him. She tore open the packet and rolled a condom down onto his erection with slow eroticism that nearly undid him. Her hands were warm and soft, squeezing him with just enough pressure to make his hips buck a little beneath her.

She stretched out on his chest, plastering her mouth against his ear. "A girl would think you hadn't had sex in forever, given how eager you are."

He wrapped his arm around her waist and rolled over, trapping her beneath him but being careful not to crush her. "Don't tease me," he growled low. "I'm of a mind to see just how much pleasure you can take without screaming out loud."

"Is that a dare?" She grinned up at him in the scant light.

"Double dare."

"You're on, big guy. Bring it. Give me your best shot at a screaming orgasm."

Laughing silently, he positioned himself and pressed home. Except it was his eyes that nearly rolled back in his head as the tight, slick glove of her body clutched his erection.

Truth be told, it was a bet he would have been happy to lose. But she had dared him. He had to at least *try* to drive her out of her mind. He set up a rhythm, much slower than he would have liked, only letting the speed and intensity of his thrusts grow by miniscule degrees. Sloane moved restlessly against him, and then surged impatiently, and yet he kept up the maddeningly slow pace. He was driving himself out of his mind, and he could only pray he was doing the same to her.

Her breathing became ragged and then devolved into light, fast pants. "More," she demanded in a bare whisper.

"So impatient," he chided.

In retaliation, she wrapped her legs around his hips, digging her heels into his thighs, and pulled him even deeper into the glory of her body. Not satisfied, apparently, she grabbed his ass with both hands and pulled even more tightly against her, seating him all the way to the hilt in her writhing heat.

She won. He surrendered. He plunged into her with abandon as she rose to meet him thrust for thrust. His breathing grew as ragged as hers, roaring in his ears. He buried his face in the pillow beside her, unable to contain his groans of pleasure any longer. For her part, Sloane buried her face against his neck, crying out against his skin.

Faster and faster their bodies joined, slapping into each other, the heat and friction provoking unbearable pleasure that ripped through him like a million volts of electric ecstasy.

He groaned into the pillow as his entire being exploded into her. Sloane surged up against him, slapping her hand over her mouth as, she, too, cried out uncontrollably. She shuddered violently against him and around him, wringing forth the very last dregs of pleasure from him before they both collapsed against the now hot sheets.

He was a very fit guy, but this woman did him in. At least she had the good grace to be limp and panting beside him. He gathered Sloane against his chest, her head resting on his shoulder.

"I'm not sure how to judge who won that challenge," he murmured.

"Hmm. I can't say, either. We'll have to try again and see who can be more quiet next time."

His chest vibrated with silent laughter. He muttered into her hair, "I like the way you think."

"I like the way you make love," she replied.

He bent his head down to kiss her, enjoying the leisurely way she kissed him back, well satisfied. He knew the feeling. No woman had ever made him feel like this. It was as if he'd found his other half, and between the two of them, they were...home. A family.

Aww, hell. He'd gone and gotten ahead of himself again. The last thing she would want to hear was that he wanted forever with her, complete with the whole white picket fence and domestic bliss thing in a small town. Sloane would run screaming, just like she had in high school, when she'd run away to the big city.

Besides. It wasn't like they could do this again when they got back to real life and Roaring Springs. Not until her blasted ex-husband was slapped with a permanent restraining order, or maybe even put behind bars for a good long time to come. If that jerk had ordered a hit on Sloane...

Liam couldn't even finish the thought. Flashes of the violence he would perpetrate on Ivan Durant were all that came to mind.

Sloane's mouth was sliding across his chest again, and the tip of her tongue was darting out to taste his skin in the most provocative way. The vixen was teasing him! So. She thought she could win round two, did she? They'd see about that...

Chapter 14

Sloane woke up abruptly, startled by something. Disoriented for a moment, she looked around a dim motel room. The wan light of dawn seeped in around the curtains, gray and muted, as if it was still snowing outside. She snuggled deeper into the cocoon of warmth encircling her. She registered a strong, relaxed arm around her shoulders, and warm, naked man chest under her cheek.

Liam.

Snowstorm.

They'd stopped at a motel when she'd been too scared to continue home to Roaring Springs last night. Always considerate, he was. Well, not always. He was a considerate lover, but he also had the capacity to be quite the demanding lover, too, as it turned out.

After the second time they'd made love, they'd declared it a tie and had to go for a third round of mind-blowing sex to declare the winner. She was a little sore this morning, but in the best possible way.

And he'd won the bet. Although she personally thought she'd gotten the best end of the bargain after a third round of orgasms ripped through her until she was a mass of quivering nerves and mindless cries.

A rustle of sound made her turn her head. Chloe rolled over, flinging a blanket off in the process. Poor Little Bug. She really had a time of it at the Durants' house. Rage bubbled up yet again that those horrible people would let their own granddaughter scream herself hoarse without once going in to comfort her. What monsters! No wonder Ivan was such a heartless bastard. He'd been raised by Carol and Niall.

She rolled over carefully, trying not to disturb Liam, and eased out of bed. She found his discarded T-shirt on the floor and pulled it over her head. Then she tiptoed over to the crib and gently pulled the blanket up over Chloe, who was sprawled on her stomach in the complete abandon of baby sleep.

She smiled down at her daughter with love overflowing her heart. She glanced back at the bed and jumped in surprise. Liam lay on his side, watching her.

Silently, he lifted the blankets in invitation, and she slipped back in beside him. He gathered her in his arms tenderly. "You're a hell of a mother. Chloe's one lucky tyke to have you."

He pushed a stray lock of hair off her face and just looked at her, studying her face intently.

"What?" she finally whispered. She wasn't used to anyone scrutinizing her like this.

"I'm memorizing your face. You're so damned beautiful I sometimes don't believe you're real."

She opened her mouth to protest, but he laid a finger on her lips. "Get used to me telling you you're beautiful. I plan to keep doing it for as long as you'll let me."

She blinked at him, shocked. Just how long *did* she plan to let him into her bed? She low-key loved the idea of repeating last night for a very long time to come. Except, ideally with Chloe in another room far enough away so noise was not an issue.

If only Ivan were out of the picture for good—

She cut off that thought before it could go one inch further. She might despise her ex, but she wished him no bodily harm. After all, he was Chloe's father. And Sloane, of all people, knew what it was like to grow up without her parents. Sure, Russ and Mara Colton had loved her and Fox and done their level best to raise her and her brother as if they were their own children. But Sloane had still felt the gap in her heart. The loss had never gone away. Never really been filled.

She would never wish that upon her own child.

"What's on your mind?" Liam murmured against her temple. "You went so still and serious."

Nor could she ask Liam to replace Ivan. Chloe was not Liam's responsibility and she wouldn't foist her baby, no matter how adorable she might be, on anyone else. Chloe was her responsibility and hers alone.

Sloane shrugged, dodging Liam's question, and then distracted him by tilting her chin up to capture his mouth with hers. She poured all the gratitude and passion she could not express out loud into the slide of her lips across his, into the little sighs of pleasure that slipped out of her throat.

Not slow on the uptake, Liam kissed her back, letting the sexual energy build between them once more.

Eyeing the crib beyond her, he rolled her onto her back and slowly, gently made love to her one last time before this stolen tryst ended.

He was so sweet, so tender with her, that tears leaked from her eyes before they finally climaxed together, their mouths clamped against each other's shoulders to muffle the sweet agony of their release.

She dozed in Liam's arms until Chloe awoke, a little before 7:00 a.m. While Liam dressed and went out in search of something to eat, she gave Chloe a bath.

Liam returned with plastic grocery bags of snacks from a gas station down the street and volunteered to watch Chloe while Sloane grabbed a quick shower. The hot water felt amazing pounding her tired muscles, and she emerged from the shower feeling like a new woman.

Liam took his turn in the shower, and they all carefully dried their hair with the blow dryer mounted on the wall. In cold weather like this, wet hair could cause dangerous hypothermia in a matter of seconds.

"Ready to continue the journey home?" he finally asked.

She took a deep breath, not relishing hazardous roads in the high mountains between here and Roaring Springs.

"I promise, I'll take it slow and be as careful as it's humanly possible to be," Liam said quietly. "I would never do anything to risk your safety or Chloe's. And I am a cop. I've had all kinds of advanced driving training. It'll be okay."

Sloane startled herself by having to dash tears away from her eyes. "I'm sorry. I'm not usually this emotional."

Liam grinned and chucked her chin. "You're authorized after the twenty-four hours you've just had. Let's get you home and get those cameras out of your house."

"Amen."

While Chloe chowed down on dry Cheerios and blueberries in the back seat, they set out. The roads were still awful, but in the light of day, Liam could at least see where he was going. And he did, indeed, crawl along at a pace conservative enough even for her. The chains on his tires were a godsend, and his heavy truck gripped the road wonderfully.

It took almost two more hours for Roaring Springs to come into view as they topped one last ridge. Sloane sighed in relief as Liam finally turned onto her street and parked in her driveway.

While she carried Chloe in and got her settled in a pile of toys in the living room, Liam headed upstairs. He emerged in a few minutes with wires protruding from his fist. He held his hand out to her, obviously interested in giving her something, and laid three small cameras in her palm. She poked at them in distaste.

"They're smaller than I expected," she commented.

"They're state-of-the-art. Expensive. Rahm Zogby said they cost thousands of dollars apiece."

Sloane frowned. "How could Ivan afford gear like this? He's broke. As in, teetering on the edge of bankruptcy."

"Are his parents giving him money?" Liam suggested.

She shook her head. "Niall is furious over the gambling and has cut him off, last I heard. As far as I know, all the proceeds of the Durant investments in Ivan's name are being put into a trust fund he can't access for several years. Ivan was livid when he found out." She remembered his towering rage well. It had been the night he destroyed her mother's china. Sloane had been certain he would turn his fury on her and Chloe next.

"Poor, abused trust fund baby," Liam retorted.

Yeah. Right. Sloane pulled a wry face. "I was no dummy. I took the full divorce settlement amount in a lump sum, and I've invested it so it will grow over time. Chloe will never want for anything."

"Ivan had to hate that."

Sloane snorted. "He tried to borrow money from me before we'd even left the accountant's office. As if I would let him touch Chloe's legacy. I told him no, of course."

"How did he react to that?" Liam asked. He sounded as if he was asking in his capacity as a police detective.

"He threw a tantrum. Threatened me. Accused me of intentionally ruining him. The usual."

"Any witnesses?" he asked hopefully.

"Not that I'm aware of. He did it in a parking lot where it was just the two of us."

"Damn. If nothing else, I have to give the man credit for covering his tracks."

Sloane replied quickly, "He's smart. Very smart. You'd do well not to underestimate him. Lord knows, I don't."

"Speaking of which," Liam responded, "I need to head down to the police station and write up a report on our little visit with the Durants and how they weren't caring properly for their grandchild."

"I really appreciate your help, Liam—"

He grabbed her hand and pulled her into the hall bathroom, closing the door behind them. He drew her into his arms and kissed her urgently. She arched up against him with equal ardor. This was probably the last time they were going to get to do this until the mess with her personal hater was cleared up.

How was she supposed to keep her hands off Liam? Keep her mouth off him, hold her body apart from his, her arms empty of his comforting warmth? A sobbing breath escaped her.

"Be strong, sweetheart. Think of Chloe. This is the right thing for her. For both of you."

"But it's not fair to you!" she wailed against his chest.

"I've waited this long for you. I can wait a little longer."

His words were quiet. Simple. Uttered matter-of-factly. But they resonated all the way down to the bottom of her soul.

"Are you sure?" she whispered achingly.

"Positive."

He kissed her hard and then stepped back abruptly, as if to stay with her like this any longer was too painful for him to bear.

She knew the feeling.

He turned and swept out of the bathroom. Out of her house. Out of her life.

Damn whomever was out to get her and his or her stupid private investigators, anyway, interfering in her life and threatening her custody of Chloe. If she weren't a kind and decent person, she would be sorely tempted to off the guy herself.

The house felt depressingly empty with Liam gone. Heck, her *life* felt empty with Liam gone. He was smart and funny and put her at ease like no one she'd ever been around, except maybe her brother. Russ and Mara had been busy people with a big family of their own and a resort empire to build. She'd been a quiet kid who didn't ask for much, and in retrospect, easy to ignore. She'd stayed out of trouble, done her schoolwork and faded into the background of the loud, boisterous Colton clan.

Most of her five cousins, whom she thought of more as brothers and sisters than cousins, were all big, dynamic personalities who'd loudly challenged her desire to curl up in a ball in the corner of life and had ended up driving her deeper into her emotional shell.

Liam was different. He saw into her corner. He joined her there, no pressure, no demands. And he'd gently coaxed her out. He made her want to live a full life; he made her believe she could find love and laughter and passion and fulfillment with him.

She'd thought she could find all those things with Ivan, too. But in fairness to herself, Ivan had put up a hell of a false front while they'd dated and first been married. It had only been later, when his gambling started to put him under severe financial pressure and she'd dropped the bombshell that she was pregnant, that the facade had crumbled.

Looking back, she had to believe he was a bit of a sociopath, without the skills to navigate relationships or the empathy to relate to others. He acted like a man who had carefully memorized a set of rules for behavior so he could pass for a normal person. But when she'd really gotten to know him, he'd been empty inside, only capable of loving himself. He'd also been fundamentally dishonest, violently egocentric and devoid of any remorse for hurting the people around him.

Liam was none of those things.

In Ivan's defense, she could see why he'd been drawn to her. She'd been as shut down emotionally as he was, going through the motions of living without really engaging with anyone around her. He must have thought she would be perfect for him. Until she had a baby, discovered what real love was and learned just how deeply she was capable of feeling it.

Thank God Liam had come along and woken her up inside as a woman, the same way Chloe had woken her up as a mother. Who knew where she might have ended up without him?

Maybe that was why she felt his absence so keenly now. For the first time in pretty much ever, she had intense, amazing feelings for a man. She actually felt giddy when she thought about being with him. Cripes. She probably should have gone through this all-absorbing crush phase in about the sixth grade. But hey. Better late than never.

Except she was beginning to suspect this was more than a crush. Much more. It was as if her entire being revolved around him when it wasn't revolving around Chloe. What was Liam doing now? Had he eaten properly when he got home? Was he safe? Who was he talking to?

More importantly, was he thinking about her? Did he miss her, too? Did he love her at least a little?

God, she hoped so.

Chapter 15

Liam walked into the No Doze Café and looked around. He'd beat Daria Bloom to their meeting, so he ordered a cup of coffee and sat down to wait for her. He opened the thick file he'd gotten from the Denver Police Department on the disappearance of April Thomas. The part that alarmed him most was a receipt for a gas purchase April had made the day she supposedly headed for Roaring Springs. The highway she'd been traveling when she'd stopped for gas led straight from Denver to Roaring Springs with no other major cities in between.

For all the world, it appeared that the young woman had, indeed, come to Roaring Springs. And then she'd never been seen again.

Daria came in on a hard gust of wind and swirling snow. She grabbed a fast cup of coffee and joined him at the booth in the corner. He'd chosen it because no one else was sitting nearby and they could talk freely.

"What have you got for me, Liam?" she asked without preamble, her gaze glued to the police file on the table in front of him.

He pushed the file over to her. "This is a copy I made for you of the Denver PD file on April Thomas."

"Quick overview?" Daria asked as she opened the thick file to browse it.

"Check out this receipt." He flipped to the photocopy of the gas chit.

Dari looked down at it for a moment and then back up at him. Her gaze was stark. "She made it here, then. And disappeared. Is it possible we've got a serial killer on our hands?"

Liam nodded grimly. "Maybe."

"We've got to keep this under wraps for now. Let me talk to the sheriff. We're going to have to reopen the Bianca Rouge case, but I'd like to do that as quietly as we can. The fewer people who know we're looking into it, the better."

Liam added, "Best not to spook the killer if he or she is still in this area. We're going to need every advantage we can muster. We've got a careful, intelligent, self-disciplined criminal on our hands."

"Pretty much a worst case scenario."

Liam leaned forward to murmur low, "Maybe we should wait to call the FBI back in. If our killer is local, he or she will spot FBI agents roaming around town and could go to ground."

Daria grimaced. "I have to call the FBI guys in Denver and let them know what's happening, but I'll ask them to hold off descending upon Roaring Springs for now."

Liam said, "I'll go through that file again and call

you if I spot any new leads or I have any brainstorms on how to proceed."

"Ditto. And thanks."

He met Daria's dark, worried stare with one of his own. It was up to them to keep any more young women from dying. If they, indeed, had a serial killer on their hands, it would be a race against time to identify the killer and catch him or her.

Chloe had a rough day. She was exhausted from the day before and Sloane wasn't about to take any chances with the child's still-fragile health. She insisted on keeping Little Bug at home and quiet all day, which turned out to be a gigantic undertaking.

It was approaching 10:00 p.m. before Chloe finally fell asleep on top of Sloane in the big armchair in the living room. Exhausted herself, Sloane wasn't about to risk waking Chloe by carrying her back to her bed. She would let the kiddo sleep here for a while, let her get good and unconscious, before tucking her into bed.

No surprise, Sloane's eyelids got heavy immediately, too. She would just take a little catnap while cuddling with Chloe...

Sloane jerked awake as Chloe coughed on top of her.

She remembered abruptly where she was. Chloe coughed once more. *Oh, Lord. Please let her not be getting sick again.* The last thing either of them needed was a relapse with that awful virus—

Sloane frowned. Why did her ceiling look so black? And why was it so warm in here?

She sat up carefully, shifting Chloe's head to her shoulder as she kicked down the footrest and sat up.

Ohmigod. That was smoke.

Had she left the oven on, or a pot of something on the stove? God knew, she'd been absentminded recently, what with Chloe's illness and Bill Gunther spying on her. She stood up, and realized a pall of smoke, several inches deep, hung near the ceiling. Cripes. How long had she been asleep in the chair with Chloe?

What was that noise? It sounded like the furnace fan was running too loudly. Which might explain why it was so hot in the house. Maybe the thermostat had broken?

She padded into the kitchen in search of the scorched, forgotten food, but the stove was turned off. Frowning, she backed out of the kitchen and headed for the utility closet in the hall between Chloe's bedroom and hers. What was going on with the furnace?

As she approached the utility room door, she halted, staring in shock. The smoke was coming from her bedroom, seeping around the door in thick black ribbons. They rolled up from the floor and crept around the sides of the wood panel, and a sheet of smoke poured down from the top of the door frame like an ethereal waterfall, and then rose to join the pall of smoke hanging even more thickly in the hallway.

She reached for the door and her palm touched the doorknob. Searing pain ripped through her hand and she jerked back in shock. Her palm was bright red and burning like fire.

Fire.

Ohmigod. FIRE!

She ran down the hallway with Chloe, as the ceiling burst into flames over her head all at once. A thousand tongues of fire licked at the smoke, orange chrysanthemum petals of flame, layered one on top of the other, devouring the ceiling in a gout of heat almost too hot to stand.

Sloane ran like she'd never run in her life, flying toward the front door, the flames right on her heels. A puff of violent wind hit her in her face. It whooshed behind her, and a deafening explosion ripped through her house. It was accompanied by a flash of heat at her back that felt as if it charred the skin off her body.

Chloe began to cough and cry, the keening of a child's terror.

Another thunderous sound deafened her, this time the tearing of wood and the scream of metal warping, as if the entire back end of her house had ripped apart. She looked over her shoulder frantically, and the crackling, hissing, breathing fire consumed her hallway and roared into her living room like a furious dragon.

She tore open the front door, heedless of the pain in her hand, and flew down the front steps. The next-door neighbor to her right was already outside, talking urgently on his cell phone.

The neighbor hurried over to her. "The fire department is on its way. Is there anyone else inside?"

"No!" Sloane cried over the unbelievable noise of her house burning.

"Let me get you some shoes and a coat. You two must be freezing."

Only then did it dawn on Sloane that she was barefoot in the snow, and that she and Chloe were wearing only their pajamas. She hugged Chloe tight and turned so her daughter couldn't see their home being destroyed.

Chloe was crying in earnest now, and Sloane realized tears were streaming down her face as well. She would never forget that explosion of flames over her head and the fear that her baby was going to die. She hadn't feared for herself, but shock was starting to set in, and she was shivering so hard she could barely hold Chloe.

The neighbor came out with a pair of rubber boots that were way too big for Sloane. But they were dry and lined with fleece. The guy draped a thick wool blanket around her and Chloe. It staved off the cold, but it didn't do a thing to slow down her shivering.

A wail of sirens, a lot of them, split the night, and in a matter of seconds chaos reigned in the street. Four fire trucks pulled up, two ambulances and a bunch of police cars. Sloane searched the crowd for Liam's face but didn't see it.

Someone led her and Chloe over to the back of an ambulance and checked them both over. A medic spread salve on her hand and wrapped a rayon bandage around it, then taped gauze over that.

Chloe was given a few puffs of oxygen from a tank, but she threw a screaming fit at the mask over her face, and the medic, laughing, declared Chloe's lungs just fine.

A fireman came over to ask her what had happened, and Sloane quickly relayed the terrifying chain of events that had transpired upon awakening to discover her bedroom was on fire.

The fireman nodded tersely and talked quickly into a radio, something about rollover fires and the back bedroom as the origin point. He warned about a flashover fire and then moved away from her.

Sloane was just about to stand up and go see how bad the fire was when a large shape loomed in front of her and strong arms went around both her and Chloe.

"Thank God you're alive," Liam rasped. "Are you two okay?"

"I burned my hand a little, but that's it."

"When I heard the address of a major house fire over my police scanner, my heart stopped. I got here as fast as I could," Liam murmured into her hair.

His heart was actually pounding like a jackhammer beneath Sloane's ear.

"Let's get you out of here," he said grimly. "There's nothing more you can do here tonight."

"But my house. Shouldn't I check on it or something?"

"The fire department won't let you near it, and when the fire burns out, I've already told the fire chief I want a full arson investigation."

"Arson?" She leaned back to stare up at him.

"C'mon. Let's get Chloe inside where it's warm. The cold can't be good for her."

That motivated Sloane to move. Liam looped a protective arm around her shoulders and guided her out of the maze of fire hoses, vehicles and people. She made the mistake of looking back over her shoulder and gaped in dismay.

Her entire house was engulfed in flames that shot up into the night like a gigantic bonfire.

"My home!" she gasped.

Liam gently but firmly turned her away from the blaze and urged her into motion once more. "It's just stuff. You and Chloe are safe and unharmed. Nothing else matters. *Nothing.*"

He was no doubt right, but that was her entire life back there. And it was gone. All of it. She had nothing left. Just Chloe. Her shock deepened until a blanket of numbness enveloped her.

Only one thought stood out in stark relief against the shock. *Thank God Chloe is safe.* She hugged her daughter close, abjectly grateful that the two of them had been in the living room when the fire started.

What if she'd been asleep in her bedroom? Would she have been overcome by smoke? Unable to get to Chloe and get her out before the fire reached Chloe's room?

She'd been so lucky not to be asleep in her bed...

The house was brand-new. How on earth had it caught on fire like that? And why her bedroom? Was it a wiring problem? The furnace? Or something else...

"I don't understand," she mumbled as Liam helped her into his truck.

"I'm afraid I do," he responded tightly as he climbed in his seat.

"What do you mean?"

"Later," he bit out. "Let's get you and Chloe someplace safe. Do you two have any clothes out at your brother's place?"

"Chloe does. She stays with Wyatt and Bailey fairly often, and we ended up leaving a few things out there for her."

"Perfect."

Sloane looked over at Liam in confusion. He sounded angry. Enough so that she reflexively retreated into her emotional shell. She'd spent too many years around Ivan and his temper, apparently.

The drive was silent, and Chloe actually fell asleep in her arms before they arrived at the ranch. Liam was back to his usual calm self by the time they pulled into the Crooked C and parked by the main house. He told her to stay in the warm truck while he woke up someone.

He banged on the door for a while, and she watched dully as lights came on in the ranch house and the front door opened. She recognized Wyatt's tall figure in the doorway. He and Liam exchanged brief words, and then Wyatt disappeared. More lights turned on as Liam came to get her and Chloe.

Liam lifted Chloe out of Sloane's arms and carried the toddler into the house. Sloane went first, leading him to a guest room and turning down the blankets and sheets in the bed. Gently, Liam laid Chloe down.

The toddler half woke and reached up to hug Liam. He hugged her back and kissed her forehead before pulling up the blankets and tucking them around her chin. Sloane fought back an urge to cry at the sight. Ivan had never tucked Chloe in, let alone hugged and kissed her.

"I scared of monsters," Chloe announced.

"I'm a policeman. I catch monsters and put them in jail. No monsters will come around while I'm here. Okay?"

"'Kay. 'Night, Lee-Mum," Chloe mumbled.

"Good night, Squirt. Sweet dreams."

As Liam straightened, smiling down fondly at Chloe, Sloane wrapped her arm around his waist in silent gratitude. He looped an arm over her shoulder as they waited beside Chloe's bed for a minute to make sure she went back to sleep. When it was clear the toddler had, indeed, crashed, Liam guided Sloane from the room and closed the door behind them.

"Snuffles!" Sloane wailed under her breath. "He was in Chloe's bedroom. She's going to be devastated if she loses him!"

"I'll take her to a toy store and buy her a new stuffed toy in the morning," Liam promised.

"Is it possible Snuffles survived the fire?" Sloane asked hopefully. Her mind knew what she'd seen, but her heart was having a hard time accepting that everything she owned—everything—was gone.

Liam didn't answer. He merely gathered her into his arms for a long hug. As if he knew exactly what she needed, he stood there with her in the hallway until she began to cry.

It hit her all again. She and Chloe had nearly died. It had been sheer dumb luck that she wasn't asleep in her bedroom when it went up in flames.

Yes. She'd lost everything. But she had good insurance and stuff could be replaced. Thank God she'd spent much of her free time last year scanning and uploading all her family photographs to an internet storage site. Her important legal documents were in a safety deposit box at a bank.

The rest of what she'd lost was memories. And she could make new ones. But having to rebuild her life from scratch was overwhelming right now, coming hard on the heels of a bad scare.

She sobbed on Liam's chest until he scooped her up, carried her into the living room and sat down on the sofa with her in his lap. She was aware of Wyatt and Bailey peeking into the room, but they prudently left her and Liam alone. She would have to remember to thank them later.

When she'd cried the worst of her shock and grief out, Liam silently offered her a handkerchief.

"Who still carries a hankie in this day and age?" she hiccuped.

"Call me old-fashioned," Liam murmured. "It came in handy tonight, though, didn't it?"

She smiled up at him as she dabbed at her face. She had no doubt she looked like a wreck but didn't much care as long as Liam wasn't frightened off. And he didn't seem to be as he gazed at her, relief shining in his eyes.

"Can you handle a little serious conversation?" he asked.

"I think so."

"I heard you tell the fire chief how the fire started. It was in your bedroom, correct?"

"As far as I can tell."

"The first firefighters on scene said it was burning like an accelerant had been poured on the floor and lit."

"Accelerant?"

"Something like gasoline or kerosene."

"You're saying the fire was set intentionally?" Sloane gasped. As soon as she said the words aloud, she knew them to be true. She didn't need to see Liam's sober nod to know it.

"Who?" she managed to choke out. "Gunther wouldn't...would he?"

"I highly doubt it. He bragged about not doing any rough stuff as a private investigator. Complained about how much more money he could make if he did. I'll have the Denver PD pick him up and find out where he was tonight, though."

"If not him, then who?" Sloane asked.

She stared at Liam, and he stared back.

Someone was trying to kill her.

She said in a hush, "I'm starting to think the SUV that jumped the curb and nearly hit us in Denver wasn't an accident."

"I never thought it was," Liam replied. "I always thought that SUV was targeting you."

"Why me?"

"That's what I plan to find out. I'm going to catch whoever's doing this and put him away for a long, long time. I promise you that, Sloane."

The grim undertone in his voice didn't bode well for her would-be killer. She threw her arms around Liam's neck and held on tightly. Eventually, she whispered, "I don't deserve you. I'm so thankful you came into my life."

"Stop with the not deserving me stuff, already."

She turned him loose enough to lean back and look into his eyes. "You're always there for me when I need you. You always have been."

"And I always will be," he added.

Did he—? Did that mean—?

"Hey, you two. I've got some food heated up if you're hungry. My mother always said there was nothing in the world her homemade chili couldn't fix."

Sloane looked up at Bailey and smiled a little. "What would I do without you?"

"Well, you'd be a whole lot skinnier, for one thing," Bailey retorted and said to Liam, "Bring your woman into the kitchen so I can feed her. I'll ladle up a bowl of chili for you, too, if you're hungry."

His woman? Sloane started to mentally protest, but then stopped. She actually loved the idea of being Liam's woman. He was the kind of man who would never ask her to be less than who she was. He wouldn't care if she was strong and independent most of the time, wouldn't be threatened by her having a career and being darned good at it. Plus, Chloe adored him, and he seemed to adore Chloe back.

Liam stood up and set Sloane on her feet. Her body slid down the length of his, and as always, she responded to him like a flower to sunlight, with warmth unfolding inside her, making her feel safe and alive. He held her long enough to drop a quick kiss on her lips.

She captured his mouth with hers, though, and asked for more. Her arms went around his neck and she leaned into him hungrily, needing the affirmation that she had really survived the fire and come out the other side. He readily gave it to her, turning the kiss into a deep, drugging melding of hearts and souls that thoroughly reminded her she was, indeed, alive.

Sexual tension filled Liam, flowing into her. Hot, molten need tightened her belly all of a sudden, and the kiss changed tenor completely, becoming urgent, a slashing of tongues and deep, hungry explorations.

Liam broke the kiss, breathing hard. "In the first place, we don't have a room here that I can drag you off to. In the second place, Bailey will be back soon to see why we didn't follow her to the kitchen. In the third place, I can't think when you kiss me like that. And I need to fire on all cylinders mentally for a little while longer."

"Why?"

"I need to formally interview you."

"Sounds fun," she flirted, need still riding her hard.

"Stop that," he chided her. "This is serious."

Her moment of levity faded. "I know," she sighed.

Fox burst into the house just then. "Sis, are you okay? And Chloe?"

"We're both fine. My house is a total loss, though."

"I don't care about that as long as you two are safe." He wrapped her up in a relieved hug.

"Do you want to stay at my place while you figure out what you're doing next?" Fox offered.

Slone smiled at him in gratitude. "For tonight, I've already got Chloe down in the guest room here. I'd hate to move her again. I honestly haven't given any thought to what comes next. Can I get back to you on that?"

"Of course. Just know I'm here for you."

Thank goodness for all her family. What would she do without them?

Using his cell phone app, Liam recorded her statement as she described the evening's events again in detail. He questioned her about the timeline of when she fell asleep—what time it was when she woke up, how long it took her to check the kitchen and make her way to her bedroom door, and how long it took the first fire truck to arrive.

Fox, Wyatt and Bailey listened in horror as Liam questioned her about who might be trying to kill her. She declined to guess, citing that anyone she named would be pure speculation on her part.

But then Liam asked, "Do you think your ex-husband is capable of hiring someone to harm or kill you?"

She looked at Liam, pleading silently for him to withdraw the question, but he stared back at her implacably.

Finally, she answered reluctantly, "Capable? Yes. Absolutely, I think he is."

"Why?" he pressed.

She sighed. Liam knew the answer, but she understood that he needed her to state the reason formally. For the record. "Ivan wants custody of our daughter. I'm convinced he doesn't actually love her or want to raise her, however. To him, Chloe is a trophy. A spoil of war. He knows she means everything to me—therefore he wants to take her away from me. It's purely spite."

Liam turned off the recorder. Bailey jumped up and rushed over to Sloane to hug her. "I'm so sorry, Sloane. I had no idea your ex was giving you so much trouble. You should have told us."

"I still have no proof he's behind whoever's stalking me," Sloane responded.

Fox piped up. "Aww, c'mon, sis. Ivan's a vindictive SOB and you know it. Always has been, always will be. Quit protecting him."

"I'm not protecting him!" she exclaimed. "But neither am I accusing him until I have solid evidence."

Wyatt spoke up. "Either way, we're protecting you from here on out. You and Chloe are staying here at the ranch until Liam and the police nail your stalker."

"I don't want to intrude—" she started.

But Liam interrupted her. "That's what I was hoping you would say, Wyatt. And Sloane is correct. The attacker might not be Ivan Durant. A young woman who matches Sloane's description disappeared a while back, and that crime hasn't been solved. I need you to be suspicious of anyone who doesn't belong at the ranch or who is acting strangely. It might even be someone you know."

"What are you saying, Liam?" Sloane asked quickly, her legal instincts on full alert. "Are you saying there's a serial kidnapper or killer in town?"

"I'm not saying that...not on the record, at least. I'm just asking Wyatt and Fox and Bailey to be extra vigilant and not trust anyone."

Sloane stared at Liam in dismay. A serial killer in

Roaring Springs? Surely not. It was a peaceful, safe town, tucked away in the mountains where things like kidnapping and murder didn't touch it. She'd moved back here with Chloe for that very reason.

Not to mention, she knew Liam too well. He was indeed implying a serial killer could be on the loose. Was that who'd set her house on fire? Was it a random stranger who'd fixated on her? Or was it something— someone—more sinister? Had Ivan finally cracked and unleashed the violence she'd feared?

Chapter 16

Liam was relieved when a steady stream of family came by the ranch over the next few days to console Sloane on the loss of her house, which had indeed burned to the ground. She needed the company, and he had his hands full trying to figure out who had set fire to her house and quietly helping the sheriff's department reinvestigate the Bianca Rouge murder and track down April Thomas's last whereabouts.

It was hard to believe that Roaring Springs had gone from a town that never had any serious crimes to being the home of a murderer and an arsonist all at once. Both investigations had him working eighteen-hour days.

Liam stopped by the Crooked C Ranch every evening to visit Sloane. It had been decided that she and Chloe would stay with Wyatt and Bailey so Bailey could help Sloane with Chloe. He usually grabbed a bite to eat and updated Sloane on his investigation of who hired Bill Gunther to stalk her. Which was going nowhere.

Her house had definitely been torched. The preliminary finding by the arson investigator from Denver was that a hole had been drilled in the exterior wall of Sloane's bedroom, gasoline had been poured through it onto the floor of her bedroom, and the pool of gas had then been set on fire. It had definitely been an attempt to murder her.

Would Ivan Durant try to kill his own daughter? Did the fact that Chloe was in the house rule out Ivan as the arsonist?

The only way for Ivan to be behind the fire was if he thought the fire department would get to the house in time to contain the fire before it burned through the utility room and hall bathroom to reach Chloe. It was a calculated risk of Chloe's life...but then, Sloane had stated on more than one occasion that Ivan didn't particularly care for Chloe. Liam had seen that himself when Ivan hadn't come to visit Chloe in the hospital during her life-threatening illness.

Jerk.

Personally, he couldn't get enough of Chloe. She was arguably the cutest two-year-old ever put on the planet. She had her mother's huge eyes, and blond pigtails that just begged to be flipped. She was a bright, loving, funny kid and a joy to be around. There was nothing quite as heartwarming as a hug from her little arms and a sticky kiss on the cheek. Ivan Durant was a complete idiot not to see all of that.

Liam couldn't cross Ivan off the list of arson suspects nor off the list of people who could have hired Gunther to spy on Sloane.

Tonight, for supper, they were digging into a brisket Bailey and Sloane had spent all day smoking. The meat was fork tender and delicious.

"Any progress in the case today?" Sloane asked him.

"Which case?"

She rolled her beautiful eyes at him.

"We spent the day at The Lodge asking the staff if anyone remembered seeing April Thomas as a guest or coming there for a job interview. It was a bust. That place has so many guests pass through it that the staff wouldn't remember her if she'd been there last week, let alone last year."

"Not to mention, a lot of the guests are young, beautiful women," Sloane added.

"That, too."

"Any word on my fire?"

"Nothing new to report. I talked to several of your neighbors, and none of them saw or heard anything that night. How are you holding up?"

Sloane nodded but her face reflected disappointment. "Life is returning to normal. The stream of visitors has slowed down, thank goodness."

Liam grinned. "That's what you get for being a Colton. You have a huge family that rallies around you in a crisis."

"And sticks its nose into every corner of my business," she retorted.

Fox spoke up. "Aww, c'mon. You know you love all of us."

Sloane smiled at her brother. "Fine. I love all of you." A pause. "Most of the time."

That set off a round of ribbing and joking that Liam mostly stayed out of. He spent the time studying Sloane while she was distracted, lecturing her brother about how he'd messed up her social life in high school, and she had yet to forgive him for it.

Her skin looked more transparent than usual, and she had violet shadows under her eyes. She wasn't sleeping well. He wished he could gather her into his arms, whisper to her that she was safe, and let her sleep about twelve hours uninterrupted on top of him. But he wasn't about to shack up with her under Wyatt and Bailey's roof or under her brother's nose. He and Fox were good friends but not that good.

"I'll go kiss Chloe good-night," he announced.

As had become his nightly habit, he ducked into the toddler's bedroom. She was waiting for him, pretending to be asleep. One bright blue eye opened and then closed again fast.

"Saw you, Squirt," he chuckled. "Were you waiting for a kiss from me?"

"Uh-huh."

"How was your day today? Did you do anything fun?"

"I fed horseys."

"Sounds fun. What did you feed them?"

"Kah-wuts."

"Did the horses like the carrots?"

"Uh-huh."

Chloe sounded sleepy, and he'd learned not to rouse the extroverted toddler too much, or it would be another hour before she went down for the night.

"Need me to check under your bed for monsters?"

"Uh-huh." A thumb went into her cherry-red mouth.

He duly got down on his knees and peered under the bed. "No monsters. And now that I've been here, none will dare mess with you. You're good to go for the rest of the night, kiddo."

Chloe held her arms out to him and he leaned down for a hug. "I wub you, Lee-Mum."

Liam froze. His heart felt full to bursting…and then it did burst, in an explosion of incredible joyousness. "I love you, too, Chloe. You're the best ever."

He returned the hug carefully—after all, she was a tiny little thing like her mother—and kissed Chloe's cheek gently. Chloe wanted to kiss his cheek back, and he turned his head for her. As he did so, he spotted Sloane leaning against the doorjamb, her arms crossed, watching the exchange. A soft smile wreathed her face.

He pulled the covers up around Chloe's ears and gave them a tuck. "Sweet dreams, princess."

He backed out into the hallway, and Sloane closed the door behind him.

"Thank you," she murmured.

"For what?"

"For being a decent male role model to Chloe."

He shrugged modestly. "She's awesome."

"I happen to think so, too."

He dropped a light kiss on the end of her nose. "You're supposed to think she's great. You're her mom. As for me, I'm an impartial stranger. So my opinion is the one that counts. And your kid is the bomb."

Sloane's lips curved up against his. "Has anyone told you today that you're pretty fantastic yourself?"

"Nope. Not a soul."

"Well, you are."

"God, I'd love to scoop you up, throw you in my truck and take you back to my place for a long, sleepless night."

She groaned under her breath. "Don't tempt me. That sounds amazing."

"Soon. I'm going to find your stalker, and then we'll catch up on everything we're missing now."

"That's a deal, Detective."

It was his turn to groan in frustration. "I'm going to leave now, or else I'm going to do something that will make your brother have to pound me senseless."

"He likes you, you know."

Liam looped his arm over her shoulder and resolutely started walking toward the front door. "I know Fox likes me. We've been best friends for twenty years."

"No. I mean he likes you as someone for me to be with."

Liam stopped in front of the door and turned to stare down at her. "For real?"

"Yes. He said so last night. He said you're good for me."

"Sonofagun. I didn't think any guy would ever be good enough for his little sister."

"Apparently, you pass muster."

"I'll take it. I gotta go work on getting rid of your stalker now so we can be together and test your brother's restraint."

"Promise me you'll get at least a little sleep tonight."

"Not a wink. I'm going to be thinking of you all night."

Laughing, she kissed him one more time and then pushed him out the front door. It was a bitter cold night and he didn't linger at the door where Sloane would get chilled. He hurried to his truck and jumped in. But despite the cold, she was standing in the door, watching him wistfully as he pulled away into the night.

Yeah. He knew the feeling. It was killing him not to be with her, too.

Soon. Very soon, he would catch her stalker. And then they were going to light up the whole damned night with fireworks.

Liam was too busy to come out to the ranch the next day, and by the following day, Sloane was totally out of sorts. She understood that he was elbow deep in several important police investigations, but she still missed his steady, easy presence. Chloe was cranky that she didn't get her good-night kiss from Lee-Mum, and all in all, it was a lousy day.

The next day dawned cloudy and gray. The clouds were heavy, and a storm was forecast for later. Wyatt and Fox rode out to do a head count of the herd and to make sure all the cattle and horses were pulled into the near pasture just behind the barns before blizzard conditions set in. A few cattle always strayed from the herd, and the guys would be busy all day finding them and herding them down to the safety of the valley near the barns.

Snow started falling in the early afternoon. It started with a few fat flakes drifting in lazy pendulum swings toward the ground. But within an hour, snow was coming down heavily, accumulating in thick piles on every horizontal surface.

Bailey stood at the kitchen sink, staring worriedly out the window, waiting for any sign of Wyatt and Fox to return.

Taking pity on her, Sloane said, "Why don't you ride a snowmobile out and see if Wyatt and Fox need you to break a path through the snow for their horses? I'll hold down the fort here until you get back."

"I hate to leave you alone—"

"My stalker isn't going out in a storm like this. I'm fine. Take care of your man. And bring my brother home, too."

Bailey nodded and flew out of the kitchen to don warm clothes before heading out.

Sloane made a big pot of stew and played with Chloe through the afternoon. Chloe went down late for a nap, and Sloane noticed the fading daylight. It was time to feed the horses, but there was no sign of Wyatt, Fox or Bailey. She would just sneak out and feed the horses while Chloe was asleep. Tucking the baby monitor in the pocket of her coat, she tromped out to the barn.

Snowflakes landed on her cheeks and eyelashes, and the Rocky Mountains were gorgeous, clothed in their winter finery. She breathed deeply of the icy air, enjoying the burn of it in her lungs. She was home. And things were going to turn out all right. Liam would catch her stalker, and then the two of them would figure out where the heated connection between them was going.

It was hard to believe that a few short weeks ago she'd been convinced she would never love again—

Her thoughts skidded to a shocked halt and she stopped in the knee-deep snow. She loved Liam.

She'd known it when she watched him tuck in Chloe and smile like his heart was breaking with joy when Little Bug told him she loved him.

He didn't care that Chloe was another man's child. He seemed to understand how precious and innocent a gift the love of a child was. He'd been humbled by Chloe's love, and obviously returned it. Sloane had heard the sincerity in his voice when he'd told Chloe he loved her, too.

He was, in a word, perfect.

She resumed walking, her own heart lighter than the snowflakes around her. She pushed open the big barn door enough to slip inside and headed for the feed room. Something big and dark jumped out at her from the shadows, and that was the last thing she remembered.

Smoke. She smelled smoke. Groggy, she registered that she was waking up. She must have dreamed about the house fire again. It had been a recurring nightmare ever since that night.

She dreamed of waking up in her bedroom, surrounded by fire, unable to break through the wall of flames to rescue Chloe. It was what the stalker had planned for her, and only luck had prevented her from living that nightmare for real.

Her eyes blinked open, and flames licked at the wooden ceiling overhead through a thick blanket of gray-black smoke. Yup. That would have been what her bedroom ceiling looked like. The searing heat on her face. The burning in her lungs—

She sat up, and the walls around her swirled wildly. Whoa.

Wait a minute. This wasn't her bedroom. It was the feed room.

And this wasn't a dream.

She tried to stand up, but her head throbbed violently, like she'd been hit with a heavy object, and she was so dizzy she could hardly sit upright, let alone jump up and run for her life. She did the only thing she could think of and screamed at the top of her lungs.

Not again.

She wasn't facing being burned to a crisp again.

She had to move. Had to get out of here, legs or no legs.

Sloane rolled onto her belly and dragged herself across the concrete floor of the feed room by her elbows. Her legs weren't entirely useless, and she dug in with her toes to push herself along. She made it almost to the door and started to feel a bit stronger. She ventured to push up onto her hands and knees, and her strength held. She crawled to the door, and remembering the burn she'd gotten on her bedroom doorknob, only briefly touched her knuckle to the metal.

It wasn't hot.

She reached up and turned the knob, and gasped as the barn alleyway came into view. The entire ceiling was on fire. It appeared that the hayloft was completely engulfed in flames. Oh, God. The horses.

Their screams and panicked kicks as they fought to get out of their stalls and run for their lives reverberated over the now familiar roar of the fire.

Sloane dragged herself to her feet using the door for support. The barn spun around her, and she blinked hard, trying unsuccessfully to clear her vision. Must. Get. Out.

Chloe.

That one word, that one thought, of her daughter, was all the motivation she needed. She felt her way along the wall, stumbling forward step-by-step toward the exit.

A black shape rushed at her and she recoiled. No! The attacker couldn't knock her out again! She *had* to get to her baby.

"Sloane!" a male voice shouted.

Fox.

"I'm here!" she called back, coughing too much to project much sound.

But it was enough. The black shape resolved into her

brother. He raced forward, wrapped his arm around her waist, and ran her toward the barn door.

"The horses!" she cried.

"Wyatt's opening the stall doors. I'll go back and help him make sure all the horses run. Get up to the house. Bailey's got a shotgun."

What? A shotgun?

Oh. Her stalker. He or she might still be here on the ranch, somewhere, waiting to make sure she died in the fire this time.

Staggering through the deep snow, falling down a few times, Sloane made her way toward the house. Obscene, bloody orange light flickered across the pristine snow, a macabre display.

Please, God, let all the horses be all right. If she was responsible for getting any of Wyatt's beautiful horses killed, she would never forgive herself. She stopped, half convinced she should go back to the barn and help save the horses. But as she turned around, she saw several of them bolt out of the barn and race away into the back pasture. Wyatt and Fox emerged from the barn, side by side, bent over and coughing.

Given that they weren't going back inside, she knew they'd gotten all the horses out.

She looked around and suddenly felt very, very exposed, standing halfway across the yard out in the wide open with nary a tree, bush or blade of grass for cover. She was tempted to lie down in the snow and use its depth for cover. Lord knew, she was feeling unsteady enough on her feet to be better off crawling.

But, Chloe.

Desperate need surged through her to reach her daughter, to hug Little Bug tight and reassure herself that Chloe was safe. Not to mention she could use the reassurance herself that she was alive and well after yet another close call.

Terror that the stalker had snuck into the house and kidnapped Chloe got her feet moving, first at a walk, then a shambling run, and then a full-out sprint.

Panicked like she'd never been panicked before, she burst into the house, breathless, raced past a grim-faced Bailey, and tore down the hall to Chloe's room. She threw open the door and charged inside, prepared to do battle barehanded with whatever monster threatened her baby.

Chloe looked up from the computer monitor. A princess movie was playing, a cheerful song chirping from the speaker.

The shock of seeing her daughter safe and unconcerned was so abrupt that Sloane just screeched to a stop and stared at Chloe for a long moment.

Time resumed its forward march and Sloane raced forward, scooping up Chloe in a bear hug.

"Cold!" Chloe squealed. "You wet, Mama."

"I know, Little Bug. I love you so much. So, *so* much. I'd do anything for you."

"Wub you, too, Mama." Chloe tolerated the hug for a moment longer and then squirmed impatiently. "Wanna see pwin-cess dance wif pwince."

Reluctantly, Sloane dropped one last abjectly grateful kiss on Little Bug's head and then turned Chloe loose, setting her back down in front of her movie.

She stepped back out into the hall and pulled up short at the sight of Bailey carrying a double-barreled shotgun like it was loaded and she knew how to use it.

"You okay?" Bailey bit out.

Honestly, it was the first time she'd stopped to take stock of her overall health since she'd woken up and realized the barn was on fire. Sloane motioned with her head for Bailey to follow her to the kitchen, but the jerk of her head sent a bolt of pain crashing through her skull.

She made it to the kitchen and collapsed into a chair at the table. "I think I got hit over the head."

Bailey went into full medical mode and passed the shotgun to Sloane, then efficiently checked out Sloane's skull. When she got to the back of Sloane's head, pain exploded.

"Ouch!" Sloane cried.

"That's a nasty bump you've got there," Bailey announced.

Sloane winced as her future sister-in-law probed the tender spot on the back of her head, pushing hair aside.

"Sit still. I need to see if it's split open or needs stitches."

It wasn't, and it didn't. But then Bailey made Sloane stare at her fingers and tell her how many she saw until Sloane finally lost patience and snapped, "I can see just fine. Yes, I'm sure I have a mild concussion, and no, I won't run around and do anything stupid until I can see a human physician. You can quit fussing over me now."

Bailey shrugged. "Liam would kill me if I let anything happen to you."

"Speaking of which, has anyone called him to let him know someone tried to kill me...*again*?"

"I don't know. When we topped the ridge and saw the barn on fire, we all took off at top speed. Wyatt yelled at me to go to the house and protect you and Chloe while he and Fox headed for the barn. I did call 911 to get the fire department out here. Although by the time they get here in this storm, that barn's going to be a total loss. Good thing it was the old barn Wyatt's been talking about pulling down and rebuilding, anyway."

Sloane pulled out her cell phone and hit Liam's speed dial number.

"Sloane? Are you all right? I heard on the police scanner that there's a fire out at the Crooked C. Tell me you're not hurt. Talk to me."

"If you'll let me get a word in edgewise, I'll tell you I'm okay. Someone hit me over the head and left me in the barn while it burned down around me, though."

"*What?* Where are you? Are Wyatt and Fox with you?"

"They're still at the barn. I think they got all the horses out, but they'll need to move the livestock to another pasture, further from the fire. Chloe and I are at the house with Bailey and a very impressive shotgun."

"I'll be there in twenty minutes. Don't go anywhere. I'm calling the sheriff's department to see if they can get someone up there faster to protect you."

Liam hung up, and momentary silence fell in the kitchen. Only the crackling roar of the fire outside disturbed it.

Bailey took possession of the shotgun again and moved over to the kitchen sink. "At least the wind hasn't picked up. Otherwise, embers could have been carried to the other barns or even here to the house."

"God. I'm so sorry, Bailey. This is all my fault."

"Stop right there, Sloane. We've got plenty of insurance. I'm just glad you're safe."

When the wail of sirens became audible, it was clear that Liam had called out the entire emergency response of Roaring Springs and the surrounding areas. Four fire trucks, two ambulances and a half-dozen police cars pulled into the ranch, floundering through the snow toward the barn.

By the time firefighters piled out of their vehicles, it was obvious even to Sloane that the barn was a complete loss. All the firefighters did was watch the roofs of the surrounding structures for embers.

Sloane, standing by Bailey at the sink, saw a tall, familiar figure peel off of the cluster of police just starting to fan out around the barn and run toward the house. She went to the front door to meet Liam.

He burst inside and swept her up against his thick shearling coat, soaking her clothes with snow and cold, and she didn't care at all. His arms crushed her ribs, and then his mouth crashed down on hers.

Long moments later, they finally came up for air.

Sighing, she laid her head on his shoulder, and even through his thick layers of clothes, she heard and felt his heart pounding wildly.

"You've got to stop scaring me like this, baby."

"Believe me, I'd love to stop scaring you."

Liam stared down at her as she leaned back enough to stare up at him. He announced grimly, "That's it. We're figuring out who's trying to kill you and taking the fight to this bastard."

Chapter 17

After reassuring himself that Sloane and Chloe were safe, Liam stomped back out through the snow to have a conversation with Sheriff Trey Colton.

"Is Sloane okay, Liam?" Daria Bloom asked as he approached the contingent from the sheriff's office.

"She and Chloe are fine. Looks like Sloane got hit on the back of the head and left in the barn to burn."

The sheriff nodded grimly. "Fire chief says this was another obvious case of arson. I have to believe that whoever set Sloane's house on fire torched the barn, too."

Liam swore under his breath at the confirmation of his suspicion.

"How do you want to proceed, Liam? This is your case, after all."

"I need some officers assigned to Sloane and Chloe around the clock. In the meantime, I'm heading to Denver to get some damned answers."

"Do you have some idea who's behind this?"

"I do. Now all I need is proof."

Daria cautioned him, "Keep your head in the game, Liam. Any evidence you collect has to hold up in court. Be a cop."

"Yeah, yeah. I know. Believe me. I want to nail this bastard worse than anyone. I'll do it by the book."

Although he was sorely tempted to find Ivan Durant and beat the crap out of him.

The rest of the night was occupied with writing up a police report on the fire, collecting preliminary evidence from the firefighters on scene and setting up a schedule of round-the-clock armed protection for Sloane and Chloe.

The problem was, with armed cops crawling all over the Crooked C Ranch, the stalker undoubtedly wouldn't show himself or herself again anytime soon. And whoever it was, the person was very careful. Yet again, the police found no evidence at the scene that could point them to the identity of the assailant. Any tracks had been quickly erased by the heavy snowfall.

Frustrated, Liam drove home in the wee hours to let the blizzard blow itself out and catch a few hours of shut-eye before he drove in to Denver. He and Bill Gunther were going to have a little conversation. And if that yielded no results, Liam was going to have a very direct discussion with Ivan Durant.

The next day saw Liam sitting in an interview room at a Denver police station with Bill Gunther. "So you swear you haven't had anything to do with Sloane Colton since I last spoke with you?"

"I swear. I completely stopped watching her," Gunther insisted. "You pulled out the cameras and I turned off the computers."

"You haven't been to Roaring Springs in the past two weeks?"

"I haven't been to Roaring Springs in the past two months. Check the GPS in my car or my cell phone if you don't believe me." He narrowed his eyes. "What's going on, Detective?"

"Someone's trying to kill Ms. Colton. Two different attempts have been made on her life recently."

"Oh, man. That sucks. She seems like a nice lady."

"Has your client had any further contact with you since we last spoke?" Liam demanded.

"Not a word. Dropped off the map like he or she never existed."

Liam swore under his breath.

"Have you got a protection detail on Ms. Colton?" Bill asked shrewdly.

"Yes."

"Your killer's not going to crawl out from under his rock again until the cops go away."

Liam sighed. "I know. But I'm not willing to risk her life by pulling the protection detail."

"I would set up a trap if I were you. Use the lady as bait. You'd have to have a place that has limited access points where you could surround yourself with cameras and trip wires so you could see the bastard coming. Arm yourself to the teeth, and be prepared to take the stalker out." Bill punctuated the declaration by drawing his finger across his throat.

Liam snorted. "Oh, I'm prepared to take this bastard out. Trust me on that. I just have to lure the stalker into showing himself or herself."

"The only bait someone like that will take is their primary target. And for better or worse, that's Sloane Colton."

Gunther was absolutely right. As much as Liam didn't like it, the guy spoke the truth. "You said you were a tech guy when you were on the police force. What kind of cameras would you use to watch a house from outside?"

Bill started talking, and Liam listened intently. After nearly an hour, they left the interrogation room with Liam a whole lot more knowledgeable regarding state-of-the-art surveillance technology.

"Detective Kastor!" someone called out across the ready room.

Liam looked up, and one of his Denver counterparts strode over to him. "What can I do for you?" Liam asked.

"It's what I can do for you. You're taking point on the Colton attacks in Roaring Springs, aren't you?"

"That's correct." He'd been sending out reports state-wide in case Sloane's stalker had staged similar attacks elsewhere. Cops kept an eye out for crimes with strikingly similar MOs, and maybe he would get lucky.

"After your report on the odd behavior of Carol and Niall Durant, we were able to get a warrant to wire-tap them."

"Really? How'd you pull that off?" Liam asked in surprise. He hardly thought suspicious behavior was enough for a surveillance warrant to go through.

"Mr. Durant is suspected of other criminal activities—financial irregularities, possible embezzlement, attempting to bribe a judge. FBI was about to apply for a wiretap warrant, too. We combined applications."

"Wow. What judge did Durant try to bribe?"

"A family court judge who ruled in their son's divorce. He reported that the Durants approached him, offering a large cash sum for their son to get full custody of their grandchild."

"Was there hard evidence? A recording or written bribe?" Liam asked quickly. "And was Ivan Durant involved?"

"It was just the judge's word, although he'd make for an impeccable witness. And no, the son wasn't involved, at least not according to the judge."

Damn.

"At any rate, we picked up something on the wiretap. Thought it might pertain to your case. We were planning to make a copy of it and send it to you, anyway. But in light of what we just heard, it's good luck that you're here."

Liam followed the detective into a small room crowded with elaborate sound equipment. A technician looked up and the detective said, "Play back that piece of tape I told you to copy for Detective Kastor in Roaring Springs. This is Liam Kastor in the flesh, by the way."

"Great timing, Detective," the technician said to Liam. "You're gonna want to hear this." The guy hit a button, and an automated male voice said simply, "Leave a message." An answering machine beeped.

But then a familiar voice filled the small room. Liam recognized Carol Durant's upper-crust accent saying, "It's urgent that you return our calls. We need you to call it off. You hear me? Call. It. Off. You nearly killed our granddaughter, you dolt!" A pause was filled with what sounded like Carol breathing heavily, as if she were upset. She ended with, "Call me back. Immediately."

The tech said, "That was recorded the day after Ms. Colton's house burned." He fiddled with a few buttons and then said, "And we picked this up about an hour ago."

This time it was Niall Durant's voice echoing through the room. "We've been trying to get in touch with you for over a week now. We need you to cease and desist, effective immediately. My wife made it clear to you over a week ago that we no longer desire you to complete the hit. You may keep the money you've been paid so far. Hell, I'll pay you the rest of what we agreed upon. But stop trying to kill Sloane Colton, you hear me? You're going to get the child killed, too!"

Liam sucked in a sharp breath. "We've got them dead to rights."

"Looks that way," the detective confirmed. "I've got my guys writing up an arrest warrant as we speak. You want to stick around and help us serve it?"

"As much as I would enjoy seeing those two in handcuffs and sputtering for a lawyer, I need to get back to Roaring Springs right away. There's a hit man out there trying to kill Ms. Colton, and I have to stop him."

The drive back to Roaring Springs was interminable. The heavy, accumulating snow and far too many idiot drivers conspired to make the trip take forever. Or maybe he was just frantic to get back to Sloane.

He called ahead, of course, to warn her security detail of who they were up against. They promised to keep her away from windows or sight lines for a sniper, and they put an extra cop on foot patrol around Wyatt and Bailey's house in an effort to scare the hit man off.

Sloane and Chloe couldn't live that way forever. At some point, he had to draw the would-be killer out and catch him. At least, from the phone messages left by the Durants, they knew the assassin to be male. That was better than nothing…but not much.

While he drove, a plan hatched in Liam's head. It could be a little risky, but based on the information Bill Gunther had given him, Liam felt certain he could minimize the risk to Sloane.

He would do largely what Bill had suggested: pick a spot where Liam controlled the approaches and use Sloane as bait to draw out the killer. He debated asking a female cop to impersonate Sloane, but they were dealing with a professional who'd had weeks to study Sloane and recognize every nuance of her appearance and movement. Liam highly doubted anyone but Sloane herself would draw the hit man out now. Particularly after the police had made a big show of protecting her. The hit man had to know the cops were looking for him.

And Liam knew just the place to set a trap using her as bait.

Chapter 18

Sloane looked around the tiny valley and the log cabin tucked into the lee of a sheer rock cliff. "Your family owns this place?" she asked.

"My dad used it as a hunting cabin and man cave. It was passed down to me when he died, but I haven't had much chance to use it yet," Liam answered as he lifted a large duffel bag of gear out of the bed of his truck. He added, "I was thinking about moving up here, but it gets snowed in a lot, and I have to be able to get to work."

"Still. It's beautiful. Peaceful." Aspens, their papery white bark bare among the evergreen of the pines, waited, dormant, for the coming of spring. Up here there had to be at least four feet of snow on the ground. Someone had plowed the driveway, or there would have been no way they could have driven right up to the front of the cabin.

"It doesn't look fireproof. Are you sure you want

to risk letting me stay here?" she asked doubtfully. "It might burn down around me."

"I'll take the chance. I've got the place surrounded with cameras and trip wires. Nobody's approaching without us knowing."

She seriously hoped so. It really was an idyllic spot. She would hate to be the cause of its destruction.

They'd left Chloe with Wyatt, Bailey and a pair of policemen at the Crooked C, and she'd come up here with Liam in hopes of drawing out and exposing her would-be killer once and for all.

She followed Liam to the covered porch, where a rustic pair of rocking chairs labored under a foot or more of snow. She could imagine sitting in one of those in the summer, watching the sun set over the mountains across the valley below.

Only the sound of the wind whispering through the pines disturbed the silence. She fancied she could hear snow falling off the needles as the wind rustled the pine boughs.

"Come on in and make yourself at home," Liam said. "It's humble, but it's warm and dry."

The interior was perfect. From the pine plank floors, to the chinked log walls, to the river stone fireplace dominating one side of the main room, it emanated rustic down-home charm. A small kitchen opened off the back of the living room, and two doors to her right promised at least one bedroom and a bathroom.

"Are the pipes frozen at this time of year?" she asked doubtfully.

"No. The pipes are wrapped and heated. My dad was the kind of man who took care of all the details."

She smiled at Liam. "So that's where you get it from, huh?"

He looked startled for a second. "I guess so." He added slowly, "I suppose I wouldn't mind becoming like my father. He was a good man."

"You're already a good man, Liam Kastor."

He turned, and she stepped into his arms as naturally as breathing. It was exactly where she belonged. Of that, she no longer had any doubt. Now, she just had to figure out if Liam was prepared to step into a ready-made family and raise another man's child as his own. If it came down to a choice between Chloe's well-being and her own happiness, her responsibility to Chloe would, of course, win out, no matter the emotional cost to her.

"I'm going to check on the cameras and carry in more firewood. The furnace works, but it can only do so much against this cold. If you want to get a fire started, feel free."

She grinned at him. "How did you know I love starting fires?"

"I remember when you were a Girl Scout. Fox complained that you would never let him start fires after you learned how."

She stared up at him. "Really? You remember something that trivial?"

"I remember everything about you. Always have."

She smiled as his head tilted down toward hers. Their lips touched, and as always, everything else fell away, leaving just him and her, existing in their own private, perfect universe.

Liam pulled away, laughing ruefully. "We're going to freeze to death if I don't bring in some wood."

She teased, "I don't know. We generate plenty of heat when we're together."

"You ain't seen nothing yet, kid."

He left, still grinning.

Sloane explored, the dreamy smile taking a long time to fade from her face. A huge log-frame bed filled the lone bedroom, leaving only enough room for a small closet and a nightstand. The bathroom was small and old-fashioned, but spotlessly clean. The kitchen was the same.

The furniture in the living room was big and comfortable and half swallowed her when she tried out the armchair. Liam must have gotten his height and size from his father.

She knelt before the cast iron insert in the fireplace, opening the doors and carefully stacking kindling and braided grass knots over several pieces of fatwood. Using a long match, she lit the fatwood and watched it carefully, blowing on it as needed until the grass caught and the first twigs started to ignite.

The whole thing was burning merrily by the time Liam burst in with a gust of wind and crystalline particles of snow. He dumped a huge armful of split wood in the bin by the fire. She added a few of the pieces and then closed the doors and opened the vents.

"Are all your cameras in good working order?" she asked.

He moved over to the coffee table and opened a laptop computer on it. "See for yourself."

She moved over beside him and saw the screen split into four views, one of the driveway, one of the front porch and two pointed at corners of the cabin, each one covering two sides of the dwelling. He tapped a key and four more camera shots popped up on the screen.

"There's a circle of trip wires all around the cabin. I laid them down yesterday, and they're buried under the snow that fell overnight. The hit man will never see them."

"I can't believe there's an actual hit man coming after me," Sloane muttered. "Let alone that Niall and Carol hired him."

"Ivan didn't become a colossal jerk in a vacuum," Liam commented dryly.

Sloane smiled up at him. "Why don't you tell me how you really feel about my ex?"

Liam grinned back. "He's the biggest idiot on the planet not to have seen what he had in you. He should have hung on to you with both hands and never let go. But, hey." He shrugged. "His loss is my gain."

"You think so, eh?"

His grin widened. "I know so. Come over here and warm me up."

"You're incorrigible, you know."

"Why? Because I like cuddling with the prettiest girl this side of the Continental Divide?"

He didn't give her a chance to answer because apparently his lips were cold and needed warming up, too. Not that she minded one little bit. He was the best kisser this side of the Continental Divide.

They roasted hot dogs over the fire, and for dessert, Liam pulled out a box of graham crackers, chocolate bars and a bag of marshmallows.

Sloane squealed in delight. "Ohmigosh! I haven't had s'mores in forever!"

They ended up feeding each other the gooey sweet

treats and getting marshmallows and melted chocolate all over their fingers. Liam took her hand and drew it to his mouth, sucking on each of her fingers in turn until they were clean as a whistle and she was having trouble drawing breath.

Her gaze met his, and his eyes were sultry, laden with a promise of more sensual delights to come.

Liam got up and brought back an armload of thick wool blankets, which he spread out in front of the stone hearth. Then he slowly stripped Sloane of all her clothes, kissing every bit of skin as he lovingly exposed it. Of course, she returned the favor. She never got tired of his big, muscular body, of his warm skin, or the way his breath hitched when she found a particularly sensitive erogenous zone.

Their lovemaking was slow and lazy as the silence and warmth of the fire wrapped around them. Sloane wasn't sure where she ended and Liam began. He was a part of her, and she a part of him. Their smiles mingled as they kissed, and their gasps mingled as their lovemaking built in intensity.

Liam kissed away the tears she didn't even know she had shed in the aftermath. She'd never known a man could treat her with such exquisite tenderness. It made even more tears come.

"Why are you crying?" Liam finally asked.

"You make me so happy, I can't help it."

He smiled, his lips pressed to her forehead. "Okay. As long as they're happy tears, I won't panic."

"You? Panic? Mr. Calm-and-in-control? Never."

He lifted his head to gaze down at her. "I lose my mind whenever I think something bad might happen to you or Chloe. You two are my Achilles' heel."

"I guess I can live with that, as long as you're there to look after us."

"About that." His expression grew serious. Really serious. As in they were about to have a significant conversation. *The* conversation.

Butterflies erupted in Sloane's stomach, and she was suddenly so nervous she could hardly stay still.

Liam launched into what was clearly a prepared speech. "I've been waiting to say this to you for a very long time—"

A beeping sound came from the laptop on the coffee table.

Liam swore and rolled away from her, spinning the laptop so he could see the screen.

"I've got movement outside," he bit out.

He jumped up and threw on jeans and his sweatshirt, and raced into the bedroom. He emerged wearing a coat and carrying a pair of shotguns. He jammed his feet into boots, shoved his arms into a coat and then—ominously—leaned one of the shotguns by the front door. "That's loaded."

She stared in dismay at the weapon.

"Lock the door behind me," he bit out.

Quickly and quietly, he slipped outside into the gathering dark, leaving her alone in the cabin with the shotgun and her far too active imagination.

She ran over to the door, naked, and threw the dead bolt. It didn't make her feel the slightest bit safer.

Sloane mimicked Liam, frantically throwing on clothes while watching the laptop. What had he seen that sent him outside like that? It had to be a person. And the only person who would be sneaking around outside the cabin had to be her hit man.

Oh, God. Terror tore through her gut, making her limbs literally shake with fear. A need to run, and keep on running, nearly overwhelmed her common sense. She was safest inside with these thick walls to protect her. Also, Liam knew where she was and could hunt her would-be killer without worrying about accidentally shooting her.

She picked up the second shotgun. As a kid, she'd shot her fair share of soda cans off fences, and the few times she'd been skeet shooting, she hadn't been a half-bad shot. But she was no expert marksman. And she would hate to shoot Liam accidentally. Still, she felt better with the weight of cold steel in her hands.

She moved over to the window and waited beside it, peeking around the curtains into the darkness. Full night was falling fast, and what little light reflected off the snow only served to deepen the shadows and make the woods seem menacing and spooky.

She thought she saw a man-size shadow move once, but then she lost the shape in the dark. Crud. Was Liam safe? Should she call his cell phone to check on him? Or would its vibration give away his position and get him killed?

She pulled the laptop over to her side and alternated looking outside and watching the screens. With each gust of wind, she heard the crystalline whisper of snow falling from the branches. It was a cold sound. Lifeless. Like the death the hit man had planned for her.

All of a sudden, one of the camera views exploded with motion. Two men grappled on screen, wrestling over a shotgun. They were behind the cabin. Frantically, she enlarged the view and saw in horror that one of the men was Liam, fighting for his life.

He couldn't die!

She leaped for the door, threw open the lock and raced outside. Momentarily disoriented as to where the camera was, she paused on the porch. Then, to her right, she heard a grunt of pain. The kind of grunt a man would let out if he'd been punched hard in the gut.

Shotgun at the ready, she ran off the porch and straight into thigh-deep snow. Running through it was like running through molasses, but she powered on, desperate to reach Liam and help him subdue the hit man. She rounded the corner of the cabin and saw tracks in the snow. She followed them into the woods, fairly certain she was paralleling the driveway. Her eyes adjusted to the low light, and she was able to make out two sets of tracks. She ran in them through the snow where the going was easier.

She made it perhaps a hundred yards beyond the cabin when she spotted Liam and the assailant struggling, well down the mountainside from her.

Liam was facing her, and even in the dim light conditions, she saw the grim determination on his face.

She opened her mouth to shout, in hopes of distracting his attacker, but instead, she saw a flash between the two men, and a deafening explosion of sound split the night.

Liam flew backward and fell on his back, disappearing into the deep snow.

No no no no...

He'd been shot.

The hit man turned to face her and charged toward her.

Belatedly, she remembered the weapon in her hands and raised it to her shoulder. Taking careful aim at the middle of the assailant's chest, she pulled the trigger.

The attacker flew backward into the snow as the buckshot hit him.

Circling wide of the downed hit man, she darted left and ran into the open path of the driveway. She sprinted down the hard-packed snow toward where she'd last seen Liam, frantic to get to him.

Please be alive. Please be alive—

She had just about reached where she thought Liam had gone down and was starting to veer toward the trees when a voice came out of the dark.

"Gotcha. Stop where you are or I'll shoot you."

Sloane skidded to a stop.

"Put your gun down and turn around slowly, Sloane."

She knew that voice.

"You?" She turned around and dropped her weapon. "You're the hit man, Ivan?"

Her ex-husband stood behind her, a handgun held at arm's length in front of him. It was pointed at her face.

"I don't know what the hell you're talking about."

If Ivan wasn't the hit man, that meant a second man was up here, somewhere, threatening Liam's life. A whole new layer of panic tore through her.

"You're coming with me," Ivan bit out.

"No, I'm not. Liam's shot and I have to get to him to help him."

"You're not helping anyone but me. I swear to God, Sloane, I'll kill you where you stand if you don't come with me right now."

Indecision froze her in place. Ivan would, indeed, shoot her if she turned away from him. At this range, no more than a dozen feet, the odds were excellent that he would hit her. Maybe kill her.

In the time it would take her to raise the shotgun and

shoot him, he would get off several shots. Nope. That was a gunfight she would lose.

Her only hope was to approach Ivan. Get the gun away from him, or get him to lower the weapon so she could make a run for it. She *had* to get to Liam.

"Drop the shotgun," Ivan ordered.

She dropped the weapon.

"Walk toward me."

She strode toward him rapidly, hoping to close the gap and get her hands on that gun.

"Stop!" Ivan barked.

Damn. She wasn't within arm's reach of him yet, and he'd backed away from her as she'd approached.

"You and I are going for a little ride," Ivan announced.

"Where to?" She had to keep him talking. Get him to let down his guard. Convince him she wasn't going to resist him.

"To get Chloe."

"Why? You know you don't want to raise a child by yourself, Ivan. I get that you want to punish me for getting custody of her, but there are other ways you can hurt me without sticking yourself with a screaming two-year-old."

"Move." Ivan gestured with the pistol, indicating that she should walk down the driveway. "And put your hands behind your head. Lock your fingers together."

She did as he ordered and started walking down the driveway reluctantly. How was she going to get out of this? Maybe when they approached whatever vehicle he had up here, she could use it for cover and make a run for it.

Except Ivan stayed directly behind her as she approached a European luxury sedan, that damned pistol undoubtedly pointed at her the whole time.

"Get in."

She opened the passenger door, climbed in and buckled her seat belt. While she twisted around to reach for the buckle, Ivan kept the pistol trained on her. Damn.

"Hold your hands out, wrists together."

She complied because that stupid pistol didn't leave her any choice. With one hand, Ivan quickly reached out and fastened a zip tie around her wrists, then gave the end a sharp tug.

Well, crap.

He closed and locked the passenger door and then rushed around to the driver's side and climbed in.

"Hands on the door handle," he ordered.

He leaned across her, the pistol's muzzle jammed into her side, and used a second zip tie to tie her wrists to the door's arm rest. It was awkward and uncomfortable, sitting with her arms pulled over to the right, and it severely limited her options for getting free and wrestling the weapon from him.

Soul-deep panic set in. Ivan was going to get away with this. And Liam was lying in the snow, God only knew how hurt. She had no idea if her shot had killed the man Liam had been fighting or not. For all she knew, the guy had survived and gone back to finish off Liam.

The idea of the man she loved being killed was almost too much for her to bear. Were it not for the gun pointed at her right now, she would have been completely incapacitated. However, that tiny black bore clarified the situation like nothing else could. It focused her mind down to a single pinpoint—survival. At all costs.

An image of Chloe came sharply into her mind, and she latched on to her daughter's face.

She had to keep her wits about her. Had to figure out a way out of this. She *had* to live.

To that end, she had to keep Ivan talking. Convince him she was no threat. Conversationally, she asked, "Who was the guy you had with you up at the cabin?"

"What guy? I came alone."

"The hit man."

"What hit man?"

"The ones your parents hired to kill me."

Ivan made a scornful sound. "My parents would never do such a thing."

She opened her mouth to tell him Liam had them on tape talking to their hit man, but at the last second, thought better of it. The object here was not to enrage Ivan.

"Where are you taking Chloe and me? I assume you have a plan since you're a thorough kind of guy."

"Damn straight, I'm thorough. I'm not taking you. Just Chloe. And I'm not telling you where I'm taking her. Someplace you'll never find her in a million years."

Her heart leaped into her throat and threatened to choke her. She managed to force out words, but it was an effort. "That's kidnapping, Ivan. You won't ever be able to come home again. Are you sure you want to do something so drastic?"

"I'll do just about anything to make your life a living hell."

She refrained from telling him he'd already done that brilliantly for the past several years.

"And besides," Ivan added, "I've got a few creditors to get away from."

Ahh. Not good. In that case, he really would leave the country with Chloe and never come back. She fell silent, thinking frantically. There had to be a way to stop him. But how?

She became aware that Ivan was driving way too fast for safety on the icy, winding mountain road. "You need to slow down, Ivan. This is a great car, but even it has its limits."

"You always were a nag, telling me what to do and how to do it."

"Please, Ivan," she begged. "Slow down a little. You wouldn't want to make Chloe an orphan, would you?"

In response, he stomped on the accelerator, and the big car roared forward.

Good Lord. They were both going to die. Just like her parents. Had this been how her parents met their end? Having an argument and her father speeding up to spite her mother? She would bet her mother hadn't been zip-tied to the door, though, or had a gun pointed at her head.

It didn't help her panic that Ivan was driving with the pistol gripped between his fist and the steering wheel, still pointed in her general direction.

She watched him warily, in between glancing through the windshield at the shiny glare of ice on the road in the headlights.

A sharp curve to the left came up all of a sudden, and Ivan threw the car around the bend. The back end skidded to the right, and he yanked the steering wheel back to the right. The pistol jerked, and she flinched, squeezing her eyes shut against the shot she was sure would come.

The car's rear end fishtailed as the road S-curved back hard to the right, and Ivan hit the brakes.

"No!" she cried out reflexively.

The car turned sideways of the road and slid across the ice, careening completely out of control. They were going to die.

Just like her parents. This was how their lives had ended. In terror and panic. With thoughts of her and Fox ricocheting through their minds.

As the car smashed through the guardrail and slid toward the edge of the cliff, Sloane screamed at the top of her lungs.

Chapter 19

Liam lay in the snow and tried to breathe, but damned if he could draw a breath. The bullet that had hit him square in the chest plate of his bullet-resistant vest had really knocked the wind out of him. Cold soaked through his body as he frantically tried to relax, and more importantly, tried to hear movement from his attacker. He had to regain control of his body and breathe again before the bastard closed in on him and finished him off.

He struggled to sit up in the snow half-burying him, grappled to draw a proper breath.

The crack of a gunshot made him jolt violently. That was a shotgun. Had Sloane come outside to enter the fray? Please, God. No. Let her be safe inside and not tangling with a professional hit man out here while he was down and out for the count.

He opened his mouth. Tried to shout her name. To hell with giving away his position to the killer. He had to get her to go back inside to safety. Barricade herself in the heavily walled cabin—

Turned out it was impossible to make sound with no air in one's lungs to force out past one's vocal cords.

Swearing up a blue storm inside his head, he forced his unwilling body to get vertical. He paused on his knees, searching the darkness frantically. No sign of the killer or of Sloane.

With a sudden spasm of his diaphragm, his lungs reengaged and he drew a ragged partial breath. The encroaching tunnel vision retreated a little. Another approximately full breath and the gray at the edges of his vision disappeared.

He tried again to shout for Sloane, but he still didn't have enough air to make more than a sigh of sound.

Grabbing on to the tree trunk beside him, he dragged himself upright. His entire rib cage felt as if it had shattered, and every breath he drew felt like an anvil on his chest. Slowly, painfully, he made his way up the hill in roughly the direction he'd last seen the assailant.

He'd slogged maybe a dozen yards straight ahead when he heard a noise to his right. Liam froze, listening hard.

Was that a male voice?

Crap, crap, crap. Had the hit man found Sloane?

He turned to race toward the driveway when he literally tripped over a body lying facedown in the snow.

Please, please, please not Sloane.

He rolled the body over and stared down. The hit man. The guy was breathing but peppered with a half-dozen bleeding holes in his coat. None of them were gushing blood as if they were life-threatening. But the guy had definitely taken some shotgun pellets.

Liam stepped over the man, who was just starting to rouse, and ran as fast as he was able toward the driveway.

He was in time to see Ivan Durant jump into a big black European sedan. The taillights went on, and he spied the shape of a passenger in the front seat.

Was that Sloane? No way would she go anywhere with her ex voluntarily. Was the bastard was kidnapping her?

The big car pulled away from him, disappearing around a bend in the driveway.

Dammit!

He ran back into the trees to where the hit man was now sitting up, putting pressure on his various wounds.

Drawing his weapon, Liam approached him. "Come with me," he ordered.

"You taking me to a hospital?"

"Eventually. Come on. I'm in a hurry."

Liam made the guy hustle in front of him to the cabin and open the front door.

"Sloane!" Liam shouted.

No answer.

"Go inside and flip the light switch just to the right of the front door. I'll have my gun pointed at you, so no funny business."

"They ain't paying me enough to get killed, man."

"They who?"

"The Durants. They want me to kill some chick so they can kidnap her kid."

Satisfaction coursed through Liam The Durants were toast. They would never bother Sloane or Chloe again.

He raced up the porch steps and poked his head into the cabin. Sloane was gone. And so was her coat. Dammit. That *had* been her out there shooting the shotgun.

"C'mon. Let's get you to town before you bleed out."

The man looked down at his torso in alarm, but Liam frog-marched him over to his pickup truck. Quickly, he yanked the guy's hands behind his back and handcuffed him. He put the perp in the back seat of his truck, and zip-tied the guy's ankles for good measure.

"Hey, I ain't gonna fight you if you'll take me to a hospital, man."

Liam jumped in the truck and gunned it down the drive. At least there was only one road off this mountain, so Ivan and Sloane couldn't disappear on him. Not for a few miles, at least. He had to catch up with them before they reached any intersections and could disappear.

He called the sheriff's department as he drove. Trey Colton answered the phone.

"Trey. It's Liam Kastor. I need one of your guys to block White Mountain Road at the base of the mountain where it comes out on Highway 192. A black sedan is coming down the mountain with Sloane Colton and her ex-husband in it. He has kidnapped her."

"Will do," Trey bit out.

Liam heard him issuing orders over a radio to the nearest units to get over to the base of White Mountain Road ASAP and block it. Liam disconnected the call to concentrate on driving down the treacherous road.

The good news was he knew the winding trail down the side of White Mountain like the back of his hand. The bad news was he didn't see headlights ahead, which meant Ivan had taken the road at a much higher speed than was safe for someone not familiar with the twisting route.

Liam came into the Kiowa Gorge and slowed down. This was the most dangerous part of the road. Sheer drop-offs of several hundred feet came right up to the edge of the road, and only a guardrail and the traction of good tires prevented vehicles from plunging to disastrous ends in the fast-running river below.

He rounded the first bend in the gorge and swore as he saw damage to the guardrail. He touched his brakes, attempting to slow down more.

Even his truck, with chains on the tires, slid a little on the ice, and then caught traction again as he crept around the steep hairpin turn back to the right.

Oh. My. God.

The guardrail was completely broken through, and the few saplings clinging to the edge of the cliff were bent and broken as if something big and fast-moving had crashed through them.

A voice in the back of his head started to scream. He eased onto the brakes as hard as he dared, and the truck finally came to a stop a few yards beyond the break in the rail. He jumped out of the truck and his boots nearly went out from under him.

The road was a solid sheet of ice.

He approached the precipice carefully and, hanging on to one broken end of the twisted metal of the guardrail, peered over the edge.

Far below, he made out the mangled shape of a car lying on its roof, half-submerged.

No one could have survived that crash.

No one.

He fell to his knees as his world ended then and there.

* * *

Sloane's right shoulder was screaming, and her right arm wouldn't move at all. Even the slightest shift of her weight sent spears of agony through the joint. Her entire right side felt as if she'd taken a beating, and she was having trouble drawing a full breath.

The snow she lay buried in was cold on her cheeks. She closed her eyes as hot tears traced down her face until they froze.

She honestly wasn't sure if she was alive or dead.

When Ivan locked up the brakes and went into that final skid toward the cliff, she'd broken through the zip ties with the superhuman strength of life-and-death panic, opened the door, and flung herself out of the vehicle.

Thankfully, it had been sliding away from her and hadn't run her over.

She'd hit the icy road hard. Really hard. She vaguely remembered rolling over and over, and then hearing a horrible crunching sound of metal impacting on metal, twisting and tearing with a terrible rending squeal.

And then silence.

She had no idea how long she'd been lying here.

The cold had felt good at first, and then had hurt so bad she could hardly stand the daggers of it piercing her body. But it felt better now. Warm almost.

She was so sleepy. It would be so nice to close her eyes. Drift away to someplace warm and safe and free of pain.

No. Wait!

Chloe's face swam in her mind's eye, and she struggled to focus on it. And there was something else—

Another face swam in her foggy brain beside her daughter's.

A familiar face. A well-loved face. A face that also represented warmth and safety.

Liam.

The name drifted through her mind, a sigh and a blessing. She loved him, too.

Loved Chloe. Loved Liam.

Didn't want to leave them.

Needed to fight.

Stay alive.

Stay awake.

Must embrace the pain.

But God, it hurt so much to live. To breathe.

One breath.

Another.

Her entire world narrowed down to that defiant act. Just breathing.

But it wasn't death.

Liam dragged himself to his feet, the agony in his heart so intense he wasn't sure he could stand it. He had to call in the crash. Get help up here.

He stumbled around the back end of his truck to approach from the passenger's side so he didn't slip and fall off the cliff.

He rounded the tailgate and saw a strange smudge on the white sheet of ice coating the road. What was that? A tire wouldn't leave a trail of rubber if it skidded on ice. Frowning, he half walked, half skated over to it.

He fumbled for the small LED flashlight on his keychain and shone it on the dark smear.

Except when the light went on, it was red.

Blood.

Where did that come from?

Had Ivan hit a deer? Was that what sent him over the cliff?

Liam's police instincts were operating on autopilot as shock lowered a dull blanket over his senses, numbing his thoughts. Must solve the mystery of where the blood came from. Maybe put an injured animal out of its misery.

He followed the blood trail to the interior side of the road, away from the drop off.

A deep divot in the snow bank indicated where the hit deer had been thrown. He waded into the waist-deep snow in search of it.

And spied a dark heap. He took a single step toward it—

And then a groan came from it. An entirely human groan.

Holy shit. He rushed forward and reached for the dark heap. That was a human shoulder—

He pulled gently, and Sloane's face turned up toward him.

He fell to his knees beside her. "Sloane. Sloane! Can you hear me? Wake up, honey. Open your eyes for me. Be alive, dammit!"

"So loud," she sighed.

His relief was so great he couldn't have stood if he tried. Gently, very gently, he gathered Sloane into his arms.

She cried out in pain, and he froze in the act of pulling her into his lap.

"Liam?" she croaked. "Is this Heaven? Are you here to meet me?"

It took him a moment to realize that she thought he was actually dead. "I'm not dead, baby. And neither are you."

She blinked up at him owlishly, as if she didn't understand.

"You're alive, Sloane. You're lying in a ditch at the side of a road, and you're hurt and dangerously chilled. But you're alive. Do you hear me?"

Her big eyes widened in surprise.

"This is going to hurt. Shout all you want, okay? I'm going to pick you up now."

She did cry out, but he gritted his teeth and stood up, cradling her in his arms as gently as he could. He carried her over to his truck and awkwardly opened the door. She cried out again as he jostled her.

"I'm so sorry, sweetheart, but I have to get you warmed up. The truck's heater is running full blast."

"What the hell happened to her?" the hit man asked as Liam set Sloane on the passenger seat.

By the time Liam came around to the driver's side, she had fallen over on her left side and passed out.

He called the sheriff's office again.

"Sheriff Colton here. Go ahead."

"This is Liam Kastor. I need an ambulance to meet me as fast as it can. I'm driving down the White Mountain Road toward Roaring Springs. Have it flag down my truck as it approaches me. I'm going to make my way toward the hospital until it intercepts me."

Trey was back on the phone in a minute.

"An ambulance is en route. You should meet it maybe

five minutes after you reach Highway 192. What the hell happened up there, Liam?"

"You've got a car in the ravine at the bottom of Kiowa Gorge. Sloane was in the car and apparently bailed out of it before it went off the cliff. She has unknown injuries and cold exposure and is unconscious on the front seat of my truck. I also have the perp who was hired to kill her in custody in the back of my truck."

"Bitch shot me," the hit man offered.

"He's been hit by multiple shotgun pellets. He's bleeding but not seriously wounded."

"You said I was bleeding out, man," the guy complained.

Clearly, he was not the brightest hit man on the planet.

"You may still die if you're not very still," Liam warned the guy. He seriously didn't need the scumbag getting any ideas about trying to escape. Not with Sloane hurt and in need of urgent medical attention.

The drive the rest of the way down White Mountain was a never-ending nightmare. Liam kept having to fight the temptation to check on Sloane, but he dared not take his gaze off the treacherous road. The best thing he could do for her right now was get her down to that ambulance coming for her.

At long last, the road's steep incline decreased and the intersection with the main road came into sight.

He turned onto the highway toward Roaring Springs and accelerated. He called Trey again. "Where's that ambulance? I'm on Highway 192 now."

Trey went away and then came back to report, "They're about two minutes from you. They want you to go ahead and pull over the side of the road and put on your emergency flashers."

Liam did as instructed, and sure enough, the wail of sirens and red flashing lights split the night.

Two EMTs rushed over to his truck with a gurney and quickly transferred Sloane into the ambulance. One of the men went to work on her in the back of the ambulance as the other leaped into the driver's seat and took off toward town.

Liam followed the ambulance in his truck.

While he drove, he demanded over his shoulder, "Did you try to run down Sloane Colton in Denver a few weeks back, coming out of a restaurant?"

"Yeah. Nearly had her, but her date knocked her out of the way at the last second."

Said date scowled into the rearview mirror at his prisoner.

"And you set fire to her house?"

"Yeah."

"And to the barn at the Crooked C Ranch after knocking Sloane out?"

"Naw. I didn't do that."

"What?" Liam blurted. "You've already confessed to enough attempted murders to put you in jail for a good long time. Why not confess to the barn fire?"

"Because I didn't do it, man."

The sounded like he was actually telling the truth.

Liam frowned. Who else could have attacked her on the Crooked C and tried to torch her inside the barn? Surely, it had to be this joker.

"What about getting me an ambulance, man? I'm bleeding bad back here!"

"We're headed for the hospital now," Liam retorted

sharply. "Shut up, stay still and don't thrash around, and maybe you'll live."

The hit man was as still a statue for the rest of the ride and thankfully didn't complain any more.

As Sloane was rushed into the very emergency room where they'd run into each other a few short weeks ago, Liam escorted the man inside. Daria Bloom met him in the lobby, and they put the perp in a hospital bed and handcuffed his wrists to the handrails on either side.

"I'll keep an eye on this guy if you want to go check on Sloane," Daria said kindly.

"Thanks. I owe you."

"Go."

Sloane had already been taken away for a CT scan to check for internal damage, and a nurse told Liam an orthopedic surgeon had been called to the hospital in anticipation of doing surgery to repair Sloane's badly injured shoulder. The real threat to her, though, was the dangerous hypothermia she was suffering from and the real possibility that she might go into shock.

As for Ivan, Liam was having a hard time summoning much sadness that the bastard was dead. Surely the fall off that cliff had been fatal.

A nurse showed Liam to the waiting room, and he began the long vigil of waiting to hear if Sloane was going to live. He had to have gotten to her in time. He *had* to. No way could he have found her after all this time just to lose her.

Fox and Wyatt were the first to arrive. Bailey had stayed home to watch Chloe. Before long, however, most of the local Colton clan had assembled in the waiting room. He wasn't sure if he was relieved to have the company or annoyed by the distraction. Mostly, he just wanted to pray to whatever deity might be listening for Sloane to be all right.

He would happily trade his soul for hers. He would give his life for her. Anything…as long as she pulled through.

Chapter 20

Sloane looked around at the recently redone tearoom at the Chateau—the elegant spa attached to The Lodge at Roaring Springs. Mara had really outdone herself this time. The room looked like a gilt-and-pastel enameled Easter egg. It was too fancy for Sloane's taste, but she had to admit the room was beautiful.

For once, Chloe was behaving herself, happily scribbling with crayons and a coloring book in her high chair. One of the crayons fell to the floor and Sloane bent over to pick it up.

A stab of pain went through her shoulder in its sling. The joint was still healing from surgery to put it back into the socket and repair a torn rotator cuff. She winced as she righted herself, and Mara looked at her in concern.

"Are you sure we didn't rush you out of the house too soon, dear?"

"I'm fine, Mom. I was getting housebound at the

ranch, and I know Chloe was more than ready for an outing."

"It's lovely having all my girls together like this," Mara said as warmly as Sloane could remember hearing her speak. It wasn't that Mara was a cold woman at all. She just wasn't demonstrative with her love for her family.

Russ and Mara's twenty-five-year-old twin daughters, Skye and Phoebe, had joined them for this celebration lunch, along with Bailey.

"It's a sad state of affairs that we're all having a single girls' day out on Valentine's Day, of all days," Skye declared.

"Don't be such a buzzkill," Phoebe retorted. "I, for one, like being single."

Bailey spoke up. "Speak for yourself. I won't be single much longer, and I bet neither of you two will, either. You're beautiful, smart, fierce women. Men worthy of you will come along sooner or later."

"It's the later I'm worried about," Skye groaned.

Sloane leaned back and let the twins' banter flow over her. They really were two peas in a pod. A person had to know them very well to tell them apart. But she'd grown up with the two of them continually switching clothes and pretending to be each other. They'd fooled plenty of teachers and boys over the years, but they'd never fooled her.

She had to admit, it was nice just to sit with her family around her. In the past few weeks, she'd become a big fan of quiet, safe and boring.

She'd barely seen Liam since the night of the accident. He'd been at her side when she woke up from her surgery, disoriented and unsure where she was. Apparently, she'd mistaken him again for an angel, and he'd had to explain for a second time that she wasn't dead, and he wasn't dead and in Heaven waiting for her.

Since then, he'd been tied up day and night writing reports and traveling back and forth to Denver. He'd been working with the Denver police to wrap up the arrest and indictment of Niall and Carol Durant, who were in jail now, awaiting trial.

When the judge had heard about their attempts to bribe another judge and kill an officer of the court, namely her, he hadn't granted the Durants bail. Which was just as well. They could get a foretaste of the prison to come.

The hit man had cooperated fully against them in return for a reduced sentence. Although he was still denying having torched the barn at the Crooked C or having attacked her in the barn. Still, he was going away for a long time for his other attempts on her life and for burning down her house. Chloe would be out of college before he was eligible for parole.

Sloane sighed. She missed Liam. She'd been so sure he was on the verge of professing his love to her before all hell had broken loose up at the cabin. But since then, he hadn't shown any interest in bringing up the subject of their relationship again.

Had getting shot and nearly dying changed his mind, perhaps? She fretted about it and really wanted to talk with him about it, but he was never around long enough to do more than wolf down a quick bite to eat at the ranch and kiss Chloe good-night before he raced back to the police station.

He and Daria Bloom were working on something supersecret, but so far, he hadn't filled Sloane in about whatever it was occupying them. If she didn't know better, she might worry that Liam was romantically involved with the beautiful sheriff's deputy. But Liam didn't even have time for her, let alone for another woman.

"Why the long face, sweetheart?" Mara asked.

Sloane looked up from her perfect tea cakes, which she hadn't tasted a single bite of, startled. "No reason. I mean, I don't have a long face."

"I know that look," Bailey announced. "She's been wearing it pretty much constantly since she got home from the hospital. She's missing her man."

Sloane sent a pointed glare at her friend. Sure enough, the twins leaped all over the remark, hooting and teasing her mercilessly about having a crush on a boy.

"Cripes. We're not in high school anymore," she complained under her breath.

The twins fell silent all of a sudden, which frankly startled Sloane almost more than their ribbing.

"Excuse me, ladies," a male voice said from directly behind her.

Liam.

Sloane started to turn around quickly but stopped abruptly as her shoulder shouted in protest.

He moved into her line of sight, wearing a beautifully tailored suit and tie. He looked like a movie star, tall and strong and clean-cut.

"Hi, handsome," she said shyly. She still wasn't used to them being a public item, but apparently, he'd made no secret of having feelings for her to her family in the hospital.

"If you wouldn't mind, Sloane, I'd like a word alone with Chloe."

"With Chloe?" Sloane echoed, confused.

Chloe was already reaching up eagerly to Liam, who

scooped her up in his big, strong arms and carried her over to the windows, overlooking the mountains.

Frowning, Sloane watched the pair. What was he up to?

Chloe squealed loudly enough that every head in the room turned to look at her. Sloane winced, but then shrugged. It had been Mara's idea to include her granddaughter in this outing.

Liam came back to the table, carrying Chloe, who was grinning from ear to ear and bouncing up and down in his arms hard enough that even he was having to work at holding on to her.

"Daddy! Daddy! Daddy!" Chloe chirped.

What on earth?

Liam dropped to one knee in front of Sloane and told Chloe, "Now. Give it to your mommy."

Chloe held out a small black object in her little fingers.

Sloane's frown of confusion deepening, she looked down at what Chloe was offering her. It was a small black velvet box.

Oh, my.

Her gaze flew up to meet Liam's. He was smiling, and the expression reached all the way down to the bottom of her heart and twisted it so tight it was almost painful.

"Sloane. I already proposed to Chloe, and she accepted my offer to let me be her forever daddy. And now I'm proposing to you. Would you make me the happiest man on earth and let me be your forever husband? I promise to make you the happiest woman in the whole world to the best of my ability. Forever."

She opened her mouth, and for once, words would not come.

"Say yes, Sloane. Please. I love you and Chloe with all my heart. You're my entire world."

The twins let out simultaneous *awww*s, and Mara was smiling widely.

Time stopped as Sloane stared at Liam and saw everything she had always wanted in her life. He was offering her love. A home. Safety. A family of her own. All of it. The void in the bottom of her heart that had been her constant companion closed up and disappeared right then and there. As if it had never existed. Yes, it left a mark behind. She would never forget her parents. But for the first time—ever—she felt whole.

"I love you, too, Liam. With all my heart."

"Is that a yes?" he asked anxiously.

"Yes. Oh, yes." She flung her arms around his neck and felt Chloe's little arm go around her as the three of them shared their first official hug as a family.

And it was perfect.

He was perfect.

Life was perfect.

And the future promised to be even better.

* * * * *

LET'S TALK
Romance

For exclusive extracts, competitions
and special offers, find us online:

facebook.com/millsandboon

@MillsandBoon

@MillsandBoonUK

Get in touch on 01413 063232

For all the latest titles coming soon, visit
millsandboon.co.uk/nextmonth